INFINITY'S FLOWER

A TALE OF 2012
&
THE GREAT SHIFT OF THE AGES

FICTION BASED ON FACT

SECOND EDITION

AS TOLD BY JACK ALLIS

Infinity's Flower: A Tale of 2012 & the Great Shift of the Ages
Fiction Based on Fact, Second Edition
Copyright© 2009 by Jack Allis. All rights reserved.

MAYFAIR BOOK PROMOTION, INC.
PROFESSIONAL PUBLISHING SOLUTIONS

For information contact the publisher:

Mayfair Book Promotion, Inc.
P.O. Box 91
Foresthill, CA 95631

www.mayfairbooks.com
prospct1@foothill.net.

ISBN: 978-1-934588-04-8

Printed in the United States of America.
Distributed by Reality Press for Mayfair Book Promotion, Inc.

WHAT PEOPLE ARE SAYING ABOUT INFINITY'S FLOWER

An epic novel that takes the reader on a journey within.

O.H. Krill
Author of "Montauk Babies"

A wonderfully written prose that certainly resonates with our modern dilemmas.

Dr. John Jay Harper
Author of "Tranceformers, Shamans of the 21st Century"

Now is the time and we are the people who are receiving the messages of truth upon which Jack Allis has based this important novel. Compelling, magical, and speaking to the intuitive heart/spirit level of the reader, 'Infinity's Flower' also serves as a guide to help us navigate through similar events in our world. This work helps teach the real meaning of "taking responsibility" for the chaos we've created, but also guides us in visualizing the world we really want, deserve, and can have...when we learn to use our intention for the highest and best good of all beings!

Vickie Karp
Co-Author, Co-Editor
"HACKED! High Tech Election Theft in America"

I am so excited about "Infinity's Flower," Jack's new novel about these extraordinary and blessed times in which we are living. This is precisely where humanity must focus, and Jack is part of a legion of conduits who will reach the masses with this vital message. The message is so simple, and yet so profound. Creating the new world starts with transforming ourselves. First, we must wake up, and reclaim responsibility for the life we create. And then, we must create that life through our vibration of peacefulness, joy, love and trust.

Dr. Michael Ryce
Founder & Director of Heartland
Author of "Why Is This Happening To Me...AGAIN?!"

Against the eternal backdrop of good and evil, Allis takes us on the ride of the century.

Carlisle Bergquist
Author of "The Coyote Oak: Burgeoning Wisdom"

If anyone is looking for a book that represents what could indeed happen if the 2012 shift is true, then this is it. It was an incredibly well written, fast paced, adventure that not only explains the spiritual changes our society has been going through, but also the various ancient cultures that have predicted these events. I can only hope that if the earth goes through such changes, the events are similar to the author's vision.

Chris Augustin
Aliens the Truth

Jack is an insightful "contemporary storyteller" with a unique ability to convey life trance-forming information in a joyful easy to understand way. His impeccable timing in bringing this story to humanity is uncanny. Don't read INFINITY'S FLOWER unless you're ready to be like "Rip Van Winkle" and wake up ...wake-up from your programmed sleep, integrate your spiritual/material values, and reclaim your true destiny of freedom and joy. INFINITY'S FLOWER will take you on an adventurous empowerment journey ... the journey to become a warrior of the heart.

Jeanine Just
Visionary Success Strategist

Jack writes with a New Age eloquence that keeps you reading until the wee hours of the morning.

Dr. Mark Brown
Natural Medicine Clinic, Pewaukee, Wisconsin

Evocative and thought provoking; an intricately crafted tale. I couldn't put it down. Jack Allis has written a timely novel, whose story-line resonated with me deeply, and whose characters have a strong voice for these times. A must-read for everyone experiencing the current planetary energies....and also for those who need to be made aware of them.

Peter Klein
Managing Director, Shamanic Astrology Mystery School
and Founder, The Manifestation Network

*For anyone and everyone interested in shifting the present world paradigm...
'Infinity's Flower' is a must read! Author, Jack Allis, creatively moves readers
into the next planetary phase with his sequel to 'Infinity's Children.' This story
unfolds like a richly textured dream! A winding, spirit driven adventure! I am
ready to join their journey!*

**Gigi Stafne
Adventure Botanica**

*"Infinity's Flower" is a fast moving tale about the impending changes that may
face humanity in the years ahead. It is chock full of truths that will reinforce the
veteran free thinker and serve as an inspiring primer for those who are curi-
ous for a point of view beyond the mainstream. Beyond that, Jack reminds us
that change is best handled with a spirit of joy, openness and trust. "Infinity's
Flower" is a seed for a fearless future.*

**Patrick Mooney
The Institute of Unlearning**

*Great fiction ... I mean 'faction.' Jack Allis's vision of how the "Great Shift of
the Ages" could occur is a spine-tingler. I had goose bumps more than once as I
read the story. I believe those of us who have been evolving through our awakening will appreciate that indeed we-the-people can empower ourselves, and use
our higher consciousness and spirituality to create the outcome whereby good
does overcome evil. What's most exciting is there is a growing audience for this
novel. "The Shift" is happening.*

**Tom Kennedy
Founder, The UsuryFree Network**

*Infinity's Flower is a magical, exciting and compelling page turner about love,
intuition and connection to spirit that triumphs when confronted with dark forces
of power, greed and total enslavement of the people on planet earth. This novel
gives us hope and inspiration that transforms and lifts our ability to deal with
unfolding earth changes, illusion, politics and the breakdown of old structures
that no longer serve us and to become proactive spiritually in co-creating a new
paradigm with higher values for the greater good.*

**Sundae Merrick
Author of "Divine Reason & Rhyme,
Access Higher Guidance and Nature's Wisdom"**

This book will move you, long after you are finished! This is one book you will not want to skip the introduction! There are ideas expressed and sources quoted worth their weight in gold. Whether you take it as "ancient wisdom" and the cosmic perspective of the black lodge, purely third dimensional, or fantasy adventure, you will find after reading it-that bits pop into your thoughts as you recognize some idea playing out before your eyes. This is a call to "awaken" and participate responsibly in the world you would like to see. When reading this book try: taking time to experience the richness through your senses, abstracting it from a physical to mental plane metaphor experience, noticing around you the daily evidence of restriction and reductions of freedom based on invoking fear and in the name of "protecting us," and recognizing the reduction in services and slowed responses from agencies and businesses.

Rev. Julie Dieterle, PT, M Div.
Member of Global Peace Ministry, Peace from Within

TABLE OF CONTENTS

Preface to Second Edition

Frequency's Rising
The Shift is Right on Schedule

It's Solstice, 2008 (December 21). Giving these dates has become necessary, as we zoom through these times of potentially monumental transformation, which were the target of so many of the ancient prophecies. Things are moving at such a fantastically rapid pace that when you read this, the world will unquestionably be very different than as I write. Yet, the metaphysics and spirituality of *Infinity's Flower – A Tale of 2012 & the Great Shift of the Ages* will be the same. They are eternal, and will not change.

It's been a little over a year since the publication of *Infinity's Flower*. What a wild year it's been! The frequency of the Earth's vital energy fields continues to rise, as she completes her 26,000 year cycle, and moves deeper into these higher frequency fields on her journey through the galaxy. The changes that accompany this are massive, and it's all playing out in our world, just as was foretold in *Infinity's Flower*. The old paradigm is collapsing, as it must, and the collapse of the world's system of money and economics, which is the hot story as I write, is only the start. We still have quite a ways to go, and I invite you to read my story to see how it will probably play out (if it hasn't already).

And the caterpillar of the new paradigm continues its metamorphosis into the butterfly of the new world of light and spirit. As the majority of people tragically cling to the destructive energies of an imbalanced and unsustainable world, all around the planet there is a great awakening or birthing, as ever-increasing numbers of people reawaken to their divine heritage as magical beings, and reconnect with their spirit essence. This is the true source of our protection in the face of these monumental Earth changes, and our power to make the dimensional shift to the new world.

And as I write, it is now four years until that providential date, December 21, 2012 – the end of the Mayan Calendar, and for so many people the target date for the end of the old world and the beginning of the new. We need not be distracted by this. The Mayans were the only ones with a specific date, and virtually all the other prophecies pointed to this time in general. The shift would not occur at a point, but within a window. And I'm certain the ancient Mayans would agree with this. And it is clear that we are now within that window.

The shift is happening, and it's happening now! Now as I write – now as you read. I invite you to join, as we ride this wave into the higher octaves of pure energy and spirit that are opening up to us.

Jack Allis
December 21, 2008

INTRODUCTION

Credits & Comments
Creating the New Paradigm
What is "The Shift?" Why 2012?
& Why Humanity Has Botched It So Badly on Planet Earth

This story is not a fantasy or science fiction, although most people would automatically leap to that conclusion. It is based upon the truth, and there are mountains of credible evidence to support every word of it. This story deals with things that are so fantastic and unimaginable to the average person that they couldn't possibly see them as true. Yet they are.

This story deals with the creation of the new paradigm from the rubble of the old, which is collapsing in a heap around us at such an alarming rate. The new paradigm is a new and totally different world, which we can only create by rediscovering our magical heritage, and reconnecting with the awesome powers of our higher consciousness and spirituality.

This story deals with that naughty "c" word, conspiracy, which to the average person usually carries the tag that you must be some kind of "nut." However, thanks in large part to the free flow of information on the Internet, we are currently in the midst of a great awakening, in which droves of people in America and the rest of the civilized world are waking up to the fact that they've been had. They've had the wool pulled over their eyes for a very long time by a small group of extremely power-hungry and elitist people. In fact, the world works very differently than we are manipulated to believe. The world we are presented with by television and the mainstream media, by the government, and by virtually the entire mainstream system, is nothing but an illusion that keeps us imprisoned inside somebody else's game.

This story deals with the fact that the version of so-called history that is fed to us by the mainstream system is a monumental lie. It is a virtual certainty that ancient civilizations, with highly advanced knowledge, existed on this planet far before what passes as the beginning of our history, on the scale of tens or hundreds of thousands of years, and quite possibly much longer.

Once you open your mind, and start going down this very deep rabbit hole of truth, the evidence also clearly points in the direction that extraterrestrials arrived on Earth during these same time frames, and have been tinkering in human affairs ever since. The proof is right before our eyes, if we just make the effort to open them.

All you need to do is look at the hundreds of ancient structures spanning the globe, such as the Great Pyramids in Egypt, the ruins at Machu Picchu in Peru, and Stonehenge in Great Britain, just to mention a few of the most well known. These structures were built according to the principles of sacred geometry, located precisely at the intersections of the Earth's crucial meridian lines, aligned with constellations and important astrological points of reference, and for which there is significant evidence that they have been there a lot longer than we are told. These could not possibly have been built by the human beings of those times, and traditional history would rather we just look in the other direction.

So, what happened to these civilizations, and exactly how do ET's implicate themselves in human affairs? I invite you to read on.

This story also deals with another immensely important feature of our world today, which you will hear nothing about on television or in the mainstream newspapers, at least not until it's too late to continue covering it up. In the alternative culture, this is commonly referred to as *The Shift* or *The Great Shift of the Ages*. I am indebted to the work of Gregg Braden on this topic, who I had the honor of interviewing in 2004 on a tele-seminar series I hosted for Stratia Corporation. *The Shift* is an exceedingly rare geophysical and astrophysical time the Earth has entered. It is the completion of a 26,000-year cycle, which was prophesized by ancient cultures spanning the globe, including the Egyptians, the Mayans and the Hopis. *The Shift* involves forces of colossal magnitude, such as the reversing of the Earth's electromagnetic field and the shifting of its other energy fields. These are forces that have the potential to change the face of the planet, and life on it, forever. The specific date that is often targeted as the turn-over point, kind of like the clock striking midnight on New Year's Eve, is December 21, 2012, which was the date the Mayan calendar ended.

There is much debate and confusion regarding these specific time frames. Many people have told me it is a mistake to use the year 2012 in my title, some because they believe it's likely to be inaccurate, and others because this does not leave me enough time to reach my audience, and sell my book. My reply to the latter is I am here to say what I must say, regardless of whether or not it is expedient. But more importantly, when you consider the multitude of diverse and ancient sources, as well as the vast length of the time periods involved, it is reasonable to assume that there is a significant margin of error regarding these predictions. Much of this information is also derived from the oral traditions of these ancient cultures, which can be imprecise. Besides, there's no reason we should trust the accuracy of our Gregorian calendar any more than anything else.

There is a school of Shamanic Astrology, which interprets *The Shift* as more of a gradual process, lasting in the neighborhood of 150 years, and that we are currently just past the midpoint. At the time of this writing, August 2007, that would seem to be the case. *The Shift* appears to be well underway. One clear manifestation of this is the dramatic increase in extreme weather, earthquake, volcano and tsunami activity. The Earth is feeling it. Another is the shocking move toward fascist world government that is taking place throughout the world, most obviously in America and Europe. The timing of this is no accident, and I invite you to read my story to see why.

People are also feeling these energy shifts in their bodies. The world feels different, more intense. Time itself seems like it's speeding up, and even the most emotionally stable among us are feeling things they've never felt before, often to the point where they feel like they're flipping their lids.

It's a pretty good guess that things are going to get quite a bit more intense in the years ahead. It's probably going to get a lot worse before it can get better, and this chaos might be just what is needed to make the necessary changes. Whether *The Shift* hits its apex on 12/21/12, or before, or after, or whether there even is an apex, doesn't make any difference. It's happening, and it's happening now, and unless we, the human race, blow it, it's going to be happening for a long time.

Which brings us to the possible outcomes of all this, and again, I invite you to read on to see one possible scenario. There are those who believe these are the end-times predicted in the Bible. Those of us who are committed to creating the new paradigm see this monumental challenge as a potential blessing, and an extraordinary opportunity to discard the old, and create a new world of higher consciousness and spirituality. It could go either way. As is invariably the case, the fate of the planet rests in our hands. The choice is ours.

Yes, the average person could only see all this as outrageous. How could anyone believe such things that are so far outside the box of our commonly accepted view of the world? The answer is exceedingly simple. The majority of Americans, as well as the rest of the civilized world, have been duped into giving their minds away. They are so mesmerized by their televisions, and by what the high priests of the system are telling them, that they've lost their ability to think for themselves.

But it's not all trickery. People choose to give their minds away. Taking responsibility for our actions, and for the lives we create, is one of our primary virtues as human beings. It is also an aspect of ourselves with which we must reconnect if we are going to transform the world.

It is basically a pact with the devil. People trade their souls in return for the promise of the material dream, and the security and protection that they are told is part of the deal. Satan promises us a job, enough money to make it all work, a spouse and 2.7 children, public education, a house in the burbs, cars, drugs for what ails us, all sorts of insurance and retirement plans, welfare if we need it, and most importantly, protection from all the boogie men it conjures up. All we have to do is follow orders, and not ask a lot of questions. The end result is a return to a feudal system, in which the government, and the hidden powers that own and control it, play the part of king and queen, and the people are reduced to the status of serfs or employees.

This split between the material and spiritual aspects of our lives, with the material being emphasized to the exclusion of the spiritual, is the fundamental reason why America has lost its way, with the rest of the civilized world close on its heels.

If we are going to create the new paradigm, it is essential that sufficient numbers of us reclaim our minds and our spirits, and take back responsibility for creating our own lives. This is the battleground upon which this great struggle must be waged. And it is the only arena in which we can win. If we choose to wage it on the turf of the old paradigm, we will lose because they have all the guns and bombs, and all the money.

There is nothing that the hidden powers can do to stop an empowered band of spiritual warriors. The challenge begins within the mind, heart and spirit of each and every one of us. These are powerful weapons indeed, with the capability of creating a world of truth, beauty and wisdom that is beyond the current reaches of our imagination.

The first step in this process of self-transformation is to break the spell that we have allowed to be cast upon us. We must wake up to how we have bartered away our responsibility and our spirit. And we must wake up to how this insidious game is played. We must not be dismayed when vast numbers of our fellow human beings, including friends, family and loved ones, choose to remain in their slumber. We must remind ourselves that it's their choice, and something they're going to have to work through themselves, or perish.

And we must be aware that it isn't necessary for everybody to wake up, and reclaim their mind and spirit, in order to create the new paradigm. It is only necessary for our numbers to reach a total that is referred to as critical mass. Once critical mass is reached, the dominoes will start to fall, and things we previously could not have imagined will begin to happen. Nobody knows at what precise point critical mass actually is. It is also something that can not be measured in the accustomed quantitative way because we are dealing with intangible, spiritual variables.

Critical mass also does not work in this accustomed quantitative way, as in whichever side has the biggest army, with the most guns, will win. It works on the basis of energetic, spiritual and magical principles, which ultimately have far greater power. It is an area, in which an entirely different set of rules apply. It is the type of power that allowed David to slay the mighty Goliath with a tiny stone. If you choose to read on, this story shows how these powers can manifest.

Critical mass can only be judged on the basis of what's happening. When we get there, we'll know. In fact, it is only necessary for a relatively small percentage of us to wake up, and reclaim our mind and our spirit, in order to change the entire world. A small group of people with a connection to the true source of their power have exponentially more impact than much larger groups with little or none.

My own personal wake-up call came in the mid to late 90's, when I attended a series of seminars at which G. Edward Griffin and David Icke were featured speakers. I've always had an open mind, and I've always lived on the fringe, dabbling with various counter-cultures, and dancing to the beat of my own drum. I was like Neo in the movie sensation *The Matrix*. I knew there was something seriously wrong with the world, like a splinter in my mind, but I could never put my finger on exactly what it was.

For me, the most perplexing question was why humanity was botching it so badly on the planet Earth? I refused to believe that human beings were inherently this stupid. In my personal metaphysics, it didn't make any sense for the universe to create beings who were so incapable of managing their own existence. And yet, I had no other answers.

The light went off in my head when I heard Ed Griffin's classic lecture, based on his book *The Creature from Jekyll Island*, in which he exposed the scam of the Federal Reserve, the income tax, and the entire American system of fiat money and credit. I didn't doubt for a second the veracity of what I was hearing. It all made perfect sense. But far more important was the question that immediately took root in my mind. If the international banking establishment and the federal government are able to successfully conspire to pull the wool over the eyes of the people in this area, what's to prevent them, or others like them, from doing the same thing in other areas?

Enter David Icke, the godfather of the current generation of conspiracy theorists. The role that David's work played in helping me to take the next step, and fit together all the pieces of this gigantic puzzle once and for all, is incalculable, as is my gratitude. I heard him speak in 1998, in Cancun Mexico. As I watched and listened, it was an epiphany, as the threads from my world, which had been splintered for decades, were tied together, one, after another, after another. I proceeded to inhale his three books *And the Truth Shall Set You Free*, *The Biggest Secret* and *Children of the Matrix*.

As David traced the conspiracy to enslave the human race back to the beginnings of human civilization, and then back to Atlantis, Lemuria and other ancient civilizations that predate "official" history, and then ultimately off planet, I was enraptured by what a great story it made. This turned out to be an important source of inspiration for *Infinity's Flower*, and its predecessor, *Infinity's Children*.

It takes balls for me to admit that David's work is such an important influence. He is a pariah, and even in the alternative community, his work tends to be taboo. He's like good pornography. Everybody enjoys it, but nobody admits it. All of which is extremely ironic because so many of David's once wacky ideas have become so woven into the fabric of the alternative culture that they are now taken for granted. He is rarely ever cited. And yet when these topics are discussed, people often refer to the "reptile" guy or that whole "reptilian" thing, and everybody knows who you're talking about.

And even the "reptilian" thing isn't as far fetched as those with their heads stuck in old paradigm thinking believe. All it takes is an understanding of shapeshifting, a common feature of virtually every primitive culture that lives close to nature and the spirit world. If you read on, you can learn about that too. Like Wilhelm Reich, and so many other original and revolutionary thinkers, perhaps David and his work will be swept into the dust bin of history, without anybody remembering. Or perhaps, when we succeed at creating the new paradigm, he will receive the credit he deserves.

And most importantly, David's work provided answers to those nagging questions that had been a splinter in my mind for so long. Human beings aren't inherently stupid or wicked. They are botching it so badly on this planet, and have lost their connection to the rhythm and flow of life, because they have been tampered with.

As soon as I accepted the premise of the conspiracy, another vital question leaped instantly into the mix. How can human beings be capable of such evil? How can human beings deceive, manipulate and murder their fellow human beings for thousands of years, all for the purpose of world domination and control? The answer: because they're not human.

For much of the metaphysical perspective presented in this book, my gratitude goes to the work of Carlos Castaneda, who departed this world on his own definitive journey in 1998. This metaphysical system was taught to him by don Juan Matus, a Yaqui Indian sorcerer from the American Southwest and Mexico. Don Juan's knowledge was passed down through his lineage, which he said went back ten thousand years, and which he referred to as the sorcerers of ancient Mexico.

To use one of don Juan's favorite terms, this metaphysical system is impeccable. It is also eerily similar to the revolutionary discoveries of quantum physics, which have recently been popularized in the alternative culture. To my knowledge, Castaneda, and obviously don Juan, had no knowledge of quantum physics. Quantum physics reached the public awareness for the first time in the mid-1970's, roughly the same time as Castaneda, with Fritjof Capra's classic book, *The Tao of Physics*.

And yet don Juan speaks the language of quantum physics to a tee. The sorcerers of ancient Mexico derived their power from their ability to perceive, in heightened states of awareness, that everything in the universe consisted of energy, and everything in this world of energy was connected to everything else by luminous, pulsating fibers. They were capable of performing their stupendous feats of magic, which defied the logical, cause and effect rules of the ordinary, third dimensional world, by virtue of their ability to see directly this world of energy, to act in it, and to merge with the mysterious powers and forces that guided it.

Castaneda does not hit the nail squarely on the head in all of his books. The ones that do are *Journey to Ixtlan, Tales of Power* and *The Power of Silence*. By the way, I choose to take no part in the debate about whether don Juan was a real person or fictional. I don't care, and it doesn't make any difference. The only thing that matters are the teachings. These connected with my spirit like nothing else. That's enough, and I trust it.

And finally, the inspiration for my characters Hibutu, Mahnya and the Togi Tribe comes from Drunvalo Melchidezek, and his beautiful little story, *The Kogi Story*. A printed copy of this was given to me several years ago by a friend. It instantly touched my heart, and started the wheels turning for Chapter One of *Infinity's Flower*. Hibutu and Mahnya are shamans with the Togi Tribe, who live deep within the jungles of South America. The Togi have never had contact with modern civilization. They have knowledge that is identical to don Juan's, as it is derived from the same source - nature. They too have powers that far exceed those of ordinary humans, powers that we are all capable of. All that is needed is to make the choice to wake up, take back responsibility for the lives we create, and reclaim our minds and our spirits.

Just imagine for a moment an army, filled with people the likes of don Juan, Hibutu and Mahnya, an army of spiritual warriors, who are determined to reclaim the planet, and change the world. There is nothing the hidden powers that control the world could do to stop them. Or us.

ONE ✿ THE SIGN

David's eyes popped open.

Kelly was nestled behind him beneath the quilt and the wool blanket. He could feel the warm flesh of her entire body nuzzled into the contours of his, like spoons.

He knew she was awake too. Much of what passed between them didn't require words. Theirs was a connection of the spirit. They often journeyed together in their dreams.

Was this it? They had known for weeks that something was about to happen, but they had no idea what. They could feel it. They could feel that the time had come for their three-year hiatus in the wilderness of South Dakota to come to an end. So they waited for a sign.

The crescent moon had disappeared hours ago. The room was pitch black. The door and all the windows of the cabin were open, and the cool, crisp September air was still, breathless.

David felt prickly sensations in the middle of his abdomen, at the center of his core, like electric charges. They danced up his spine, and then shot to the crown of his head, and to his fingertips and toes.

David and Kelly shifted onto their backs, like they were one person, and took each other's hand. He knew she was feeling it too.

David rolled his eyes back in their sockets, and looked out the window behind them. The sky was ablaze and frothy with stars. The energy around them was palpable.

They were not alone. There was a presence in the darkness of the cabin around them.

They waited, breathing as one, enveloped in a sea of darkness and silence.

Time was suspended. Their world was reduced to the simple act of waiting, trusting that the time had come, and their message would soon arrive.

It came in through the window behind them, like one of the massive stars had taken flight, and cruised in. It looked like a firefly, which they both recalled from their days in the Wisconsin countryside. It passed over them on a straight and steady course. They sat up together on their bed on the wooden floor, as if it was pulling them with a mysterious force. The tiny spark of light then gently landed on the thick wool rug at the foot of their bed.

It rested there for a moment, and went out. The room was dark again.

Again, they waited, and breathed.

Time, again, stood still.

The space in front of them started to faintly glow, in a semi-circle around where the spark had landed, like a halo, several feet off the floor. The halo began to slowly swell into a flickering luminous band, casting shadows that danced around the cabin. It reached a crescendo a few inches wide, pulsated for a few moments, and then contracted again back to its glimmering halo, like the thin shell of a luminescent cocoon.

David's scalp and spine prickled again at what he saw next. Air gushed involuntarily into his lungs.

Inside the halo, there was a man, sitting cross-legged on the rug in front of them, with his hands folded in his lap.

The light was just enough to illuminate his features. He appeared to be a native from either Central or South America. He was small in stature, perhaps less than five and half feet tall, with short, thin, straight dark hair that hung loosely around his head. His round face, with high creek bones, was smiling serenely. His dark brown skin was satiny smooth, and his narrow, dark eyes were glittering in the luminescence around him. He was wearing a reddish-brown sleeveless shirt, with a v-neck, made of course material, like burlap, a necklace of small, multi-colored beads or stones, dark pants made of a thin, cotton-like material, and sandals.

He sat perfectly still, and his sparkling eyes glanced back and forth from theirs.

David and Kelly knew instantly what to do. It felt like it was coming to them in waves from the little man, extrasensory signals beyond the scope of words.

They didn't even look at each other. It was a perfect understanding. With their eyes fixed on his, like magnets, they let go of their hands, tossed the covers off to the side, and mirrored the position of their visitor, crossing their legs yoga-style, and folding their hands in their laps.

They were both naked. It didn't matter.

The little man's angelic smile turned upward in obvious bliss. His eyes continued to go back and forth between them, holding one for a few seconds, then going to the other.

His eyes shined into Kelly's, then moved away, and gazed at a point directly between her and David. His eyes were more glazed, like they were taking possession of something in that space, or something was taking possession of him. He held it briefly, or it him, and closed his eyes. His entire torso, from his waist to the base of his neck, expanded with air, raising his shoulders. He then exhaled forcefully out his nose, dropping his head and his shoulders, like air rushing out of a balloon. Silence again. Raising his head, and expanding his chest, he again fixed his twinkling eyes at the point in between them, his face beatific.

The names popped into David's head, as if from nowhere. Yet, there was no doubting it. It was unmistakable. His mind had been in a blank trance-like state. Now, these two names had been inserted, names he didn't think he had ever heard before.

David and Kelly turned, and looked at each other. They spoke the two names in perfect unison.

"Hibutu. Togi."

Again, without saying a word, they had perfect understanding. The little man was known as Hibutu. And his people were known as the Togi, or the Togi Tribe.

They also perfectly understood that this was not the language they were going to use to communicate with Hibutu. These words were mere reference points, and they were not essential. And this was not something they were figuring out as they went along. This knowledge too had been inserted into them by Hibutu. It had passed between them on waves of energy, and was picked up by receptors other than those in their brains. Theirs was to be a language far more universal, and precise.

David and Kelly looked back at Hibutu, sitting like a Buddha, smiling serenely inside his luminescent shell. His supercharged, yet peaceful eyes again passed back and forth between them. It was much more than just a mere look, though they had no idea what. Not yet. David and Kelly could feel that he was tenderly taking hold of them. Something mysterious was shifting around them. They trusted it, and acquiesced.

Hibutu returned his eyes to the space in between them, and nodded his head reassuringly.

He closed them again, tilted his head back, and his torso inflated again, with his shoulders pointing into the air.

"Ahhhh," he sighed, barely above a whisper, relaxing his shoulders, his mouth open in a slight oval. The sound resonated with his look of serenity. It was both a sigh and a moan, coming from deep within his depths. It exuded both great calmness and primal ecstasy. It was the sound of divine creation.

David felt its vibration ripple through his entire being, like a soothing cosmic breeze blowing through him.

David and Kelly knew exactly what to do. Thoughts and words, again, were not necessary.

"Ahhhh," they replied simultaneously, mirroring his rapturous tone.

Hibutu opened his eyes, and returned his twinkling gaze to them, back and forth. His breathing remained deep and even, but it accelerated, his chest heaving in and out. He began to tilt his head from side to side, and fixed his glowing eyes on them more intensely, with a slight squint, and a furrow of his brows. It was a look of yearning, of strong desire, a reaching out of one heart to another, like a beckoning to merge with him.

"Mmmmm," he moaned beseechingly, looking back and forth at them.

David felt a pleasant tingling in the core of his abdomen, and then a soft pressure in the middle of his chest, like invisible hands were taking hold of him.

They again replied in unison, their cadence matching each other perfectly.

"Mmmmm."

Their tone was indistinguishable from his.

Hibutu's dark, round face beamed with his etheric smile, and his glassy eyes returned to the space in between them. He sat in total silence and stillness, like a statue. His eyes gazed deeply into space, trance-like. It was as though he had left his body, like he wasn't there anymore.

Once again, time stood still. It was either an instant that passed, or an eternity. It didn't make any difference.

David's eyes were open wide, yet his vision was glazed, like everything was fusing, like he was seeing everything and nothing at the same time.

His skin felt sensuously cool, and his body light, feathery. His head was dizzy. It felt odd, yet intoxicating and alluring. He too felt like he was going away, like he was merging with his surroundings, with the world around him.

The halo around Hibutu started to pulsate and swell again. The room in front of David's eyes was slowly brightening, glowing. He too was a part of this. The space inside his head, behind his eyes, was glowing. In his yoga position, he could make out the outline of his arms, his hands, his legs and his feet. They were all glowing. Kelly's silhouette, next to him, out of the periphery of his vision, was pulsating with light. In front of him, Hibutu's physical features were no longer discernible. He was immersed in light. The boundaries of his body were giving way, and blending with the halo around him, transforming him into a luminescent ball. David's boundaries too, arms, hands, legs and feet, were fading, merging with the sea of energy enveloping them.

Soon, there was nothing left of David's physical body. The only thing that remained was his breath, like a wind blowing through the ether. That too blew away, and was gone.

All was light.

In this sea of infinite light, the only thing remaining of David Rhodes was his awareness. He hadn't disappeared, and he wasn't sleeping. He was aware that he was a part of this. He was it, and it was he. He was also aware that he was moving. And he was not alone. Kelly and Hibutu, at least their awareness and their life force, was there with him. And they were traveling, traveling through a dimension beyond the scope of the third dimensional, material world.

There was no sight, sound, touch, taste or smell. And no time. Just energy and consciousness. The creation reduced to its most primordial essentials.

And unity. Everything in this world was a part of everything else.

Light. Timeless energy.

First, David's breath returned. Then his heartbeat. He could feel its thumping. Then, the rest of his body started to slowly congeal, and come to life, like sails filling with the breath that blew through the void. He could feel the warmth of his blood, and warm, damp air on his skin.

The light began to break up. Colors started to emerge. A vast sea of amorphous green started to take shape on the bottom half of the screen of light, and a field of light eggshell blue on the top, like the sky. The world of form was condensing in front of his eyes.

Sounds came next – the screeching and high pitched whistling of birds – big birds, lots of big birds.

The sea of green materialized. It was a huge, thick jungle, stretching as far as he could see. David was looking down upon it from a perch high in the air. He seemed to be flying; yet he had no sensation of the air moving around him. He could feel the muggy air, but it was still. It was like no experience he had ever had before, not even when he dreamed. He could feel his body, but he couldn't see it. The world below was a vast panorama, and it was moving slowly, but he didn't will this. It was as though he was looking out the window of an invisible airplane, or watching a movie. It was like he was looking out of somebody else's eyes.

The scene below moved to his left, and a gigantic river came into view, meandering, like a snake, through the jungle all the way to the horizon. It reminded him of the films and pictures he had seen of the Amazon, the Nile or the Mississippi.

The lens through which David was seeing all this shifted down, and started to follow the river. He was flying directly over it. The river was multi-dimensional, like a chameleon that adopts the shades and the moods of the world through which it moves. It was like a living creature that encompassed all of life's elements. At times it glittered like a jewel in the glorious sunshine. At others it was a deep blue or a steely gray, reflecting the sky above, or the emerald green of the verdurous growth at its banks. But mostly its murky brown tones spoke of the earth from which it sprang, and the teeming life within its depths.

The lens kept following the river, and up ahead David spotted a large clearing in the massive trees on the right bank of the river, and what appeared to be a primitive village. It consisted of numerous hut-like structures, with thatched roofs, which were built in a series of concentric half-circles, their open ends facing the river, like it was the center of their universe. Most of the structures were simple, one-story bungalows. At the center of these half-circles, and closest to the water, were the two largest edifices, both about the size of an old-fashioned barn on an American farm. They were circular, with conical thatched roofs. The one closest to the water was open at the sides, and bordered by a wall of thick bamboo. The other was covered with a siding of thin logs, placed vertically to the ground, with several windows, which were simply square openings. David thought these must be temples or meeting places. In between the first and the river was a huge circular black pit, surrounded by large stones.

As he moved closer, the lens shifted down, and directly below him in the dark mass of water David spotted the tiny outlines of several brown boats, with pointed bows and sterns, and thin dark strips at their sides that appeared to be oars.

The lens shifted up again, and stopped, with its focus on a point in between the temple closest to the river and the first bungalow in the inner half-circle. It remained there, and didn't move, the image locked in place, like a photograph. A surge of energy shot through David's body. He felt even lighter. Then, it was as though the shutter on the lens blinked, and when it went up, David had been instantaneously transported to that spot, on the ground, in the village, facing the bungalow.

He felt like he was more a part of things, a part of this world. He could feel his feet on the earth, and the tropical heat, and the heavy damp air on the skin of his face and arms. He could now also see, or at least sense, the outlines of his body. Yet, he knew this body wasn't his. Nor was its volition. He was inside Hibutu's body. As far as he could understand, he was there strictly as an observer, or at least his consciousness and his life force were. He also knew with certainty that Kelly was there with him. He could feel her in the space around him.

The bungalow was slightly larger and more formidable than most of the others. He took several steps toward its entrance, a rectangular opening, about six-feet tall, in a wall of bamboo or wood strips. He stopped, as two women came out. The first appeared to be about Hibutu's age, perhaps in her mid-fifties or sixties. The second was quite a bit older.

The younger woman resembled Hibutu in many ways. She was very short, with the same round, dark brown features, and angular dark eyes. Her skin was smooth, and her cheeks were plump and rosy. Her black hair, with the slightest hint of gray, was tied back, and she was wearing a headdress of bright, multi-colored feathers that came to a point on the top. She was wearing a fluffy white blouse, with half-sleeves, and a round neckline, showing the brown skin at the top of her chest, and a plain dark skirt. Wrapped around her neck was a thick, multi-coiled necklace of tiny gold beads. She was also wearing two other necklaces of larger multi-colored beads and stones, one that came to a point in a red heart shaped stone in between her breasts, and the other that was draped all the way down to her upper thighs.

The older woman was dressed much less ceremoniously. Yet, she was just as elegant in her own way, dressed in a plain dark blue dress, and brown sandals strapped around her feet. Her long, thick steel-gray hair was tied back in a ponytail. Her dark eyes shined with a vibrant glow, and she was grinning peacefully, with deep wrinkles around the corners of her mouth that were carved in the same shape as her smile, giving her a look of enduring joy. David thought she must be in her mid-nineties, possibly older. Without his customary frames of reference, it was impossible to figure.

The bungalow was built on a wooden platform about a foot off the ground. The women went down the single step, and gracefully walked toward him.

As David watched them, he became aware of the noises and the activity of the other members of the community, milling around, apparently going about their normal business.

David then noticed that he too was moving, apparently walking in the direction of the women. He had no volition to move this body. He could only observe, and experience, and feel.

When she was a few feet from him, the younger woman stopped, and placed the palms of her hands, one on top of the other, over the red heart-shaped stone in between her breasts. Smiling serenely, she closed her eyes, and bowed her head. When she looked up, her dark eyes were twinkling into David's. She extended her hands, with her palms up, and moved closer to him.

Again, he moved too. David's hands, which were Hibutu's, reached forward into his field of vision, and took the woman's hands. The older woman was standing at her side. Though this body wasn't his, he could feel all its sensations as if it was. Her hands were tiny, yet her grip was firm and resolute. He could feel the warmth of her skin.

As they held hands, her sparkling eyes were locked into his. She smiled broadly, flashing her white shiny teeth. Then her chest swelled with air, raising her shoulders, and she tilted her head to the side, with a furrow of her brow. It was the same intense look of yearning and longing he had seen with Hibutu, like she was reaching out to him with her heart, and inviting his soul to merge with hers.

"Hah," she sighed, in a delicate, melodious tone.

David was transfixed, inert. He had that same feeling that he was going away, blending with her, and everything else around him.

Once again, words popped into his head. They were not sounds, but were more like pictures that he could feel. And he experienced them as much in his body, in his gut and in his heart, as in his mind. They spoke so much more than plain words ever could.

"Mahnya. Welcome. Togi people. Earth love. Earth changes. Thank you."

David instantly knew what this meant. He didn't have to think about it. He and Kelly had been waiting for these messages for three years. They just didn't know what form they would take. As soon as he heard it, it all fit together like the pieces of a spectacular cosmic puzzle. He also sensed again that Kelly was right there with him, taking all this in too. When they returned to their physical bodies in third dimensional reality in South Dakota, they wouldn't even need to discuss it. They would, but they didn't have to.

Mahnya was her name. As she stood before them, holding their hands, her eyes shining into theirs, with the same look of yearning and merging, she continued to paint her picture inside the totality of David and Kelly.

This is what they saw. She and Hibutu were married. They were both shamans with the Togi tribe, located somewhere deep in the jungles of South America. The Togi were a self-sustaining and autonomous people, unknown and untouched by outside civilization, and retaining virtually all of their tribal knowledge and traditions going back thousands, if not tens or hundreds of thousands of years, perhaps more. Though civilized people would call their lifestyle primitive, their consciousness and their sensitivities were highly evolved. They lived in total harmony with nature, and their spirituality was derived from their intimate connection with the earth, including the jungle where they lived, as well as the planet as a whole, and the universe beyond.

The Togi knew, on the basis of their connection with the forces of life, that there was something seriously wrong with the world, and that there were human beings, or other creatures, on the outside, who had lost their connection with the divine spirit, and who presented a serious danger to the planet they loved so dearly. So, they set out to learn about these people, or entities, to see if they could help.

The Togi knew that the material world that people perceive with their five senses in third dimensional reality is only one of countless worlds that are available to human perception. None of these worlds is any more real than any other, and yet the Togi knew that the foundation of everything in the universe was a world of pure energy, governed by an unseen intelligence or spirit, in which everything is connected to everything else. They knew how to connect with this world, how to see this world, and how to act in this world, thereby transcending their physical bodies, and transcending the rules that govern material, third dimensional reality. From the limited perspective of everyday life, this gave them unimaginable powers, among which was the ability to travel inter-dimensionally.

This was how they chose to study the human race, by traveling inter-dimensionally, and observing, undetected, the world outside their village. They learned that the planet Earth was a stage for an intergalactic battle between the forces of good and evil that had been going on for millions of years. The Earth had been visited and inhabited by extraterrestrial beings since far before what has become known as "official" history. The extraterrestrials were of two types, benevolent and malevolent, and the differences were very simple and basic. The benevolent ones chose to live in harmony with the universal laws that governed all life. The malevolent ones didn't. The benevolent ones also had a strict policy of not directly interfering with the affairs of indigenous beings on other planets. The malevolent ones followed no such policy.

The malevolent ET's were involved in a form of rebellion against the creation. This consisted of attempting to usurp the power of the source of creation, the divine spirit, and recast the universe according to different laws, which were of their own making. In other words, they wanted to rewrite the universal laws that were responsible for the universe being created in the first place. To put it bluntly, they wanted to become god, and they believed they could rule the universe according to a different plan, their own.

The complete domination and control of the planet Earth and all of its people was a centerpiece of this project, which they called *The Great Work of the Ages* or the *New World Order*. Throughout the galaxy, Earth, with its rich resources and abundant organic life, was considered a very special place, and to some, quite a prize. The malevolent ET's interbred with the indigenous people of the Earth, creating a race of genetic hybrids, part ET and part human being. These hybrids were also able to shapeshift, which meant they have the ability to appear in either form, much like the shamans and sorcerers from many indigenous cultures, who could transform their bodily form into those of birds, animals, or virtually anything else they chose. Due to their vastly superior intelligence, the hybrids, in the form of the Caucasian or white race, assumed all the major positions of power, including economic, religious, political and educational, and they have been covertly ruling the world for thousands of years. They are commonly referred to as *the global elite*, at least by those who are aware of them.

The global elite own everything, which gives them the awesome power to orchestrate world events, such as wars, financial collapses and ecological disasters, thereby keeping the world in a state of continuous chaos. This is also the primary means by which they maintain their control, as they use it to deceive and manipulate the people of the world into giving up their power and their freedom to them, or at least to the puppet governments that serve them, in order to protect them from all the horrendous chaos, which they have created to begin with.

The ultimate objective of *the global elite* is the *New World Order*, in which their complete ownership and control of the entire planet and all of its people would be complete. This would take the form of a world government, with a world army, a world currency, and all the people of the world would be micro-chipped, and tracked by a global central computer – all of which would be controlled from behind the scenes by *the elite*.

Human beings were important to the malevolent ET's for one other essential reason. They served as food for them. The malevolent ET's fed off the energy or life-force that each human being is born with. In this way, people were farmed, at least those who were slaves to the *New World Order* agenda, much like chickens in chicken coops were farmed by people. This was the age-old pact with the devil. When humans allowed themselves to become slaves, they bartered away their soul in return for the material comforts and the security and protection that the devil has duped them into believing they need.

As people matured, their energy would be mostly consumed, and they were no longer of much value. Children, especially newborns and infants, were particularly important to the malevolent ET's because their energy was fresh, and had not yet been tapped. The ET's could stir up the energy of older people by stimulating negative emotions, such as fear, hatred and aggression, which were natural by-products of all the wars and crises they manufactured, but this recycled energy wasn't as nourishing, or tasty.

Those human beings, like David and Kelly and the Togi, who were free from this bondage, and who had not given up their power, were of particular interest to the ET's because they retained their original energy in all its purity. To put it bluntly, what the ET's were after was the essence, or the soul, or the spirit of humanity. That was their sustenance.

The Togi also learned that there was a deadline to this *New World*

Order scheme, and this coincided with major Earth changes that the Togi knew were soon to occur. These cataclysmic changes occurred periodically over vast periods of time, on the scale of tens of thousands of years. They were able to calculate and predict them based upon their advanced knowledge of the Earth and its cycles, and their oral history, which dated back to the last time such changes occurred. These stories told of the sun rising and setting again on the same spot on the horizon on the same day, of the sun changing directions in the sky, of torrential winds that destroyed everything in their path, and of a great tidal wave that came from the sea, and flooded all the land. The malevolent ET's also knew about these vast geophysical cycles, and they believed their plan had to be complete before they occurred. Otherwise, they would be dealing with forces and variables they didn't understand as well, and the outcome would not be assured.

David was suddenly aware again of the damp jungle heat, and of the birds screeching and the whistling around him. It was as if he was waking up from a dream, but in this case, he was moving from one dream to another.

He looked at Mahnya. Her eyes were fixed on his, but they were glazed. She too appeared to be in a trance. David knew she had communicated all this to him in a way he didn't understand. And yet he knew it all, and he knew it instantly, and completely.

A strange thought popped into his head. Strange because it was his own, separate from Mahnya and Hibutu. During this journey, most of his thoughts were those of another mind. He thought of the year 2012, specifically December 21, 2012 (12/21/12). This was the date that had been prophesized, or calculated, by the Mayans, the Hopis, and so many others, as the turnover point in the great cyclic, cosmic shift. This sounded like what Mahnya was alluding to. The date was now September 2011, and every indication was that the secular powers that ruled this world were rushing, almost desperately, to complete their *New World Order* agenda.

The bubble of David's musing was popped by the sound of laughter and voices. He turned, and saw three young women, perhaps in their mid-twenties or late teens, and a little girl and boy approaching from the direction of the river. They had the same dark features and small round stature as Hibutu and Mahnya. They were wearing plain, thin, gray and brown dresses, and the little boy, a toddler, was naked. Two were carrying baskets filled with wet clothes, and the third was carrying an infant boy.

As they joined them, all eyes were fixed on David, and Kelly. They reminded David of children for whom smiling and laughter was a natural and irrepressible state. No words were spoken. They didn't seem to be necessary, and neither were formalities. They seemed to know and understand each other perfectly, without saying anything, even the infant, who couldn't have been more than four-months old, and whose peaceful, vibrant eyes beamed into David's, as he smiled blissfully. It was as if David belonged in his perfectly safe and ordered world, just like everything else.

After a moment, two young men, perhaps in their twenties or thirties, and a teenage boy emerged from behind the hut. They were wearing only loose fitting shorts that covered their midsections, sandals, small necklaces made out of beads and bones, and plain, functional headbands. Their smooth muscular brown skin rippled and glowed in the hot sunshine. They joined the circle, and locked onto David and Kelly, and the others, with the same look of calm and quiet peacefulness and joy. David felt like they all knew who he was, and why he was here. He felt like he had known them forever, and like he belonged, like they were his people.

David's vision became unfocused and blurred, and he gazed at all of them peripherally, like they were one person. Once again, he started receiving a message, a message without words, a message that he felt in his body, and saw as pictures. But this time it didn't come from Hibutu or Mahnya. It came from all of them. They were all one channel, one mind, one spirit.

"There are many more, like you, like us. Children of the light. Children of the spirit. Children of the new world. We have found them, as we found you. We know who they are, and where they live. And we know what special gifts each has to give to create the new world. It is our job to join with you, and help in the only way we can. It is our job to unite you, and so to move things along. Our role at the current time is a limited one. It is limited to what we are doing now. If you, and the others, fulfill your tasks, then our role will be enhanced, which is what we desire. We are of one mind, one body, one spirit. And our goal is the same. Our goal is to play our part in saving the Earth from the forces of darkness in this time of sacred change. Our goal is to use the forces of this apocalyptic time to create a new world, a world in harmony with the universal laws of the divine spirit. Our goal is to restore the Earth to its rightful place in the galactic union of celestial beings."

David heard the birds in the jungle again, and the world came back into focus. Many other Togi people had joined the circle - men, women and children, of all ages. A pleasant din arose from them, and all eyes were on him, as they smiled and giggled playfully and serenely. And again, these sounds were not words, and yet their meaning was crystal clear.

"Ah." "Mm." "Ha."

David felt like he was immersed in a pool of communion and love.

He was also reminded again that his body was not his own, and its actions were not his. Out of these eyeholes, he saw two brown-skinned arms reach in front of him toward the crowd, like they were his, with the palms held up. Those who were close enough reached out, and tenderly clasped these arms and hands. The others reached as far as possible in his direction. Those who were alongside him patted and stroked his shoulders and back with their hands and fingers. David felt all this as if this body was his. He felt himself slipping away, disappearing into them, like they were one body.

"Ah." "Mm." Ha."

The chatter started to fade, and the Togi people started to glow, as did the hands and arms held in front of him. It was happening again. The shapes and the colors of the material world were blurring, and everything, the Togi, the thatched huts behind them, the tangle of jungle, the thick puffy clouds in the spectacular blue sky, was merging back into the realm of infinite light. Just like before, it all slowly dissolved. Soon all was silent. All there was, was light and awareness. They were traveling again. Timeless traveling. Traveling on beams of light through dimensions we cannot see, hear, touch, taste or smell. That was the only awareness, the only reality there was.

David's breath and heartbeat started to return, and the world slowly started to take shape again. The air was cool and moist this time. As the colors and forms congealed, he was again perched high in the air, flying in the invisible flying machine. An immaculate dark blue sky came into view above, and a vast city below that stretched as far as the eye could see, with a skyline of massive skyscrapers, and a huge lake in the middle, with several large islands protruding. The blue-gray water, dotted with sailboats, ferries and fishing boats, rippled like a giant washboard in the wind below. The terrain was green and undulating, almost mountainous, and numerous steep hills poked through the expanse of the city. Then, David spotted something that pinpointed undoubtedly where he was. He'd seen this countless times. It was a massive bridge, cluttered with traffic, with an elaborate series of arches and cables, extending from one coast to the other.

The Golden Gate Bridge. San Francisco.

Again, the shutter went down over the lens that was viewing all this, like the blink of an eye, and David found himself inside a studio, which upon closer examination was a scientific laboratory of some kind. The room was brightly lit by the radiant sunlight that shined in several open windows. Curtains fluttered in the cool breeze. Scattered about in a state of considerable disarray was a vast accumulation of electronic and laboratory paraphernalia – monitors, disassembled computers, circuit boards, glass vials and beakers, gas burners, and gadgetry of every kind. There were wires and tubes and sockets and connectors and devices everywhere. There were also several mechanical contraptions lying about that were unlike anything David had ever seen before, and he had no idea what they were.

In one darkened corner, with the shade pulled over the window, sat a man at a desk, his back to them, in front of a computer monitor, typing at a keyboard. The desk around him was cluttered with papers, folders and pamphlets, and on either side of him were tables that were stacked high with books, several of them open. The lens scanned the room, and the entire lab appeared to be makeshift, thrown together with cheap, plain tables and furniture, the bare essentials. David thought that this man had either just moved in, or was using this as a temporary shop.

The lens shifted back to the man, and as if on cue, he stopped typing, and looked up into the space before him. He rolled back on his swivel chair, swung around, and glanced quizzically around the room, and up and down. It was as though he heard something, as though he sensed he was not alone. But he didn't look directly at them. He didn't know they were there.

His face was round and full, and his expression was soft and gentle. His thick dark brown hair was just over his ears, thinning slightly in the front, and he had a thick, neatly cropped half-beard. The first strands of gray were showing on his temples, and the tip of his beard. He was wearing round, thin-framed, scholarly glasses, through which his sparkly brown eyes shined. He had on a gaudy, blue Hawaiian shirt, with white fish printed on it, khaki shorts, and old, worn white tennis shoes, with no socks.

David liked him instantly, and felt a strong affinity for this man, whoever he was.

The man got up, and strolled to the middle of the room, stopped, and looked pensively around him. He closed his eyes, and took a deep breath, folding his hands upon the middle of his torso. He was grinning placidly, the lines around his eyes and forehead smooth, and like the Togi people, he was the picture of serenity.

He opened his sparkly brown eyes, and glanced around the room again with a playfully suspicious smirk. He reminded David of somebody who was about to arrive at a surprise birthday party that he already knew about. David felt certain he sensed their presence. He wondered whether Hibutu had been to visit him before, and whether they had journeyed together.

The man walked to one of the open windows, leaned his shoulder against its frame, and peered out. He squinted as the bright sun lit up his face. A puff of wind blew in the window, like it was on cue, and rustled his thick brown hair.

David had that light and blurry sensation of going off again, and once again, thoughts were inserted into him. Like before, no words, but suddenly, they were there, in place, a part of him, and he understood completely.

"You must watch all this closely because at this point we are limited in what we can tell you. This man has his task to perform, his particular skill, as do you, as do we. We are all of one mind and spirit in saving the Earth from a dark fate. There are others, and you must meet, if we are to succeed in this great endeavor. There are forces that will take you to him, and to the others, but you must be awake to them. This is no easy task, as these forces are inexplicable to your rational mind. You must be impeccably alert and vigilant, and you must trust the mysterious path that the divine spirit places before you. The new world we will create together will be completely different. You do not yet understand the magnitude of just how different. This we will show you."

David was in a trance as he played all this back in his head. His eyes were open, but he didn't see anything. All his energy was devoted to the message.

When the message was finished, he popped out of this state, and the world before his eyes came back into view.

What he saw was completely different, just like the message had said.

The lab, the windows, the curtains, the makeshift furniture, and all the techno paraphernalia was still there, but now its materiality looked fainter, and it appeared as though it was in the background. It was as though it was there, and yet it wasn't. In the forefront of this vision, the entire world was a spectacular lattice of luminous lines or fibers, which appeared to be shimmering or pulsating, as if they were alive. This dimension of energy appeared to overlap that of the material world. It was an indescribably intricate spider web of luminosity that extended everywhere. Even the walls of the lab now had a kind of translucency, and the lattice spread through them into the world outside, and beyond. This luminous lattice also had the appearance of something David clearly saw, and understood in his altered state of consciousness, but which had no precedent in the everyday world of linear logic. All these fibers crisscrossed in every conceivable direction, and yet none of them intersected any of the others. It was like they were all simultaneously connected and disconnected.

The man at the window, the only organic form of life in the room, no longer had the physical appearance of a human being. He was a luminous, egg-shaped ball, approximately the same height and width as before, and surrounded by an iridescent hue. At the midsection of this luminous egg, there was a point, about the size of a dime, like a belly button, through which a countless number of the fibers passed, and again, contrary to all logic, without touching each other. Toward the top of the egg, on the opposite side, there was another point through which countless fibers passed in the same manner. This one was larger, about the size of a tennis ball. If the egg still had its human form, it would have been at the height of the shoulders, about a foot from the body.

Within the lab, there were two other places where the fibers converged or flowed in this manner. One was a small bottle of water on one of the tables, and the other was a small refrigerator on the opposite side of the room from where the man had been sitting, where there were several points through which the lines flowed. The other material objects in the room also had luminous configurations, but they were not as vivid and distinct as the luminous egg of the man.

The magnitude and intricacy of this magnificent lattice was unfathomable, beyond rational comprehension, beyond the scope of words to describe. Through the translucent walls of the lab, David could see several large trees outside on the street. They too had their own configurations of energy, and points through which the fibers flowed. Beyond them he could not discern any other people or distinct material objects, but he could see that the entire cosmos, in all its dimensions, consisted of configurations of energy, and points through which the luminous fibers flowed, all within this grand, infinite lattice, where everything touched everything else, and yet was distinct at the same time – so complex, and yet so perfectly simple.

Outside the translucent walls of the lab, David could see beyond the limits of his customary vision in the normal world. He saw the lattice of fibers extending to the horizon of the Pacific Ocean, where a thick bank of fog rested. He saw it stretching over the surf and the rugged shoreline to the north. He saw it reaching into the deep blue sky, and again in an image of overlapping dimensions, he could see it extending into the star and galaxy-blotched blackness beyond.

David's eyes popped open.

He was in his bed of quilts and blankets on the floor in his cabin in South Dakota. It was morning, and the sun was shining in the open window.

Kelly was nestled up behind him, like a spoon, her naked flesh warm against his.

He was totally wide-awake. He didn't feel like he had even been asleep. He had the strangest sensation that his physical body had just been placed there. He had received his sign. The journey was complete, the message conveyed, and he had been transported back to his bed in the blink of an eye – no wasted energy.

He turned over, and put his arms around Kelly.

She too was wide-awake, her eyes wide open.

They looked into each other's eyes, and breathed together.

They both knew. David felt like he did when the messages were inserted into him. It was all there, complete and perfect. They didn't need to say anything.

Kelly took a deep breath, and sighed.

"Togi people," she whispered.

He nodded.

"San Francisco," he replied, mirroring her.

They breathed together in the total silence of the cool morning, their eyes locked together, waves of electricity passing between them.

"*The Shift*," she whispered again. "The new world."

"Forces will show us the way," he echoed.

She smiled, stroking his back.

"We're going to be leaving here soon."

He knew this was true, without knowing what form it would take.

Just then, a vivid sound broke the silence, off in the distance. They both heard it at the same time. It was faint, but unmistakable. It was the sound of automobile tires grinding along the dirt and rock road that led to the shack, and the hum of an engine.

Nobody ever came there. Nobody knew they were there. The only visitor they ever had was Robert Flying Hawk, the young native shaman, who had taught them so much. Occasionally he was joined by his grandmother, Kathy Spotted Deer. The only other people who knew they were there were several of the other natives from the town of Sanderson on the Reservation. None of them would have told anybody that they were there.

This was definitely not Flying Hawk's truck, which was an old pick-up that rattled and clattered, the engine grumbling, as it bounced along the pot-holed road.

"Who the hell?" David muttered, shaking his head.

Kelly raised her eyebrows and grinned, like the wild twists of fate amused her.

"Let's go see."

TWO ❀ ACQUIESCENCE

Florida.

The license plates on the silver Mercedes said, "Florida."

David and Kelly were standing in the sunshine in the open doorway as it drove up. The day was quickly warming up. He had thrown on a pair of maroon volleyball shorts, and she khaki cutoffs and a yellow tank top.

They recognized the car immediately. How could they ever forget? It had been their getaway car.

"It's them!" David blurted exuberantly.

Kelly giggled impulsively.

It had been a little over three years since they had seen Peter and Janice Hoagland. Peter and Janice were the ones who rescued them from the volcanic eruption that decimated the tiny Caribbean island of Martinelle, in which thousands died. They took David and Kelly by their private yacht back to their home in Florida, and then drove them to the Pine Ridge Reservation in South Dakota, where they could hide out, and be safe. That seemed to be the only way. David and Kelly were in too much danger otherwise.

As they pulled up to the shack, they honked the horn loudly and jubilantly several times. Janice was poking her head out the window on the passenger side, and waving excitedly.

"Hi-eee!" She shrieked like a teenager.

David and Kelly were laughing uncontrollably.

They parked next to the rusty, old, red pickup truck in front of the shack. David and Kelly slipped on their sandals next to the door, and went to greet them.

"Surprise!" Peter bellowed, as he opened his door.

"Not waking you up, are we?" Janice chimed in.

They looked like they were born to be together. They were both darkly tanned from the Florida sunshine, wearing fashionable sunglasses, with clean, slightly faded blue jeans, with a crease, and white, designer sneakers. He was fiftyish, and she mid-fortyish. He was bald on the top, and his neatly cut silver hair, combed meticulously back on the sides, gave him a distinguished and elegant look. She was the female version of him, or perhaps it was the other way around. She was wearing a red and black Tampa Bay Bucks cap, and her poofy brown hair hung out the hole in the back in a ponytail. They were both wearing neat, clean T-shirts, tucked in. His was plain black, and hers was white, with an exotic and brightly colored sun on the front, advertising some festival. They were both very physically fit.

The couples came together, and hugged and kissed.

"What are you guys doing here?" Kelly chirped.

"Well, we're taking a little road trip," Janice replied. "And we wanted to pop in, and see how things were going."

"Actually, it's a little more than that," Peter added, more soberly. "When this trip came up, we both just knew we had to come see you. It was just one of those things. And we both felt it so strongly we didn't even bother sending word to your friends in Sanderson. We just knew."

"And we knew you'd be here too," Janice piped in. "Dig that."

"Hmm. Hmm." David chuckled. "Then we'll be finding out why very shortly."

Peter's eyes gazed past them at the shack and the space around it. It was a one room log cabin, with a steep pitched roof covered with slabs of tin and sheet metal that looked like it had been gathered from the local dump or wrecking yard. There was a huge stone fireplace and chimney on one end, and a round metal chimney, with a crown, for a wood stove, sticking out of the roof on the other. Adjoining the cabin, next to the stone chimney, was a makeshift lean-to green house, covered with panels made from sheets of thick, clear plastic. Behind the cabin, on the far side, there was an old dilapidated wooden barn, and behind that an old-fashioned, one-seater out-house. Next to the barn was a gigantic pile of firewood. On the other side of the barn was a large pen, in which there was a small herd of goats. It was fenced in on the sides and the top with chicken-wire and in the back there was a small wooden lean-to shed. Inside the open door you could see clumps of fresh hay and grass and weed clippings. Next to the woodpile, there was another pen, almost identical to the other one, except smaller and with a smaller shed. This one was filled with chickens.

Behind the woodpile and the chicken pen, there was a huge resplendent vegetable garden, at the late stages of summer maturity, and bursting with growth and vitality. It was surrounded by a wood frame fence, with chicken wire tacked to it. In front, leaning against the fence, there was a row of giant sunflowers, their petals withered, and their massive heads drooping with age. Inside was a thick tangle of verdurous leaves, of every shape and size, grown in raised beds and clusters, and overgrowing the narrow, packed-mud paths that separated them. The soil surrounding the plants, at least where you could see it, was covered with thick layers of mulch, consisting of decayed straw and weeds. Within this mass of life, Peter could discern beans climbing up tall wooden poles, peas entwined in the chicken wire fence, and tomatoes drooping from their vines.

"Wow. It looks remarkably the same," Peter commented, "and remarkably different. You guys have really done a lot. That funky old roof's the same though."

"That is the best roof ever built by the hand of man," David crowed. "Three winters, and no leaks. Not a drop."

Janice was busy looking too, but she was looking more at them than their surroundings.

"We might say the same thing about you guys," she said. "You look the same, and yet totally different."

She shook her head bewilderedly.

"Something's different. You look fantastic."

Standing before Janice were the two most remarkable people she had ever known. Kelly was one of her oldest and best friends, going all the way back to childhood. She had only known David for a few months, meeting during their ordeal in Martinelle, but what a power packed couple of months that was.

Looking at them now she felt an intense closeness and connection with them, and yet the strangest sense they were now from another world. Kelly was a strikingly beautiful woman, a few years younger than Janice, with big blue eyes, and a large mouth full of big shiny teeth. Yet her beauty had become as raw and rustic as the South Dakota wilderness surrounding them. There were no pretenses. Her thin, straight, sun bleached, brown hair flopped randomly about her forehead and shoulders. The skin of her entire body was dark brown, just a few shades below black. Like the sun rising over the tall trees, her beauty was beyond esthetics. It was in the glow of her eyes and toothy smile. It was in the sweet melodious tone of her voice. It was in the smooth rhythmical movements of her lean, hard body.

A glance at David told the same story. This was a young man who belonged to the earth, the wind and the sun. He was younger than the rest, in his mid-twenties now. His dark brown shade was the same as Kelly's. His build was slight, but his muscles were wiry and well chiseled. The most remarkable thing about David's features was how unremarkable they were. Everything about him, his nose, his mouth, his cheeks, his chin, his ears, was plain and normal. Nothing was too big or too small, too sharp or too round. Everything was so average that it was difficult to decide if he looked boring or classically handsome.

His straight brown hair was parted in the middle, and down to his shoulders. The only thing that stuck out about David was his bright blue-green eyes that sparkled like pools of water in the morning sunshine. His eyes changed everything. Looking into his eyes was like looking into the depths of infinity. You could get lost in his eyes.

"Have you guys been here the entire time?" Peter asked.

"We just got back from South America," Kelly quipped, grinning.

She and David looked at each other, and giggled.

"It'll take some explaining," David said. "We'll get to it, but yeah, we've been here the whole time."

"How much do you know about what's going on on the outside?" Peter added.

"We know," David said. "They bring us a paper every once in a while, about every month, or so. We read as much as we can stomach. Last one was about two weeks ago."

"You're pretty up on things then," Peter nodded.

"We have some other ways too," Kelly said, "some other sources, but we'll get to that too."

"I'll bet you do," Janice chuckled. "Remember who you're talking to here, honey."

"It's so much bigger than that," Kelly continued, soberly. "So much bigger than you guys realize, than what you read in the papers, or see on TV. This is really, really huge, huge beyond your wildest imagination."

"Nothing you could do or say would ever surprise us anymore," Janice said. "Ever since that day on the boat. We know there's more. We just have no idea what. That's what we need you guys for. We knew there was a reason we had to come here."

The three years that David and Kelly had been in South Dakota had been the most momentous in the history of the world. The United States Government and the State of Israel had instigated a full-scale world war in the Middle East by dropping nuclear bombs on Iran and Syria. They claimed that this was preventive due to definitive proof that terrorist cells were about to launch an attack on them with biological weapons. Validation of this alleged proof was never provided for security reasons. At least that's what they said.

This forced the other major nations to take sides. China and Russia allied themselves with the Muslim nations of the Middle East. With the exception of Great Britain, the nations of the European Union opposed the US's actions, and stayed neutral, as did the EU as a whole.

This amounted to an act of war, but not of a military nature. It was a money war. The battle between the US dollar and the euro became tantamount, as they competed for supremacy in the world financial markets, and top dog as the world's reserve currency. The first domino to fall was when China decided to totally cease funding the US debt by purchasing US bonds, and switched to the euro for its purchases of oil and other international transactions. Russia was next to follow, and soon there was an international stampede away from the dollar. The US economy quickly went into a state of hyperinflation, and it was not long before the dollar collapsed totally. However, the US economy, particularly its purchasing of foreign goods and services, had been the prop holding up the global economy for too long, and when it caved in, the entire global economy collapsed. Soon all the world currencies were close to worthless.

A global economic depression unparalleled in the history of the world followed. No nation was untouched. Social and political chaos, lawlessness and crime, hunger and starvation were rampant, and millions of people around the world died. The US was impotent to continue the war, and those American soldiers who were stranded in the Middle East without lifelines were soon easy targets.

The United Nations in New York City had never been formally disbanded, and the leaders of the major nations, The EU, China, The US, Russia, Japan and India, decided to hold secret, top-level meetings to try to find a solution to this global disaster. The actual attendees of those meetings were never disclosed to the public, but a plan did emerge, and the decision was made to use the structure of the United Nations to implement it.

The cornerstone of the plan was financial. It involved the elimination of all the world's currencies, both paper and those backed by precious metals, and replacing them with a global system of money that would be cashless and electronic. To protect the system, and for purposes of security, at least allegedly, any person who wanted to participate in this system had to consent to become a member of a global central data bank. This meant receiving a medical examination, relinquishing all of one's personal information and history, and receiving a microchip implant for the purpose of scanning any time a financial transaction was made. Personal computers were modified to include this scanning feature. There was no more use of credit, debit or ID cards of any kind, including driver's licenses and passports. Everything was done by electronic scan. The microchip was implanted in the back of the wrist, just above the base of the hand.

The plan also eliminated all national sovereignty. People were told that this would eliminate wars, and that the existence of separate nation states was the cause of most of the world's problems. The United Nations was now the supreme authority, and its name was changed to the United Union. Nations were now called regions, and the former nations were joined to form the new regions.

There were five regions: the American, European, Asian, African and Australian. The American Region consisted of the US, Canada, Mexico, Central and South America. The eventual plan was the elimination of these regions too, and the merging of all of them into one global union. The United Union was referred to as just the Union, and the microchip was affectionately called the *uni*.

"Doesn't seem like it's affected you guys much, "David said. "Same car. Same sun tan. Same smiling faces. Same old lovable yuppies."

"Hasn't," Peter said, with a shake of his head. "Everything's the same. I'm with the same firm, doing the same thing. Things were very bad for a while there, when things first crashed. It was like back to the Stone Age. Boy, can we tell you some stories. Very scary. But then things returned to normal, at least for us."

Peter was an attorney for one of the most prestigious corporate law firms, representing many of the largest banks and companies, both domestic and international.

"It's still pretty awful in a lot of places," Janice nodded. "Especially the cities, and the inner cities are a total disaster. They're a jungle, a war zone, definitely not safe. Dead bodies on the street, that kind of thing. At least that's what we're told, and we're not about to check it out. But out in the burbs, life goes on pretty much as usual."

"In a weird way," Peter added, "people with means have been bought off, and the rest have been left to die. And hell, it's way beyond us. We don't know what to do about it."

David and Kelly looked at them in silence. This was their first flesh and blood exposure to the world they had left nearly three years ago, and all the pieces weren't fitting together yet. In particular, there was one missing piece that was sticking out, like the proverbial 800-pound, purple gorilla. They didn't even need to say the words.

"We got chipped," Janice said bluntly, as if she was reading their minds. She extended her hand.

"See. There's the little fucker you're probably wondering about."

It looked like a tiny white bead, like a miniscule pearl, in the soft spot on the back of her wrist, barely visible.

David and Kelly were speechless. They didn't know what to think.

A twinge of fear shot through David's body, like electricity. It was like a reflex that had been conditioned by all his previous experiences with those outside forces, which had almost killed him. Suddenly all this garbage was stirred up, and swirling around in his head, like bad dreams. He trusted Peter and Janice totally, and yet far stranger things had happened, things that he still had no rational explanation for. Just when he thought he was beyond their reach, they would pop back into the picture, again and again.

Again, he didn't need to say the words.

Peter reached out, and gripped him affectionately by the shoulder.

"Don't worry, you guys," he said softly, his eyes flipping back and forth between them. "We're flying completely beneath the radar. We wouldn't have come here otherwise. You know that. They're not watching us. They don't suspect us of anything. They think we're one of them."

Pieces were still missing. David and Kelly waited, silently.

"We all have our part to play, right?" Janice added, filling in the vacuum. "At least that's what you told us when we brought you here. It made sense. We believed you. Except then none of us knew what our parts were. All you knew was you had to get away, and hide out for a while. And we…well, we didn't know what to think. We didn't know diddly. Now we do."

"Somebody had to be spies," Peter said. "It might as well be us."

He paused.

"There's two worlds out there now: those who are chipped, and those who aren't. There's a lot of people like you, who said no. And now they're in deep shit. They've basically had to go underground. Cant' buy anything. Can't conduct any business, except on the black market, which right now deals strictly in barter, no money. And the cops have become total pigs; busting people for anything they want. It's not against the law not to be chipped, but it might as well be. And those people need a go-between. That's where we fit in."

"And it's a good fit," Janice chimed in. "We're perfect. We just look like a couple of well-to-do yuppies, who want to keep living the good life."

She took a deep breath, raising her eyebrows.

"You know we care just as much about all this as you do."

She caught herself, and laughed.

"Well, maybe not as much as you guys, but you get what I mean. We know what's going on, and we want to do the right thing. This is where we can do the most good, like with you guys."

"Us?" Kelly asked.

"Yeah. We took you to David. We got you off that island, sort of. And we got you this far. And now…well, we just knew we had to come."

Kelly looked at David, and back at them.

"The timing does seem perfect for us too," she said. "We've known for awhile that our time here was coming to a close. And last night we had this incredible experience, which confirmed all that. We'll have to tell you about that. And now this morning, presto, here you are."

Most of the pieces for David had settled into place, but a few did remain.

"Help me out a little bit here," he said. "Can't they track you wherever you go, put thoughts into your head, and control how you feel, even how you perceive things?"

"Can, but don't, and won't," Peter replied. "They've got bigger fish to fry. They're not worried about us - don't give us a second thought. They already think we're brainwashed, that we believe all their shit. And we've been playing our part well. And even if they do track us to an Indian reservation in South Dakota, so what? Just a couple of liberal, do-gooders, who want to help the Indians. We can tell. I'm still me. She's still her. And there's nothing to worry about."

David reached a point he had reached many times during the last four years, ever since that fateful day he had crossed the line, and cracked over into that world that average people can't see. He was dealing with forces and powers he didn't understand, and if he allowed himself, it would be easy to never trust anybody or anything ever again. But if he was to move forward with what was most important, and that was living, and playing his part to try to rid the world of this evil, then it was imperative to make choices regarding what he trusted, and what he didn't. And invariably, he always fell back upon the one thing he knew he could trust above all else: his intuition, and how he felt in his gut. It had guided him this far, and he was exactly where he needed to be. There comes a point where the rational part of our mind hits a wall, and beyond that we must use the other parts of our totality, the totality of our mind, body and spirit. And here, his gut, his heart, and his higher self told him it was OK.

He and Kelly looked at each other, and their look said it all. She was on the same wavelength. He knew it. She knew it.

"You guys hungry?" She chirped.

"Starved!" Janice exclaimed.

"Let's rustle up some breakfast. I hope vegetables and eggs are OK. If not, tough shit."

She laughed.

"We'll whip you up a feast you'll never forget."

The boys went to the chicken pen to gather eggs, and the girls to the garden to pick vegetables. When they were finished, David split some wood, and he and Peter made a fire in the pit outside the front door.

The girls went down to the creek, which babbled through the tall trees next to the shack, to wash the dirt off the vegetables. The boys could hear them sloshing and laughing, and then Janice's piercing squeal when it sounded like she fell into the chilly water.

They frolicked up the bank of the creek, chattering like teenagers, with a load of potatoes and onions and a huge wooden bowl of green beans. One of the legs of Janice's jeans was totally soaked.

"How about scrambled eggs, fried potatoes, and steamed beans," Kelly playfully proclaimed. "A breakfast fitting these city folks."

Their mirth was contagious, and spread instantly to the boys.

"Awe shit!" Peter barked. "Not scrambled eggs and fried potatoes again. We're on vacation. No eggs Sardeau and Hollandaise?"

They all laughed.

"Hey hon," Kelly went on. "That corn is done. Can't wait any longer. Let's have some tonight, along with one of our killer salads."

Each had their task. There were potatoes and onions to slice, beans to cut, and eggs to whip. David continued to add wood to the fire, and when a bed of coals had formed, he placed a large metal grate over it. Kelly took one of the steel pots down to the creek to get water for steaming, and when she returned she also had a glass bottle that was half filled with milk, and a glass container with a chunk of butter inside.

"This stuff is really precious in the summertime, without any refrigeration," she said. "But we still do it. It's just a lot of trouble. In the winter we can use the snow, and make our own ice, and just keep things outside."

"The world is just one big refrigerator," David joked.

"How much of all this do you do yourself," Peter asked, shaking his head.

"Everything, just about," Kelly replied. "We cheat sometimes. Flying Hawk and Kathy and some of the others bring us stuff from time to time. Rice and bread, stuff like that. Old clothes and blankets. We haven't learned how to do everything for ourselves yet, but with time, we will. And of course, the goats and the chickens. They got us started with that. And they bring us a bail of hay every once in a while."

"Red Cloud and Kathy had lived here a long time, and when we first got here, the place was pretty well stocked with pots and pans and dishes, and everything we needed for the garden and the house, like tools and watering cans. There were even a couple of hoses and a big trough they used to collect water, and irrigate the garden by running them down the hill. And they brought us the wood stove. Boy, was that ever nice. And the plastic for the greenhouse and some two-by-fours."

David and Kelly moved to the Pine Ridge Indian Reservation in Sanderson, South Dakota because they didn't know where else to go. They knew it was the correct thing to do, but at the time, they had no idea why. Little did they know what a perfect fit it would turn out to be.

David knew about Pine Ridge from an internship he had done as a pre-med student several years earlier. He attended a small, liberal arts college in Ohio, where he received college credits for working at the infirmary on the

Reservation. He had always wanted to be a doctor, and he was just becoming aware that he had special gifts as an intuitive healer, as his mother, a psychic and spiritual medium, had been. At that time, David didn't understand how he did the things he did. All he knew was when he instinctively followed nature's laws, as he understood them, and went with the rhythm and flow of things, as he felt them, miraculous things seemed to happen. He always believed he was the way he was because he was born and raised by such an extraordinary mother. The bond between a mother and child is a mysterious and powerful connection, and he still felt his with her.

One day at the infirmary, David saved the life of a man who was bleeding to death from a chain saw accident. There was not enough time to call the nearest hospital, and if not for David, he certainly would have died. There was no rational explanation for what he did that day, other than he had possessed this man with his spirit, and imbued him with the faith to stop his own bleeding. As a token of his gratitude, the man took David to meet his great grandfather, a shaman and sorcerer named Red Cloud. Red Cloud lived in the shack where David and Kelly now lived, together with his daughter, Spotted Deer, also known as Kathy to the white people. The shack was located in the wilderness, in a remote part of the Reservation, about a half-hour drive from the actual community of Sanderson. Nobody, aside from their immediate family and a small group of insiders, knew they were there.

David's meeting with Red Cloud was a major turning point in his life, and the first in a series of monumental and mysterious events that were to become the norm from that point on. David's mother, Celine, had been murdered when he was four years old in ritualistic fashion by what appeared to be a satanic cult. Her heart was cut out, and she was hung from a bridge in downtown Chicago, where they lived. Just prior to her murder, she wrote a letter to David, which she mailed to her sister Dorothy. She wrote that she was in danger, and she feared she was going to be killed. She instructed Dorothy to give the letter to David when he was old enough to understand.

Dorothy took custody of young David, who was extremely precocious, like an adult in a child's body, and gave him the letter when he was thirteen. In it, Celine expressed that she was in grave danger because her psychic abilities had given her the power to see into a dimension that was beyond the scope of perception of normal human beings. She didn't yet understand any of this, but she was beginning to see an evil, alien presence that was masquerading in human form. These beings could also see that she saw them. Hence, her plight.

Celine also believed that these evil forces had tampered with humanity, its natural development, and its history. This explained how humanity had allowed itself to go so far off its natural course, and why the world had been transformed from the paradise nature designed it to be into a place of such chaos and misery. She also implored David to continue her quest to uncover these truths, and to break the chains that held humanity in bondage.

"What can you tell me of the forces of evil in the world?" David asked Red Cloud, five years later.

Red Cloud instantly saw that David was a white man with special gifts. He also told him that his appearance was an omen that he had been waiting for that day. He then shared information that had been passed down from his ancestors over many thousands of years, and which filled in the gaps in his mother's letter. He told him that the white man's world was a trick, a lie, which had been perpetrated by evil beings who came from flaming ships in the sky many thousands of years ago. The purpose of this trick was to keep the human race enslaved. It was also a simple matter for humanity to defeat this plan, but it depended on one crucial factor. Human beings had to truly want to be free. Reclaiming responsibility for their own lives, coupled with waking up to the truth about how they had been scammed, would create an environment that the evil beings simply could not tolerate, and they would go away, in search of other worlds to infest. Red Cloud also told David that he might be the one to set his people and the world free.

When Red Cloud died, Kathy returned to Sanderson to be with the rest of her family, and the shack was left vacant for two years. It was also about two years after his meeting with Red Cloud that David slipped into that same dimension as his mother, and started seeing the alien beings. He was in his first semester of medical school in Chicago. His descent into this dimension was far more abrupt and drastic than his mother's, and he was in immediate danger. He had several sightings on his first day, and they knew who he was, and that he posed a threat to their cover.

David's sightings varied in their appearance, but there were a few common traits. These beings were still humanoid, but with a reptilian quality. Their skin took on a greenish hue, and often there was the same greenish aura around them, particularly around the head, like a mist. The most predominant characteristic was what Red Cloud referred to as the evil eye. Their eyes were wider and rounder than normal humans, and the pupil was a narrow, black, vertical slit. This made the whites of their eyes more prominent, and gave them a cold, piercing, and flashing look. Another common feature of these sightings was a sickening feeling of revulsion and repulsion that David felt in his own body when he was in their presence, which were totally unprecedented for him.

David immediately dropped out of medical school, which was infested with these beings, and fled to rural Wisconsin, where he hoped to hide out, and be safe. Here, guided by mysterious forces and circumstances, he met Kelly.

They instantly knew they were soul mates, and he moved into her small house in the woods on Hickory Lake. He lived with her there in apparent anonymity for a little over six months, until destiny ripped them apart. The evil beings had somehow discovered his whereabouts, and on a hot, full moon lit night, when Kelly was away visiting friends, they appeared at Hickory Lake to eliminate him, as they had his mother. Again trusting the unfathomable power of his higher awareness, and with the guidance of nature spirits, who had recently contacted him, he made a miraculous escape. The nature spirits had shown him, for the first time, the world of light beyond form where spectacular feats are possible, and he was able to use this new power to make his escape. So now, he was not only capable of seeing into different dimensions, but he had also acted in one of them.

Knowing he had to stay away from Kelly because they obviously would be watching her too, David fled to the mountains of Colorado, where he rendezvoused with an underground author, David Reich. Reich was attempting to expose the scam perpetrated by the evil forces in his books. Knowing they kept a close eye on Reich, he and David, along with Reich's circle of friends and associates, hatched a plot to use David's power to see the evil beings to capture one of them, and expose their scam to the world on film. They planned to do this at a conference on the tiny Caribbean island of Martinelle, at which Reich was the keynote speaker.

Meanwhile, Kelly knew about David's plans to meet with Reich, and if he was alive, which she strongly sensed he was, she knew that was where he would go. Obviously strongly impacted by her time with David, shortly after their estrangement, she also slipped into that dimension where she could see the evil beings. Now she was in the same danger. She also tracked Reich's speaking engagements on the Internet, and she strongly suspected that David would be with him in Martinelle. So, she contacted her two close friends, Janice and Peter Hoagland in Florida, and made arrangements for them to take her on their yacht to Martinelle for the conference.

When the time came, their sting at the conference in Martinelle was working exactly according to plan. However, unbeknownst to them, the evil forces were one step ahead of them. They had knowledge and power that far exceeded anything human beings could even imagine. During the sting, while Reich was on stage, and as David was doing his part from the control room, the tiny island was struck by a violent earthquake, and its dormant volcano erupted. Two of the evil beings appeared in the control room, and attempted to kidnap David, but Kelly appeared, as if by magic, and rescued him, shooting one of them, as the other vanished with the aid of a high tech device. This turned out to be the most dramatic sighting for either of them. When it was dead on the floor, this being transformed entirely into a lizard-like creature, complete with course scales covering its body, claws for fingers and toes, horn-like nodules coming out of its head, and wings that folded over its chest. Then, it too vanished.

The conference center was total mayhem, and it was crumbling around them into a heap of rubble. Their only hope of escape was to once again trust the awesome power of their higher awareness and their newly discovered inter-dimensional capabilities, which David didn't yet know Kelly had. Just as Hibutu had transported their energy bodies on the wings of pure light to the jungle of South America, and again with the help of the omnipresent nature spirits who watched over David, David and Kelly transported themselves out of the conference center, and off the island. When they materialized, they were on the deck of Peter and Janice's yacht, as it fled the volcanic devastation. Kelly had told them about David, and many of the extraordinary things she was experiencing in her life. It was a stretch, but they knew her well enough to know there must be something to it. When she and David popped in out of nowhere, they became true believers.

There were practically no survivors on Martinelle. David Reich, who had become another of David's soul mates, his wife Linda, and his entire entourage, of which David had become a part, were killed that day.

The vegetables were cut, the eggs whipped, and the fire ready. Kelly plopped a hunk of the butter into a large cast iron frying pan, and placed it on the grate.

"Hon, would you get me the salt and pepper, and the spatula," she asked David. "More cheating. What a luxury it is to have salt and pepper."

"What about in the winter?" Peter continued, shaking his head again. "What do you guys do?"

"David heap big hunter," Kelly laughed. "We eat a lot of meat. Rabbit. Quail. Deer. Plus, a lot of eggs, milk and cheese, of course. Flying Hawk taught David how to hunt and trap. We've also gotten real good at stretching out what we grow in the garden, and freezing and drying some of it. We mulch the potatoes and carrots so heavily that they keep even when there's snow on the ground. And we eat tomatoes as late as January because we've learned how to ripen the green ones real slowly inside."

David had returned.

"Survival," he said bluntly. "That's why we're here. To learn how to survive independently in the world. To learn how to take care of ourselves, and our basic needs, without being dependent on civilization to do it for us. We didn't understand that when we first got here. But pretty soon it became clear."

He spread out his arms, and shook his head from side to side, his eyes rolling around in the top of their sockets, to indicate the vast expanse surrounding him.

"That's why this place, and these people, are so special. And why we were drawn here. When the world out there falls apart, somebody's got to have the knowledge, the know how, to build it back up again. And do it properly this time. We're going to be starting from scratch. And we're going to be creating a completely different world. One that's governed by a totally different set of rules. One that's completely beyond our imagination. And one where people take care of themselves, instead of government and the system doing it for them. Kind of like the dolphins. Dolphins don't need government. They're completely in the rhythm and flow of things, and once people return to that state, life won't be a problem."

He nodded at Kelly.

"We think that's what our role is. That's the part we were meant to play. The bridge between two worlds."

They were silent. The potatoes and onions were crackling. A flock of chickadees were fluttering and twittering in the tops of the tall trees alongside the creek.

"Flying Hawk was an apprentice of Red Cloud. He's an impeccable warrior and sorcerer. He seemed to know why we were here instantly, way before we did. He took me, Kelly too, under his very broad wings, and has endeavored to teach us everything he knows. These indigenous people, they know, at least the warriors, shamans and sorcerers. They know exactly what's going on out there, without ever being a part of it. They pick up the vibrations. The Earth tells them. The spirit world tells them. They even check it out themselves sometimes by light travel or inter-dimensional travel or dream journeying, or whatever you want to call it. We learned a little more about that last night. We still have to tell you about that. And they know that in order for things to change, it's up to us, the white people, to take the lead, to take the first step with our own kind. Once we do, and once we get through that crack in the door, then they'll be able to join us, and incredible things will start to happen."

He was sitting on a stump, with his arms on his thighs. He patted his thighs with his hands, and tapped his feet on the ground.

"Both in this dimension, and the others. That's where things are really going to happen. That's where we have our greatest advantage."

Soon the food was ready. Kelly scooped a bean out of the pot, and sampled it.

"OK, let's eat."

David and Kelly were sitting next to each other. They took each other's hand, and extended the other to their friends. Peter took David's hand, Janice Kelly's, and then Peter and Janice clasped hands, forming a circle. David and Kelly closed their eyes, and took a deep breath. The creek babbled quietly. The chickadees sang above, and a goat baaed in the distance.

Then they ate. The atmosphere was serene and contemplative.

"Flying Hawk's practical knowledge is just incredible," Kelly continued. "You'd be amazed at the stuff that's out there, in nature, that people can live off of. Practically everything. Summer's a piece of cake, with all the leaves, and herbs and flowers. But even in the winter, he taught us about lots of roots, and nuts and berries from the trees, and even the sap. Powerful stuff."

"And seeds," David added with deliberate and passionate emphasis. "We've learned how to cultivate most of our own seeds from the garden. And that's something too that's going to be very necessary, when we start over to build the new world. Like everything else, the seeds that grow our food have been corrupted, most recently genetically corrupted. I have the strangest feeling that the seeds we've developed here are vitally important. That somehow they're going to be the starting point in giving birth to new generations of healthy seeds to grow the food for the new world. Kind of like Adam and Eve, except in a totally good way."

When they were finished eating, they took their pots and pans and dishes down to the creek, and put them into a tub to soak. Then they went up to a spot in the shade on the bank above the creek, where several old, hand-made wooden chairs were arranged around a massive stump. Tall grass gone to seed, dandelions gone to seed, and an assortment of weeds flourished around them. The cluster of tall trees was one of several that dotted the prairie-like South Dakota wilderness, like islands. It formed a canopy above them, and the chickadees continued to frolic in its leaves and branches. The day was cloudless, hot and still. The creek continued to play its eternal, ethereal melody.

"This is where Red Cloud and I talked," David said. "He told me this spot was sacred. Actually, he was sitting in the chair you're in, like a king on his throne."

He pointed at Janice.

She playfully rubbed the arms of the chair with a big grin, like she might be able to absorb some of its magical powers.

"He also told me he was going to be buried here," he went on. "But I found out later they never found his body. He just vanished. That's the way it is with all of the most powerful sorcerers. They don't actually die. They just vanish. Poof. Here one day, gone the next. It's called the definitive journey. But I think I know what he meant by that. I've always been able to feel his presence here."

He looked back and forth at them, his eyes shining.

"It's here now," he nodded.

"Can you feel it?" Kelly asked them softly.

They looked at each other, and nodded.

"Yes," Peter said softly.

"I feel it around you," Janice added. "Around this whole place."

They savored the moment in silence.

"Do you still…see em?" Peter asked.

"Haven't seen anything in almost three years," Kelly answered. "Ever since we've been here. But then again the only people we've been around have been the Indians, and they're genetically clean. Just like all the other indigenous people. It's the white people you've got to really look out for. They're the ones who've really been messed with."

"It's been a nice break," David added. "For three years we've been completely focused on food, shelter and heat. Nothing else. Except each other, of course, and staying on the path. Keeping our connection with the divine spirit. That's the most important thing. Without that, none of the rest of it matters."

"So what's next? Janice asked.

They looked at each other. Kelly spoke.

"Don't know. We're pretty certain our time here's up. We just don't know what that means yet. We could live here, and be perfectly happy for the rest of our lives. No problem. But that's not part of the plan. And you guys. We've got to figure out what you're doing here. "

"And we had an experience last night that completely reinforces all this," David added. "We had a visitor named Hibutu, who took us on a little journey to his village in the jungle of South America."

They told them all about Hibutu, Mahnya, and the Togi people, and everything they'd seen, and been told.

"We haven't even had time to talk about this yet," David said. "Things are really moving at warp speed. This truly is a time of incredible shift. A once in a millennia kind of thing. What's happened so far, the crash, the chip, the world government, is all man-made, and it's just the start. There's something much bigger brewing."

"And there are others we're supposed to meet. We each have our part to play. And once we do, an opportunity's going to exist for us to take a shot at evicting the forces of evil, and creating the new world. Have no idea what form that's going to take yet, only that it will. And like I said before, once we get our foot in the door, then indigenous folks from around the world, like the Togi and Flying Hawk, can join us too, and play their part. And the spirit world, they're part of this too. They have their part to play, and they want to help. They're just waiting to follow our lead. When it all comes together, it'll be an amazing thing to behold."

"And after that he took us on a little trip to San Francisco," Kelly added.

"It appears there's a man there we're supposed to meet, a scientist. Don't know who he is yet, but we know what he looks like. We saw him working in his lab."

Before she even finished, Peter and Janice both twitched, like their bodies were struck by a bolt of lightening. They looked at each other, their eyes bulging out of their sockets. Peter burst into a fit of uncontrollable laughter, very unlike him. It was infectious, and Janice joined him. Peter's eyes were glassy, and he was holding his stomach. It took them a moment to settle down.

"What?" Kelly squealed.

David had once learned that even free will is an illusion. Human beings, all organic and inorganic beings in the universe for that matter, are, in fact, in the midst of an infinite sea of forces that they could never possibly comprehend, at least not with their reason. Reaching the highest levels of awareness, then, means learning to be open to these forces, and to acquiesce to them, so allowing them to perform their magic, and to be a part of it. It's both yielding to them, and joining them. This was the key to people being able to perform unimaginable feats in life. This acquiescence, another in life's splendorous array of paradoxes, is simultaneously, then, an act of abandonment and control.

And once again, in this perfect moment, here it was.

"Well I guess that answers that question!" Janice shrieked. "What we're doing here."

"It didn't seem that important in the context of all this other stuff," Peter bellowed ecstatically, his arms spread like a big bird. "I didn't even think of mentioning it until now. But that's where we're going," Oakland."

THREE ✿ RE-ENTRY

"Good afternoon, Tom."

The two men approached the counter. They were both wearing plain dark gray suits, with white shirts, black ties, and black shoes. They were the same height, about 5' 11," and with the same athletic physique, with bony cheeks and thick muscular necks. One was totally bald, and the other had straight, short, brown hair, parted on the side.

"Well, well," the man behind the counter replied good-naturedly. "If it isn't my two favorite police officers, Agent Smith and Agent Smith."

David was standing off to the side with his back to them, pretending to look at the merchandise, waiting for the store to clear out. Tom was obviously tipping him off that these were cops.

"Mind if we have a look around?" The bald one asked in a monotone. "We don't have a warrant, but we can get one quick enough. You know that."

"Sure, no problem. Wherever you like. Got absolutely nothing to hide."

Tom gave the genuine impression that he enjoyed playing this game of cat and mouse with them. Either that, or he was the world's greatest actor.

"What are you boys looking for this time? Guns?"

The one with hair glared at him hostilely, then looked away.

"Just make sure you don't plant anything. I should be able to search you guys first for drugs. OK if we do a quick pat down?"

They ignored him.

The bald one walked behind the counter to where Tom was standing, and stood at his side, staring at him. Tom stood his ground, continuing to look straight ahead, his hands on the counter, like he wasn't there.

"Move from behind the counter, please," he sternly hissed.

Tom put his hands in the air.

"Yes, sir."

He moved around to the front, and turned around to watch.

There were rows of drawers both in the front and in the back, several cupboards along the floor beneath them, and a large cabinet, with swinging glass doors, along the wall in the back.

The bald cop opened everything that could be opened. His facial expression was fixed, cold and vacant, like a snake. The drawers and cupboards were cluttered with papers and all kinds of junk. He rummaged through everything, leaving nothing unturned, while making only a token effort to put things back in their place. After he had gone through everything, he made a mock display of tidying the final few items in the last cupboard, and delicately closed the door, with a gentle tap of his fingers.

Tom had been watching this whole display. The bald cop walked around the counter to him, and faced him with the same blank stare.

"That concludes our investigation. We'll be leaving now."

The other one walked up, and stood at Tom's side, with the same look. It was like they had been cut from the same diabolical mold.

"We know what you're up to," he said, with the same monotone. "Don't get too comfy. You will slip up. It's only a matter of time."

They eyeballed each other like three gunfighters for an instant, which seemed like an eternity.

Tom's face broke into a smirk.

"You gentlemen have a great day, all right."

While this search was being conducted, the cop with the hair wandered around the store, and looked at things disinterestedly. Unlike the other, he wasn't looking for anything in particular - just killing time, and snooping. Aside from David, there were no other customers in the store. A couple of times he came close to David, and on one occasion, he stopped, and David could feel his eyes staring at his back. Then he resumed pacing, and snooping.

David was doing his best to be inconspicuous, but he felt like it was impossible. After all, this was a pawnshop that was loaded with every conceivable kind of second-hand junk. It wasn't that interesting. Plus, he didn't look like everybody else, no matter how he cut his hair, or what kind of a disguise he wore.

And he couldn't look in their direction. He felt it right away. He couldn't make eye contact with them. That was crucial. He knew what he would see, and he knew that they would see him.

He was having that same feeling he had come to know so well, the same feeling he had every time he was in their presence. It was unmistakable. Revulsion. Repulsion.

He felt sick to his stomach, and he felt the urge to get away from them as fast as he could. He never felt this way any other time.

David had no idea what they saw when they saw him. Did he look different to them, different from other humans? Or was it simply that they saw that he was seeing them. He was only certain of one thing. They did.

He thought about just walking out of the shop without looking, or saying anything. But he didn't. He didn't know what he was dealing with here. Maybe that too would look conspicuous. Besides, he was here for a reason. Meeting Tom was a major breakthrough. And he knew Tom well enough to know that he knew what he was doing. He knew how to play the game, and beat them at it. That was the key to his success. David's best bet was to keep his distance, and stay out of the way.

They stared Tom down one last time, and left, without another word.

They closed the door, and David looked up for the first time. Tom stood still in his spot, and waited, his eyes on the closed door. A moment passed. It was eerily silent. Tom took a deep breath. It was as though he had come to life. He turned, and walked behind the counter, examining the mess. It had been a mess before. Now, it was more of a mess.

"Assholes," he grumbled.

David and Kelly had been in Oakland now for four days. Their return to the outside world had been smooth sailing, at least to their knowledge, up until now. They hadn't found the man they were looking for, and nothing much of significance had happened, until they discovered The Chip-Free Zone, a pawn and barter shop, located in a seedy part of Oakland, close to Berkeley. It was owned and operated by Tom Brantweiler, a renegade, who refused the chip himself, and who refused to buckle to the pressure of the new monetary system. Prior to the crash, it was a traditional pawnshop, and afterwards it was strictly barter. Tom owned the building, and lived on the second floor, making him quite self-sufficient. The only thing he needed the new money for was to pay his utilities, and he had numerous contacts who did that for him, either as part of a trade, or charity. People would trade him food, and often simply donate it because they believed in what he was doing. His shop also became a hub for the underground, and for those who refused to be a part of the new system, which also made him a prime target of the authorities.

Finding the scientist David and Kelly were looking for was beyond the proverbial needle in the haystack. They had virtually nothing to go on, other than what they had seen on their journey with Hibutu - his physical appearance, and the appearance of his lab. Once again, it was a matter of going with the flow, and trusting the path that the divine spirit placed before them. They had been living their lives this way a long time now. They were getting quite good at it.

It was so profound, and yet so simple, once you got in the groove. Trust the path. Of course, it takes a good deal of learning, discipline and practice to acquire the awareness of the path, but once you do, that becomes your compass, and it will never lead you astray, in good times or in bad. And it's always there, right before you, never changing. It's all in how you look. The universe is an infinite sea of mysterious and unfathomable forces. Higher consciousness means being open to these forces, and acquiescing to them, flowing with them, like a surfer on the crest of a magnificent wave. This is the path. This is how David and Kelly lived each and every day. This is how they intended to find their man.

And Peter and Janice were proving to be invaluable allies. Clearly, they were an indispensable piece of this whole picture. They too, in their own way, had learned to acquiesce. They also consistently showed that they understood their part, and they were playing it, to all appearances, superbly.

Away from their sanctuary in South Dakota, David and Kelly were in constant danger. They always had to be on the alert. They could never take any chances. The alien beings were everywhere, hiding behind their human mask. For hundreds of thousands of years they had thoroughly permeated the human gene pool. Though their strongest concentration was the white race, they were present in all the races, particularly in the elitist and ruling hierarchies. They also tended to be more prevalent in the more populated urban areas, which are the primary seats of power, and here again, they are more abundant in places of affluence.

In general, the farther up the pecking order of the socioeconomic ladder you go, the more of them you find. The higher echelons of bankers, corporate executives, lawyers, politicians, law enforcement, intelligence agencies, medical doctors, and the like, are crawling with them. And very importantly, in relation to the population as a whole, the vast majority of these genetic alterations are very minor, and most of those who are affected aren't even aware of it. David and Kelly are able to see it, but the people who have it can't even see it themselves.

But that small percentage, who understood the game, and who could knowingly shapeshift back and forth between human and alien form, were sufficiently plentiful to put David and Kelly constantly on guard. And their numbers were growing all the time.

David also had no idea what his status was with them, and Kelly knew even less. Prior to his disappearance from Martinelle, he had definitely been very high on their most wanted list.

He had learned through hard and painful experience never to take anything for granted with them. They had knowledge and power, at least of the technical and scientific kind, that was far beyond his imagination. He was tempted to assume that since he had been completely undisturbed for three years in South Dakota that they didn't know his whereabouts. But he had no idea whether or not they still believed he was alive. In his gut, that place he always trusted, he strongly suspected they did, and that he had not fallen off their radar screen.

And what did they know about Kelly, other than the fact that she was his girlfriend, and she too had disappeared without a trace? Did they know she was the woman who rescued David in Martinelle, and killed one of them? It was at least questionable because she had bleached her hair blonde, changed its style, put on gobs of makeup, and done an expert job of changing her appearance. David was not even able to recognize her at first. However, there was the other alien being, the one who witnessed the shooting and vanished, and the entire incident was probably observed and recorded through two-way computer monitors and other advanced, high-tech surveillance equipment. They could put one and one together as well as anybody, and analyze this woman from all of their other records.

It always came back to the same thing: they were dealing with powers they didn't comprehend, and they could never take anything for granted.

There was not much to worry about on the drive from South Dakota to Oakland. They took three days to do it, stopping each night at motels in the boonies to eat and sleep. The only potential trouble spots along Interstate 80 were Salt Lake City, Reno and Sacramento, and they made a point of not stopping at any of them.

They did stop at the first Wall Mart they saw, and bought clothes for David and Kelly, so they didn't stand out so much – nothing fancy, just a casual, unpretentious, everyday wardrobe, and new sneakers. Now they looked like the average Joe and Josephine - at least as much as possible.

While they were in the car, they both also cut their hair. David had been a fugitive for so long that he had tried every possible disguise, from totally bald to shoulder length hair and full beard, and he had been detected in each. So, he decided to go with a traditional haircut, intermediate length, parted on the side. He also bought a Colorado Rockies baseball cap and a new pair of sunglasses.

They had last seen Kelly as a floozy blonde; so she stuck with her natural brown, and cut it extremely short, like a man, and let it flop naturally around her head. David didn't think he would like it. He was pleasantly surprised when it made her natural beauty stand out even more. She also got a new pair of sunglasses, and a yellow hat, with a brim turned up in a circle all the way around, like a sailor.

They were both such extraordinary people, with such a healthy and vibrant glow, that it would be difficult for them to blend into any crowd, any place, any time.

Peter and Janice were staying at a luxury hotel in Oakland, where Peter's business meetings were being held. While they were en route, they managed to make a reservation for a separate room for David and Kelly. They were only scheduled to stay for a week, before they headed back to Florida, and, of course, they were willing to help out financially in any way they could, and in any other way too. So, David and Kelly didn't have much time to figure out what they were going to do.

They spent their first day at the hotel, getting oriented to Oakland, the bay area, and the world in general. Peter was tied up in meetings, but Janice was free, and she stayed with them. She also had the car in case they needed to go somewhere.

They started by getting every local newspaper and magazine they could at the hotel gift shop. It was a challenge being on the outside, particularly in this affluent, urban hotel, and even with their caps and sunglasses, they made sure to keep their eyes diverted, and not look directly at anybody. Whenever a purchase needed to be made, or there needed to be any kind of personal interaction, Janice would take care of it.

David and Kelly agreed that the hotel didn't feel particularly good. They could always tell when there were alien beings around by the rotten way it made them feel. And during the course of the day, while they were out in public, these feelings came and went. There were times when it was quite intense, and others when they felt normal. Whenever the feelings were strong, they would quickly move away, and go to an area that did feel OK. And again, they had no idea what they were dealing with, and whether these beings could feel their presence in some way.

They spent the second part of the day back in their room scouring through all this literature. It was of virtually no assistance. It was all mainstream, and nothing but propaganda. There wasn't a single shred of what they were looking for. All it did was reinforce the illusion of the *New World Order*, and the view of the world the controllers wanted people to see.

The Yellow Pages also got them nowhere, even in areas like health care, where previously naturopaths, homeopaths and other alternative healers had at least some representation. In the *New World Order*, most of these types of alternative healing modalities had either become extinct, or been driven underground. The only exception was chiropractic, which had become so big and popular that it couldn't easily be eradicated. However, the licensing guidelines had become so strict that virtually all chiropractors had been forced to sell out to the system, and now they were really no different than the physicians.

The world, as Peter had said, had indeed been split in two – one with the chip that toed the party line, and the other without it, which was very difficult to find. David and Kelly quickly realized the futility of this, and gave up. In order to find what they were looking for, they were going to have to explore the world outside the hotel.

They had an early room-service dinner. Even though the hotel restaurant was first-rate, they had to eat light and very carefully, as their systems had grown very unaccustomed to so much processed and chemically filled food. They agreed that their first order of business the next day would be to find a health food store, where they could stock up on natural food, and possibly get closer to the kind of people they wanted to find. A tour of all the local health food stores might prove very helpful in their search.

After dinner, they decided to see what they could discover on the television. Television in the *New World Order* had been transformed into *univision*. The world government had essentially taken over the television industry, and regulated it as tightly as the United States Government previously had regulated industries such as the airlines, banking and insurance. Everything was by satellite, and free, public television now consisted of one worldwide channel, the *unichannel* or UC, which was 24-hours of news and features.

Those who had the chip could access a menu off of the UC, from which they could select from a wide spectrum of programming, some free and some paid. The major networks still existed, as did many of the cable channels from the pre-*univision* era. The main difference was the viewer was no longer restricted to a fixed programming schedule, but had complete freedom of choice of what they wanted to watch, and when they wanted to watch it. All the latest movies were available on paid UV, making traditional movie theaters obsolete, and any sporting event could be accessed from anywhere. Those who had the chip could also do virtually all of their shopping by UV.

David and Kelly had already watched UV several times in the motels while they were on the road. TV before, and UV now, had always been the best medium for them to observe the alien beings and the true state of the world, without being detected themselves. They quickly learned that the world had become far more infested during their three years in South Dakota. Either that, or their ability to see the beings behind their human mask had sharpened. Perhaps it was a little of both, but they agreed that it was obvious that the presence of the alien beings had become far more pervasive.

They had numerous sightings, and just like before they left for South Dakota, it was a simple matter to find where to locate them. It was no shock that the UC was exclusively alien beings. Aside from that, the best source was the major network news broadcasts. All the news anchors were alien beings, as were the President of the US, his entire cabinet, and virtually all high-ranking federal government officials. Any person in a position of significant power, either inside the government or outside, was an alien being. Another area of surprising concentration was Hollywood and major market movie and UV stars. Country western music stars were also particularly well represented. And in general, the more local and rural the UV station, the less prevalent they were. David and Kelly had several sightings on the local Bay Area channels. They saw nothing in Rock Springs, Wyoming.

The next day, Janice drove them to Berkeley. They planned to visit several health food stores, where, in addition to getting some food they hopefully could eat, they intended to check out the scene, and the literature and bulletin boards. Janice, who was familiar with the health food scene in Florida, wasn't too encouraging, telling them they would probably either find people with more of an open mind, but still chipped, and who believed that the new system was acceptable, and definitely better than the alternative, or hippies and drop-outs, who were mostly losers, and who couldn't possibly be any help to the cause.

They also intended to explore the State University in Berkeley, or at least the outskirts of it, which had long been one of the primary hubs of the underground and the alternative culture in the US. However, they had to be exceedingly careful. David had learned the painful lesson, in his experience as a medical student at North Central University in Chicago, that state universities are also bastions of the alien beings, particularly the upper echelons of the administration and the faculty, and the graduate programs in law, medicine and finance. But David and Kelly were mostly interested in checking the bulletin boards and any underground activity they might discover in the general environs of the University.

It was here that David and Kelly had their first real exposure to the other side of the new world, and the ravages that the crash had heaped upon massive numbers of people. They drove around Berkeley and Oakland, parked several times, and walked the streets of what had once been a flourishing community of artists, intellectuals, musicians, flower children, and a distinguished center of non-conformity. Now it was more like a poverty stricken third world nation or a blown-out ghost town. Office buildings and storefronts were abandoned and in disrepair, with broken windows, and their exteriors blackened with soot. Garbage of all kinds was strewn around the sidewalks. Even large items, like computers, televisions and refrigerators, had simply been left there. Automobiles with flat tires and smashed windows were left in their parking spaces.

Some stores and businesses were still open, and were scattered here and there around these old neighborhoods – a corner grocery store, a coffee shop and restaurant, a second-hand electronics and appliance store, a used bookstore, a thrift shop selling used clothes and all kinds of other junk, a corner magazine stand, a public grade school. They were primarily mom and pop operations, with metal bars and grates over all the doors and windows. It was painfully obvious that this was a dying world, and the rare few, who could afford to stay in business, weren't doing it here.

These streets were also crowded with people, people of all shapes, sizes, ages and colors. No one was spared – disheveled men and women, children with dirty, frightened faces, mothers carrying infants, entire families huddled together. People with nowhere to go. People with all the life sucked out of them. People with vacant eyes and stiff, hungry bodies. Some wandered aimlessly, like zombies. Others sat on the sidewalks, their backs against the wall. Many were sleeping, or unconscious. They didn't see any dead bodies, at least they didn't think so, but they might as well have. It was only a question of time for so many of these folks.

With no money, the face of begging had clearly changed. David and Kelly had nothing to give, and it was a good guess that Janice was the only person among this throng with a chip. A few people asked them for food, or if they could just help out in any way, but for the most part, these people appeared to have given up. They were waiting to die, or for a miracle. Perhaps David and Kelly could help them with the latter.

It was a helpless and horrible feeling. Of course, Janice could have bought some food, lots of food, and given it to some of them. But where do you start? Who do you pick, and who gets left out? They couldn't assume the responsibility to feed them all. It was way too much to even begin thinking about.

And besides, they were on a mission. They had some rather urgent work to do, even though they didn't know what it was yet. They believed they were going to help these poor people in a far greater way.

Strangest of all, David and Kelly felt safer than at any time since they arrived in Oakland. As far as the alien beings were concerned, the vibes here were as clear and clean as on the Reservation in South Dakota. There were none of them here in this squalor. The only people they needed to be wary of were the cops, but there were none of them to be seen, at least not in squad cars or in uniform. David and Kelly could walk these streets with their heads held high, and look these poor, pitiful people straight in the eye, if they wanted to. Their bodies were free from that sickening feeling that the presence of the beings triggered. There was no danger, at least on that score, here.

And Janice was right. The health food stores were of little help. There were several in this area, particularly as you got closer to Berkeley, where there were still pockets of suburban-like affluence and mini-malls, to cater to the students and professors who were chipped. However, even the natural food and more alternative thinking magazines and literature had been diluted and contaminated by *New World Order* propaganda. There was none of the anti-establishment vigor and fiery iconoclasm of days gone by. Even student rebellion and the battle of the generations, hallowed traditions of the American family and educational system, were now mere tokens, transparent masks behind which glared the immutable eyes of the *New World Order*. The subliminal message had raised itself to the level of non-subliminal, there for all to see. Resistance is futile. Join or perish.

Hibutu, Mahnya and the Togi had told them there were others, and even shown them one, others who they would meet to work together to make *The Shift* to the new paradigm of consciousness and existence. They knew this was true. But where? If there was another world, and they knew there was, it was very well hidden. And totally separate. They couldn't see a shred of it anywhere.

They had to hang onto the one thing they knew for certain. They had to trust the path. They knew they were in the right place, at the right time, doing the right thing. They had to be patient, and keep flowing with it all. The divine spirit reveals itself in mysterious ways. The unfathomable powers and forces, with which we must merge to be shown the way, always seem to manifest themselves in the ways we least expect. It's almost like the divine spirit likes to have a good laugh from time to time, and invites us to laugh along, reminding us that this lightness of heart and spirit is part of the whole deal. Without it, everything crumbles, and we can't see the way.

As if on cue, they saw it. They had quit for the day, and were about to head back to the hotel. It was right in front of where the car was parked, in the lot of one of the health food stores, several blocks from the University. It was stapled to the opposite side of a thick utility pole. They could have seen it hours ago, but they just weren't looking in the right spot. It was a poster on thick, rugged paper, like cardboard, that read:

THE CHIP-FREE ZONE
Dealing In Only Real Money
Money Is A Store Of Value – Not An Electronic Impulse
Unis Not Accepted – Barter Only
High Quality Merchandise - We've Got It All!
Food Accepted
Tom Brantweiler, Proprietor

They instantly knew they would have to check this out. It would have to be the next day because it was in a dumpy part of Oakland, and it was already approaching closing time. They decided that David would go by himself because Kelly and Janice had to take a drive down to Santa Cruz. Kelly had a powerful dream the night before that took place on a huge rock that jutted into the waves and surf on the coastline north of Santa Cruz. She had never even been to Santa Cruz before. Clearly she needed to check this out, and see where it fit in. Janice rented a car for David to use, which would also allow them to split up again if they needed to.

David arrived at the Chip-Free Zone around mid-morning. First, he wanted to scope the place out, and get the feel of it. He also wanted to check out this guy, Tom Brantweiler.

David browsed around the shop for awhile, trying to be as inconspicuous as possible. There were always other customers there, and people milling around, mostly middle age and older men. It did appear to be a hub of sorts. Mostly everybody knew Tom, and they were all on a first-name basis. Not everybody came to trade. Many of them were simply there to hang out, and shoot the shit about what was going on in the world. And they didn't like it.

This place had a totally different feel to it. For the first time since he arrived in Oakland, David felt as though he was in a different world. These people weren't slaves to the *New World Order*. They talked a different language, and they didn't seem to be afraid. They saw through the scam, and knew how the game was played. And David felt comfortable here. He felt like he belonged.

There was also some local literature, handouts, flyers, those sorts of things, and a bulletin board. Many of them dealt with community groups and meetings, and people who were attempting to start businesses like Tom's, which didn't depend on the new money. They were all fairly tame in nature. After all, in a fascist state, people need to watch what they say in public. However, the general theme was the same. These people opposed the *New World Order*, and were not going to buckle under to it. They were not afraid to speak out, and they were looking to create alternatives.

Tom was a real character. He was perhaps in his mid-fifties, robust, with lively green eyes, and a full head of course white hair, cut in a crew cut, with a stubbly gray non-shaven face. He was wearing old, worn blue jean overalls, with suspenders and lots of big pockets and loops for tools, and a white T-shirt. David was drawn to him immediately. He was a perfect blend of feistiness and friendliness.

They all noticed David, but it didn't matter anymore. These folks were OK, and he even made small talk with several of them.

"Help you with anything, young fella?" Tom hailed.

"No thanks. Just looking. Quite a store you got here."

"Not from around these parts, are ya?"

"Nope. Just visiting."

"That's quite a sun tan you got there. Where you from? Africa?"

Everybody laughed, David too.

"Nope. South Dakota. I'm a farmer."

David quickly remembered there weren't any farmers anymore, at least not that kind.

"Yup. Work on one of them big farms in South Dakota."

"Well, you look all you want, and let me know if I can help you find anything."

David knew he wanted to talk to Tom privately, but it didn't look like he would ever get the chance. There were way too many people hanging around, and coming and going. So, he decided to leave, and he returned at around 5:45. 6:00 was closing time.

When David returned, there were still a few people in the store, but things seemed to be winding down.

"Just couldn't stay away, huh, young fella?"

"Nope. Had to come back."

"Close in ten minutes. Gettin' to be my dinner time."

David pretended to occupy himself with the merchandise again. At a couple minutes to six there was one woman left in the store, at the counter, making a trade. The time looked to be right. David picked up a desktop fan, and stood behind her.

They finished their deal, and she left.

Tom and David were alone.

"Got anything to trade?" Tom asked, his eyes still playful.

David peered deeply into Tom's eyes - with a purpose. Back in his days as an intuitive healer, he had learned to use his eyes as a tool to touch a person's spirit. He was also trying to read, once and for all, whether this man was a true ally. The eyes are the window to the soul.

Tom's were clear, honest and alive. This was a good man.

"Actually, no. I was hoping I could have a few minutes of your time, privately."

Tom crinkled his eyebrows, and shook his head.

"You a cop? Don't look like a cop."

"No, I'm not a cop. I think you know that."

They looked at each other.

Tom too was an excellent judge of character. He was also trying to gauge what he was dealing with. This was unknown territory for him. The radiant young man before him was totally unlike his usual clientele. Like David, he always had to be on his guard. The authorities would like nothing better than to set him up, and shut him down. As a matter of fact, David was unlike anybody he had ever seen in his life. But he had his attention.

"What do you want then?"

David had reached that point again, the point he knew so well, where it was necessary for him to throw caution to the wind, and trust what he was feeling in his gut. He sensed he could be totally honest with this man. He was going to just let it fly, and see what happened.

"This place bugged?" David asked, his eyes darting around the room. "Are we on Candid Camera for big brother?"

"No," Tom shook his head decisively. "Not unless they're doing it by satellite, or some crazy thing."

They eye balled each other again.

"It's kind of hard to know where to start," David began. "I'm looking for somebody – a scientist. Can't tell you much about him – not even his name. All I know is he's in the Bay Area, and I know what he looks like. Probably got some radical ideas that would blow their system apart, if they ever became known. Probably hiding out, part of the underground. Thick brown hair - starting to bald - starting to turn gray - kind of long, just over the ears. A half–beard, with gray at the tip. Brown eyes – wears glasses, with thin, metal frames. Pleasant looking fellow. When I saw him, he was wearing a blue Hawaiian shirt, with white fish on it, khaki shorts, and tennis shoes, no socks."

Their eyes were stuck together.

"Can you help me out?"

Tom was close, but he wasn't quite there yet.

"Maybe. Not much to go on."

"I understand," David nodded.

He took a deep breath. Enough dangling your toes in the water, he thought. Time to jump in the deep end.

"My name's David Rhodes, and I'm a marked man," he said softly. "They definitely want me out of the picture. I know too much, and see too much. Three years ago, I was definitely at the top of their most wanted list, until I managed to give them the slip. You've probably never heard of me. I wasn't a celebrity or anything. Flew totally beneath the public awareness. But perhaps you've heard of one of my colleagues, the late David Reich?"

Tom's eyes widened, his brows popping up, with a tilt of his head.

"Sure. The conspiracy guy – the UFO guy – the reptile guy. I've read some of his stuff. Used to have some of his books in here, until it got too dangerous to have them around. They've probably all been banned by now anyway. Seems like most of what he was saying came true. And he got killed in that volcano down in the Caribbean."

"He was murdered," David stated bluntly, with another penetrating gaze of his eyes.

It sounded so crazy it just might be true. Tom was hooked. Besides, those who had opened their eyes to the *New World Order* scam had learned a long time ago to accept the inconceivable as conceivable.

"They blew up that volcano. They killed all those people. It was all by design."

Tom's eyes were glazed over, like he was in a spell.

"I don't know how," David went on. "We're dealing with some awesome powers here. If you buy the fact that they're all from outer space to begin with, then it goes without saying that they have technological capabilities far surpassing anything known to us, normal human beings."

Tom was still.

"I was down there too. And killing me, or at least kidnapping me, and locking me away forever, was part of their plan too. But by some bloody miracle, actually a couple of them, I managed to escape. Reich and me and his whole team had come up with a plan to capture one of them, film the whole thing, and expose them for the entire world to see. And it was working beautifully. Some amazing things were happening, and lots of people in that audience were witnessing them. And we had it all on several different cameras. But little did we know they were one step ahead of us the entire time. Don't understand that either. Like I said before, we're dealing with some awesome powers here. But we got too close, and that's when they decided to blow that island up, and everybody on it. Make it look like a natural disaster. As Reich was so fond of saying: just a coincidence – nothing to worry about."

David smiled beatifically, his eyes still planted deeply in Tom's.

Tom's eyes came back into focus. Then, with a twitch, like he was waking up from a dream, he took a deep breath, air gushing into his lungs like a big balloon, his shoulders shooting into the air. He turned abruptly, walked resolutely to the front door, and locked it. He returned to where David was standing, and walked past him, not even looking at him this time.

"Come," he commanded. "Come with me, upstairs."

David obeyed, not even thinking.

The clomped up the dark wooden stairway in silence.

The second floor was one large, dimly lit room, with only two windows overlooking the street in front, and an adjoining bathroom. It was like a studio, with all the basic necessities lining the walls, and no frills whatsoever - stove, refrigerator, kitchen sink, dish cabinet, bookcase, computer, TV, stereo, bed, dresser. Nothing was state-of-the art. It was a hodgepodge from past generations – a trip back in time. In one corner, there were a few wicker chairs, with cushions, and a small couch arranged around a coffee table, and in the middle of the room was a solitary dinning table. There were no pictures, no lamps, no plants, and just a few overhead lights in the ceiling. The tables and counters were mostly bare. It was as stark and bleak as the downstairs was gaudy and cluttered.

Tom was like a different person. He was now all business, as opposed to the gregarious gadfly he had been with his customers downstairs.

"Have a seat," as he glanced at the couch and chairs. "Beer? I think I got a couple left."

David had his first beer in several months the night they arrived in Oakland, and he savored every drop of it. He loved an occasional brew or two. In South Dakota, Flying Hawk would occasionally surprise him with a six-pack.

"Sure. That'd be great."

Tom opened a couple bottles of Corona, and joined David. He extended his bottle, and they clinked.

"Pleased to meet you, David Rhodes."

They each took a drink.

"So what are you going to do with this scientist when you find him?" He asked bluntly, like the thread from downstairs had never been broken.

David broke into a bemused grin.

"Hm," he chucked. "Don't know exactly. I know this all sounds very far fetched, but all I know is I'm supposed to find him, and we're part of a group of people…"

He stopped. The thoughts and words were getting all jumbled up in his head. There was so much. So much had happened in such a ridiculously short period of time, and it was all such a stretch. Just say it, he thought to himself. You've come this far. Don't make it more complicated than it has to be. Just let it flow.

"We're part of a group of people, who are going to have a very rare opportunity to change the world. And I don't even know who they are yet. This scientist is just the start. And this is all going to be happening very soon, probably within the next year or two. Maybe sooner. And I don't know what form any of this is going to take either, or even if we're going to succeed or fail for that matter. All I know is there will be an opportunity. There are some very powerful forces at work here, and I'm not talking about the man-made kind. I'm not talking about the *New World Order* scum that's jerking around the human race, and pulling all their shit. Although they too are aware of these forces. But the forces I'm talking about are the kind that act upon the entire planet. They're geophysical and astrophysical, things like the shifting of the north and south magnetic poles, and the shifting of Earth's energy fields. Happens every 13,000 years or so. This stuff has already started happening, and we can feel it, but most people have no explanation for it because they don't understand any of this. They have no frame of reference. They just have this vague sense that they feel different, weird, like time speeding up, or slowing down, or like one minute everything makes perfect sense, and the next minute they're losing their fucking minds. And when all this hits its apex, it's going to throw everything completely out of whack, to say the least. Even the *New World Order* goons, with their superior technical knowledge, don't know what to expect. That's why this time is so important. That's why the Mayan calendar ends on December 21, 2012. Somewhere in all this there will be an opportunity for us to completely transform the world, but we've got to be ready. We got to be prepared to grab that cubic centimeter of chance."

Tom was once again spellbound.

Everything swirled around in David's head again. He took a deep breath, and it all popped back into place.

"How do I know all this, you might be thinking?" He went on. "It'd be impossible to tell the whole story in a short period of time. Let it suffice to say I can see things that normal people can't. My girlfriend, Kelly, can too. We're in this together. That's why they want me, us, out of the picture. If everybody saw what we do, it'd blow their scam right out of the water. And more recently, certain information has been…channeled to me, for lack of a better term. Like the information about the scientist, and the fact that I know he's in the San Francisco area. That came to me from…a higher source."

David took a gulp of his cold beer.

Tom took a deep breath, and leaned back in his chair.

"For all I know you're supposed to be a part of this too, Tom. I don't know yet. I don't know where you fit in. All I know is I've been in the Bay Area for four days now, and, other than Kelly and the two folks we came here with, you're the first person I've talked to about any of this. You're the first person I've felt comfortable enough with. You're my one and only lead, so far."

Tom grinned, and the look of cockiness he had downstairs returned to his face.

"I'm not the smartest guy in the world, but I do know how to judge people. You were right to trust me, kid. And you're not blowing me away with any of this. I've heard most of it before – a person in my position. I've just never talked to anybody who's right in the middle of it, the way you are – channeled information and seeing things nobody else can - you being a marked man - stuff like that."

David extended his bottle. They clinked again, and drank together.

"I don't know your scientist. But if he's in this area, I can probably find him for you. I'll put some of my feelers out. Check with a few of my contacts."

David asked him about his contacts. He told him about their search through the newspapers, magazines and bulletin boards, and that they had found nothing.

"No, you won't find anything that way," Tom said. "Not that what you're looking for doesn't exist. It does. There is an underground. There's a lot of groups, and lots of literature, on every conceivable topic. And just like everything else, most of it is totally nuts, and a small portion of it is very solid and reputable. I don't have any of it here, obviously. It's all very carefully hidden, where big brother can never find it. And what I don't have, I can get. You're talking to the right man, kid."

David tried to explain to him the nature of their search, and that they were trusting divine guidance as much as anything else. In addition to the scientist, their channeled source had told them there were others, but they had no idea who they were, or what they did, or whether they already knew each other. All they knew is they shared a common mission. In some strange way, it was David and Kelly's job to bring all these parts together into a whole unit. They were the final piece that would make the whole thing go.

"We really need as much as you can possibly bring us. We're not just looking for people, and leads. I know it sounds weird, but we're following forces, omens, like what brought us to you. And sometimes the most important thing is where you least expect it, like right in front of your nose. We really have to keep our eyes open for everything."

"Tell you what, kid. You come back here tomorrow at about the same time, about fifteen minutes to closing time, and I'll have a pile of stuff that'll make your head swim. It'll keep you busy for a month – a year!"

David smiled.

"I don't think we've got that much time," he chuckled.

They said good-night. It was getting late. The sun had set over an hour ago. Kelly might be getting concerned about him.

He drove back to the hotel, and he and Kelly had dinner in their room, as usual. The next day they decided to change their tact. Now that they had discovered Tom they didn't see any point in wasting any more time on magazines and bulletin boards. He was their bulletin board.

Kelly wanted to take him to Greyhound Rock, about 60-miles down the coast, outside the little town of Davenport, which was about ten miles north of Santa Cruz. This was the place she had dreamed about. She and Janice had been there the day before. She had never been there before, but she recognized it instantly, as they drove down the Pacific Coast Highway. It was exactly as she had seen it in her dream. Like their journey with Hibutu, this was no ordinary dream. She, or some other aspect of herself, had actually journeyed there. It had been just as real as the world of everyday life. And she had been guided there by higher, etheric powers. They didn't understand this totally, but they weren't meant to. All they knew for certain was that these powers did exist, and they were their allies.

- 53 -

It was a spectacular setting, with massive sandstone cliffs, a huge crescent-shaped sandy beach, and an immense rock, its ridge shaped like the back of a greyhound, jutting into the rolling surf. Kelly took David out to the end of the rock, overlooking the majestic Pacific Ocean, where the waves crashed against the rocks below, sending spouts of water into the air above them, like geysers, and the cool, moist ocean breeze showered them with a delicate mist. They sat down, the huge rock trembling beneath them, the surf exploding, and the whole scene rolling and swaying before them, above them and below them, like the entire world, and all its elements - fire, earth, air and water - consisted of waves, not matter, waves that were inviting them for a ride.

David felt it immediately, just as Kelly had the day before, and in her dream. This spot was special. It too fit into the grand design of the path they were on. They sat there peacefully for several hours, as nature serenaded them with this spectacular, celestial chorus, and they immersed their total selves, mind, body and spirit, in its magic. This was clearly one of the things they were meant to experience in their journey all the way from South Dakota. There was a message here. They didn't know its meaning yet, only that they must listen, and merge, and, in time, they would. David had spoken to Tom of following omens. Here was another.

They stayed as long as they could, soaking up as much of this as possible, until it was time to drive back to Oakland, knowing they would return.

"Fucking assholes," Tom growled again, as he thumbed through some papers in one of the drawers that the cops had messed up.

David was numb. He felt like an animal that had been playing dead. He looked at the door out of the corner of his eye to make sure it was closed, and they were gone. He didn't know enough about what just happened to know what to think.

He took several steps in Tom's direction.

Tom turned his head with a jerk, like he had forgotten David was there. His eyes darted to him, and stayed fixed, opened wide. David felt like he could practically hear the wheels turning in Tom's head. Then Tom beckoned him with a wave of his hand to come to the counter.

David approached the counter, and stood before him. Tom leaned forward, placing his face a few inches from his.

"Sorry, kid," he said in a whisper, shaking his head. "This changes everything."

David's heart thumped. He could feel Tom's breath against his face.

"What do you mean?" He echoed his whisper.

Tom took a deep breath.

"You gotta act like just any customer," he continued in the same whisper. "Just take something, anything, that fan you had yesterday, and leave, just like that's what you were after the whole time, and go about your business – just another day in the park."

David was frozen in his spot. Like a switch had been flipped, his senses were coming back to life. He was no longer on automatic pilot. His thoughts started racing around. And he became aware of a feeling that he hadn't felt in almost three years. Possible danger might be close at hand. He was afraid.

He stared at Tom blankly.

"They don't just come and go," Tom whispered again. "They hang around, and make real pests of themselves. I've gotta cover my ass, and you've gotta cover yours. They noticed you. They know you're here. And you're very noticeable - trust me, with than suntan of yours. If you hang around, or if you leave here with a bunch of suspicious looking stuff, they'll be all over you. They might be all over you anyway. Or maybe they're gone. I don't know. But we can't take any chances."

Every fiber of David's being was going on full alert.

"Enough talk. You gotta go, now. If they don't see you walk out that front door, they'll just have more questions. And that's not good for either one of us."

Tom gripped him firmly by the bicep.

"God bless you, kid."

David nodded. He understood.

"I'll be seeing you again," David said impulsively, placing his hand upon Tom's.

He didn't know why he said this. The words just popped out.

David turned, and started walking toward the door. His vision and thoughts started to narrow, like he was going down a tunnel. His eyes fixed on the floor, he instinctively started forming maps in his head of what he might be heading into. The cops might be waiting outside. He was certain what he was dealing with. He had had those sickening feelings while he was around them. It was unmistakable. If they were there, he had to try not to look at them. He couldn't make eye contact. If he saw them, if he saw the evil eye, as Red Cloud called it, and the green hue, then they would see him too. That's the way it had always worked, and there was no reason to believe this would be any different. Under these circumstances, in this setting, in this neighborhood, that would certainly mean his undoing, and probably Tom's too. As soon as he walked out that door, he had to not directly look at anybody. He didn't know where they might be, or what they might be doing. They could be anybody. He would have to look at the world with unfocused eyes, out of the periphery of his vision.

"Kid," Tom's hushed voice broke through his reverie. "The fan."

Not thinking too well, David thought.

David turned, picked up the fan, and headed back toward the door.

New maps started forming at lightening fast speed. In a few seconds he would be outside. If they were there, he would have no time to think – just act. He had to be ready.

If they confronted him, maybe he wouldn't see them, see the evil eye. There was a chance – slim, but who knows? He could simply show them the fan, tell them he traded his old watch for it, and they would let him be on his way – too small a fish to bother with. If they asked for identification, he didn't even have a chip. Just another bum, hanging around the pawn shop. Which also meant he shouldn't be driving.

Slow down, he thought. Getting too far ahead of yourself.

Or maybe they had left. God, that would be wonderful. Or if they were there, and he did see them - run like hell – no talking - no time for twenty questions. They would be more surprised than him, and this would give him a split second advantage. And then trust that the divine spirit had one more miracle for him, at least.

He arrived at the door, and turned the latch.

Time seemed to be slowing down.

He walked out onto the sidewalk, and into the cool night air. The car was parked two blocks away, one block off the main street, in a residential neighborhood. So, he had to walk to the end of the block, turn left, and walk one more block to the car. The distance seemed interminable.

The street was dimly lit, with so many buildings empty, and the traffic was light. It was like a ghost town. The daytime crowd had thinned, but there were still pockets of homeless people and lost souls. But to David, with his eyes fixed on his course, they were all just silhouettes. All he could hear were the mumble of occasional voices, and the hum of the city in the background.

His footsteps seemed to echo clamorously in the quiet street. As he walked, maps continued to form. Each step seemed like an eternity, as he scrutinized his surroundings out of the corners of his eyes – each building, each alley, each doorway, each window. With each step, his destination seemed more reachable.

He heard two car doors open, and shut. Then, other footsteps on the pavement behind him rattled the night.

He kept walking, fixed on his course.

"Excuse me, sir – you with the fan."

David stopped. He didn't turn around. Time stood still. He waited for what was next.

"We're police officers. Could we have a word with you please?"

Their tone was courteous, much different than they had been with Tom.

He had already mapped this out. He knew what he had to do - turn around, and see what he was dealing with. That was his only option.

He turned around. There were the two cops in their dark gray suits, the bald one, and the one with the short brown hair.

David only glanced at them for an instant, back and forth, from one to the other. He saw it instantly: the evil eye. They each had it.

When they looked at him, their eyes popped into full circles, and appeared to flash, the pupils' thin vertical slits extending from top to bottom, like a lizard or a snake. They looked shocked at what they saw, whatever that was. David had seen that look before. There was no mistaking it. The skin of their faces also had that light green, almost iridescent, hue, which extended around their heads like a mist or an aura.

They glanced at each other. They didn't need to say anything. They both knew instantly, like telepathy.

By the time they looked back at David, he was already gone, darting down the sidewalk. He had that split second head start.

"Freeze! Freeze!" The shouts burst through the night air behind him.

There was an open doorway in a dark, abandoned building a few feet ahead. He had mapped this too, and he bolted toward it, like he'd been shot from a canon. He hurled himself though the doorway, and instinctively dove to the floor.

Shots rang out.

David rolled on his side, flinging his arm over his closed eyes, as bullets sprayed above him, showering him with fragments of wood and stone. He glanced over his arm. He had landed right next to the edge of the open door. He grasped it, and slammed it shut.

Another volley of shots came. The door was made of thick, hard wood, and blocked them, but not for long. He could hear the bullets tearing into the wood.

He looked up, and spotted what might be one of those miracles. The metal latch that locked the door was intact. He reached up, and turned it. Click. It worked. This would buy him time, but only seconds.

He heard footsteps clattering toward the door.

It was dark. He rolled over onto his stomach. The only light he could see was through two windows that appeared to be down a long, narrow hallway, and several open doorways on each side before that. He scurried for a few feet on his hands and knees, then sprang to his feet, and sprinted toward the windows.

The building appeared to be an old hotel, with doorways spaced at even intervals all the way down the hall.

There was a smash against the door. It sounded like they were trying to break it down by kicking it or battering it with something. It sounded like it held. Then more shots. They were going to shoot their way through it.

David couldn't see the floor where he was running. He had to trust. He raced down the hallway, arms pumping furiously, and spotted a faint light, through a wide opening on the right side. Maybe it would lead to an exit, and he could give them the slip. Whatever it was, that was where he had to go. He hardly knew where he was. How could they know, other than by the sound of his running?

The shots and the pounding on the door continued.

Just as the door crashed open, David grabbed the frame of the opening, used it for leverage, and swung himself through it into almost total darkness.

They were inside the front door. He heard their footsteps in the hallway behind him. They didn't shout any more warnings.

In the darkness, David had to slow down. He saw a faint glimmer of light reflecting off a wall above him. And below that – two steps. It was a winding staircase. Too late to turn around – he had to keep going – no choice.

Their footsteps continued to clatter down the hallway in his direction.

He felt his way with his feet, shuffling them, until they hit the first step. He leaned forward into the darkness, and found the steps with his hands. Other than the light and the two steps on top, he could see nothing. Bracing himself with his hands, he went up the stairs on all fours, like an animal, trying to be as quiet as he could.

He stopped in the darkness, on his hands and knees.

He couldn't hear their steps. Maybe they had lost track of him.

Silence. All he could hear was the hum of the city.

He couldn't hide from them – not here. That was a losing proposition. They had guns and phones. He had nothing. And time was crucial. He had to keep moving.

He crawled up the next step, slowly, carefully, trying not to make any noise. The old wooden steps betrayed him, and creaked loudly. The sound rattled down the stairway, like dominoes.

They heard him.

"There! Up there!" Shouts came from the hall below him.

Their footsteps again pounded down the hallway in his direction.

David scurried up the final few steps to the landing, where the stairway turned to his left, and went up in the opposite direction. It was better lit, with light coming from another opening at the top. He could make out the faint outline of the steps, and the walls on either side.

He jumped to his feet, and bounded up the steps, covering two or three of them with each stride. He felt like he was speeding up, gaining on them.

He could hear them banging around below him. It sounded like they were stumbling and faltering in the darkness at the bottom of the stairs.

He reached the top, where two hallways intersected at right angles, one straight ahead, and the other to either side. There were windows at the end of each, with light coming in from the outside. Ahead of him he also spotted several open doorways. He sprinted in that direction.

He could hear them clomping up the stairs behind him, with an occasional grunt or groan.

He raced down the hallway, and picked the third open doorway on the right. He stepped inside, and quietly shut the door.

The cops were just reaching the top of the stairs. Their racket stopped. They had two hallways to choose from, and lots of rooms. It was eerily quiet.

David didn't lock the door. He didn't want to risk the noise.

It was an old abandoned hotel room, with two windows on the opposite wall, overlooking the street below.

Their footsteps started up again, and the sound of them thrusting doors open. They had split up. One was working each hallway. They had probably figured out David wasn't armed. They didn't need to be too careful with their search.

There were a lot of nooks and crannies where he could be hiding in each room. They had to check these out.

More time, David thought.

He stepped to the windows as quietly as possible. They were sheets of thick glass, with wooden panes. They couldn't be opened.

He was cornered. He knew what he had to do.

Another door slammed open, moving closer down the hallway, and the sound of rustling around inside the room.

Time seemed to stand still.

This was so odd. David had done this exact same thing on two previous occasions, while fleeing from the alien beings. Except those times were so different. One was in Martinelle, after Kelly had rescued him, when the convention center was crumbling around them in the volcano. The other was that night at Kelly's house on Hickory Lake in Wisconsin, when the alien beings surprised him in a plot to kill or kidnap him. But on those occasions, he received divine guidance. At Hickory Lake, the nature spirits spoke to him, and guided him as he fled through the dark forest. And on both occasions, as with his journey with Hibutu, he had seen the light, and immersed himself in it, transporting him away from them.

This time there were no voices. And no light, at least not so far. He was all alone in a dark hotel room.

This time he felt something that was very rare for him. He felt a twinge of doubt. Maybe he was out of miracles. Maybe he wouldn't make it this time.

He had to continue to trust the path. He had to acquiesce to the forces that were there in the room with him.

He knew what he had to do.

He stepped quietly to the door. He waited for the next time they made noise. They were only about two rooms away now. When the cop started banging around again, he flipped the lock.

Click. It worked again.

He moved briskly to the window.

He took a quick peak out, and saw a dimly lit sidewalk and street below. It was the beginning of a residential neighborhood.

He bent over, untied his right tennis shoe, and pulled it off. He shoved his right hand all the way up into it, reached back, and smashed it against the window with all his strength, aiming his blow at the wooden pane that ran across the middle. It made a dull thud and a splitting sound – not very conspicuous.

The pane bent, and the window cracked down the middle, but didn't break. It was very sturdy.

He smashed it again in the same spot. The pane snapped, and some of the glass shattered. The remaining panes were bent, but mostly intact, holding much of the glass in place.

"Got him! He's over here!" Came from the room down the hall.

David took several crisp steps backwards, and then ran at the window at top speed. He clenched his hands into fists, put his arms in front of his face, and dove through the hole in the window. Shards and splinters of glass and wood ripped his skin.

As he sailed through the air, he visualized doing a front flip, and landing on his feet on the ground below. He had no experience at such things, but he had tried this at Hickory Lake, and to his total shock, it had worked.

But this time, he quickly lost control of his body. He tried to regain his balance, but he was flying wildly, thrashing his limbs, through space. The world was a dizzying whirl in front of his eyes.

The last thing he remembered was the sound of more shots being fired.

FOUR ❧ RENDEZVOUS

There was light – light on the back of his eyelids, making a yellowish-orange glow.

He felt a gentle puff of cool air against his cheek, and heard the sound of a distant lawn mower.

David's eyes popped open.

A bright white wood paneled ceiling came into view. He was in a bed, on his back, his head on a pillow, with the sheet neatly folded over a blanket that covered him from his armpits down.

Where was he? He had no sense of time. He knew who he was. That was about it.

He didn't recognize anything. His mind skipped around. Was he in his dorm at college in Ohio? Was he at his Aunt Dottie's in Chicago?

Kelly. He remembered Kelly. He was alone. She wasn't beside him. He definitely wasn't in South Dakota.

His heart thumped. Kelly always slept beside him.

He tried to lift his head, and pain shot through his eyes and down his neck, like an electric shock. He couldn't move. He clenched his eyes shut, and his head fell back on the pillow.

He was dizzy. The world was whirling behind his eyelids, and his ears were ringing, like an army of distant crickets. He felt like he might fall back into the blackness.

A squeaking, creaking sound broke through the din. Footsteps on the floor.

Someone was there with him.

He took a deep breath to gather strength. That seemed like the only part of him that was still working.

He opened his eyes again, slowly this time.

A shadowy form was moving toward him, on his right.

He didn't know what to think, what to feel. It could be anybody.

Without moving his head, he glanced at it out of the corners of his eyes. It was him!

This he remembered instantly, the first piece popping back into place. His heart thumped again, faster this time.

It was the scientist!

He was walking calmly toward him, a placid smile on his face. He looked just like in his vision, even the blue Hawaiian shirt with white fish on it.

Then, it all caved back in on him like a gigantic landslide – Oakland, Peter and Janice, The Chip-Free Zone, Agents Smith and Smith, the evil eye, the abandoned hotel, diving out the window.

He had only one other thought, one feeling, and he knew it for certain. He was safe. He had no idea where he was, or what was happening, but he knew everything was going to be OK.

He closed his eyes again, and grinned, laughing through his nose. This hurt too, his head throbbing, but he didn't care. Nothing in his life surprised him anymore. He just trusted it – all of it.

And he knew he wasn't dreaming. He knew what he just saw, and he knew that this was happening in the reality of the material, third dimensional world.

He opened his eyes again.

The scientist came to the side of the bed, and stood over him. His sparkly brown eyes were impishly playful, and kind. They shined through his thin, metal-framed glasses into David's.

"Don't worry. You're safe here," he said in a soft and soothing voice. "You've been out for quite awhile. You've had a nasty bump on your head, and some pretty nasty cuts, particularly the one on your side. But my doctor friend came right over, and we've got you pretty well patched together. And there's nothing else wrong with you, other than that ding on your head."

The scientist reached down, and placed his hand next to a spot on the right side of David's skull, about an inch above the temple.

"Right here."

David could feel the pain in that spot, but so many other things were swirling around in his mind that it didn't seem to matter.

He wanted to speak, but he wasn't sure he could. His throat was parched. He licked his lips, and tried to swallow, but he couldn't.

As if reading his mind, the scientist walked across the room, and returned with a small plastic bottle of water. He put it up to his lips, but David found the strength to reach out from under the covers with his right hand, take hold of the bottle, tilt his head slightly forward, and take a drink.

He dropped his head back onto the pillow.

"It's you," he forced, in a raspy tone, his voice sputtering. "I know you. I've seen you. I've been looking for you. I came all the way from South Dakota to find you."

The scientist shook his head, and chuckled, with a look that was a blend of astonishment and disbelief.

His eyes narrowed, and sparkled deeply into David's.

"I don't know what the hell any of this means…but I believe you. You came flying out that window…and it's almost like I was waiting for you. I knew what I was supposed to do. There wasn't any doubt, not even an instant of hesitation."

David took this in. He was silent, and still.

Thoughts were sorting themselves out in his head. There was so much here. He didn't want to jump ahead of himself. He knew he had been as good as dead, and in a miracle of manifestation, this man had saved his life. There was so much more yet to know. But he couldn't let himself get lost in it all. This was still a matter of life and death. He had to get everything in the right order.

He took a deep breath, and emptied his mind.

Instantaneously, it popped into the void.

Kelly! She had to know.

The thought deflated him, like air going out of his sails.

He closed his eyes, and took another deep breath, to gather strength.

"How long have I been out?"

He almost didn't want to hear the answer.

"Almost a day. You crashed onto the sidewalk early last night. It's about five o'clock now."

Not too bad, he thought. She'll still be at the hotel, with Peter and Janice.

David took another drink. His voice was coming back.

"There's somebody I've gotta tell, somebody who's gotta know. They're gonna be real worried. Our situation is very…precarious. They could be thinking all kinds of bad stuff."

The scientist chuckled again.

"With good cause, or so it would appear."

David stirred under the covers, moving and feeling his body for the first time. He stung all over from scrapes and cuts. There was a large bandage on his side, next to his liver, that was held in place by tape that was wrapped all the way around his midsection, and another, smaller one, around his forearm. But he could move his arms and legs just fine. He was OK.

Another thought popped in. He'd been spotted. They would figure out it was him. He knew it for certain. He knew how they worked, and they had their ways. They would stop at nothing to find him, and they would put one and one together as far as Kelly was concerned. She was in even more danger than before.

He put the bottle of water on the table next to the bed, and placed his hand against the spot on the side of his head. He felt a lump about the size of a half an orange. He pressed against it ever so gently, and it sizzled with pain that crackled across the top of his skull.

He clenched his eyes shut - then forced them open, and looked back up at the scientist.

"I've gotta talk to her – get word to her. If I don't, they might do something…rash. And she's in more danger than she even knows. And I can't just call her. We don't use phones anymore. It's got to be face to face."

The scientist placed his fingers gently on his shoulder.

"OK. OK. Just slow down. We'll figure it all out. Sherri, Dr. Tennyson, made me promise that you stay put when you came to. She wants to check you out again before you get back on your feet. I'll give her a call. She's right down the street. Makes house calls. You stay put. I'll be right back."

David closed his eyes. He knew he was right. A little time wouldn't make any difference, even a few hours. It's only been a day.

He had an irresistible urge to think about all this, put all the pieces in place. He took another deep breath. It was way too much. Let it come to you, he thought.

The scientist returned after a few minutes.

"Left a message. She'll be here shortly – a couple hours max, probably sooner."

He pulled his chair over to the bed, and sat down.

They looked at each other, and grinned, like two Cheshire Cats.

They were total strangers, and yet they felt like they'd known each other forever. Neither of them had the faintest idea what was happening.

The moment had them both tongue-tied.

The scientist broke the silence.

"Who are you?" He asked, with a shake of his head.

"David. David Rhodes."

"Donald Morrisee."

He extended his hand, and David shook it.

"You're a scientist, right?"

"You've heard of me?"

"No, I told you. I've seen you – in a vision, kind of like a dream, a spiritual journey – kind of hard to describe. You were even wearing that same shirt. I was living in the wilderness in South Dakota, on an Indian reservation, and I was guided here by a shaman from the jungles of South America to find you."

David was looking at him like this was the simplest thing in the world.

Don's eyes were blazing into his, with his ever-present impish grin.

"Damnedest thing," he said in a hushed voice. "You know why I was waiting there for you? I had a dream the night before. It wasn't about you, and most of it's totally silly. I can't even remember a lot of it. But it took place on that street corner, at night. And when I woke up, that street corner was echoing in my head. Evans and Fountain. Evans and Fountain. It wouldn't stop. I had to go there. Something important was going to happen on the corner of Evans and Fountain, and I was supposed to be a part of it."

David chuckled.

"Hmm. Things are really coming together, aren't they?"

"You know these kinds of things don't happen to me," Don shook his head again. "I don't even dream that much – nothing out of the ordinary. And never anything supernatural – no premonitions, or anything like that. Just your basic Freudian kind of garbage. And now this!"

He extended his hands, gesturing toward David.

David squinted back, crinkling his forehead.

"What did happen?"

"I told my wife, and she and I drove to the corner of Evans and Fountain, parked the car, and waited to see if anything was going to happen. We made sure to get there right around dusk. That was part of it – Evans and Fountain in the evening. We saw the cops, and then them yelling, and shooting their guns. And then all the commotion inside that old building, the hollering, doors slamming, and more shooting. We got scared, and ran back to where the car was parked. We didn't want to get shot. Denise was all set to drive away. But I just couldn't get in the car. I couldn't leave. I had no idea what was possessing me. And then you come flying out that window, like you think you're Superman, and crash headfirst into the sidewalk. You almost landed on the hood of my car, for Christ's sake – missed it by a few feet – me too, for that matter. And I didn't even think. I scooped you up, threw you into the back seat of the car, and we sped out of there, like Bonnie and Clyde. Denise was half out of her frigging mind, but I really didn't give her much of a choice, did I?"

"What about the cops? They were right on my tail."

"Never saw em. Heard some more shots inside after you flew out. Then some more after we had driven away. I think they may have taken some shots at the car from the window, but we were too far away. And I'm sure that by the time they got back to their car, it was too late. We were long gone."

"The door must have held better than I thought. It's a good thing I locked that door before I jumped."

David closed his eyes, took another deep breath, and sighed.

"The divine spirit keeps watching over me, keeps guiding me on this path. It's been this way for over four years now."

Birds fluttered and chirped in the tree outside the window.

"You never answered my question, David," Don continued. "Who are you?"

David's thoughts had picked up their momentum. It was almost like he hadn't heard him.

"What kind of a scientist?"

"What?" Don laughed. "You don't know?"

They laughed together.

"No," he smiled. "I just saw you in your lab, at your computer, with all your gizmos and gadgets. The whole thing lasted about a minute or two. That's all I know."

Don was beyond shock. There was nothing David could say at this point that could surprise him.

"Energy," Don replied. "I'm an energy guy. Cold fusion, zero point energy, stuff like that. Alternative sources of free and infinite energy, so they can no longer use it to enslave us."

"Figures. It all comes back to energy, doesn't it, regardless of what level you're on?"

Don was studying him, calmly, patiently.

"Who are you, David Rhodes?" He slowly enunciated with exaggerated emphasis.

It got through this time. David was ready.

He reached for the water, and took another drink.

He told him his story. He didn't struggle with it in the slightest, like with Tom. He didn't concern himself with the proper chronology, whether it sounded too outrageous, or whether Don knew what the hell he was talking about. He knew he was meant to be with this man, and that was all that mattered. The particulars would sort themselves out as they went along. He just let it go, stream of consciousness style. He started where he started, and ended where he ended.

Don was enthralled, riveted on every word. His sparkly brown eyes never wavered from David's. The impish grin never left his face. He never interjected. He didn't ask any questions. He sat serenely, and soaked it all up, like warm sunshine. He too had a strong sense that this was exactly where he was supposed to be, and this the man he was supposed to be with. He knew that this story was vitally important. And he knew that he was a part of it.

It was getting dark when David reached the end.

"So how do you fit into all this? Or perhaps I should say, how do I fit in with you?

They held each other with their eyes. It was like beams of energy binding them together.

"I get it," Don replied, shaking his head. "It's as clear as a bell. You'll see. At least the first step is. We're having a meeting tomorrow night. Obviously, you're supposed to be there. There's a group of us. You're a perfect fit. We're a bunch of rebels. Rebels against the current system. Rebels against the *uni*. Rebels who understand how the game is played, and with a vision of a better world. Most of us have been drawn here, just like you...."

He broke into a broad grin, and burst into laughter.

"Well, not quite that fantastic! I was living in small town outside Boston. And the guy who owns this house, a big-wig geologist from Berkeley, who had heard of me and my work, got a hold of me through the grapevine, and told me I had to come here, and be a part of this. So here I am. Like you, the *New World Order* turned me into kind of a gypsy. Lost my house. Me and my wife had to go underground, just like you and Kelly."

He laughed again. His laughter came from deep inside his chest. It was melodious and resonant.

"Not on an Indian reservation in South Dakota, but you know what I mean."

Don looked off into space, like he was getting lost in his musings. His eyes regained their sharpness, and returned to David's.

"Yeah, we're quite a group. But you'll fit right in. We've got just about all the bases covered. Scientists – geology, physics, astronomy, new energy. Some of the foremost experts on *The Shift* you're talking about. Natural food and sustainable farming. There's an economist, with a specialty in how real money works, and private money. A former politician, a Libertarian, ran for President in 2004. There's a UFO and ET guy – had a bunch of sightings and contacts. A survivalist, who knows all about underground shelters, and how to survive if the worst happens when the poles shift. Writers and musicians. A doctor, who'll be here shortly, and a couple of other natural healers, energy healers. We've even got a full-blooded Hopi Indian, who knows all about the ancient prophesies. And tomorrow night, our two main computer geeks have something they want to announce, something big. They've been keeping it completely under wraps. I don't even know what it's all about. Nobody does."

David had only one thought, one feeling. He felt it in every cell of his body. Perfect – it was all so perfect. This was why he never doubted the mysterious workings of the divine spirit. All he had to do was live up to his side of the bargain. All he had to do was keep the connection intact, and things always worked out with such absolute perfection.

Don's eyes were surveying David pensively.

"Yeah, we've got most of the bases covered, but you definitely add something, something major, particularly with your sightings, and your...light travel...other dimensional travel, and with...your connection with the tribe in South American, and the whole indigenous thing. That's huge. I've heard people talk about this kind of stuff, but you're actually doing it. That's some powerful stuff, big medicine, as Black Horse, our Hopi, would say. If we could enlist that, we can do amazing things."

There was noise downstairs, like a door closing - then footsteps on the stairs.

"It's me, Don," a pleasant female voice rang out.

Dr. Sherri Tennyson entered the room. She was fortyish, with lively green eyes, a bright smile, with shiny white teeth, and short, straight dark-brown hair, fashionably styled, with bangs just above her eyebrows, and curling around her ears. She had the look of a casual professional, with a red blouse, white pearl necklace, a black swishy skirt, just above the knees, and flat, black, slip-on shoes.

She examined David, taking his vital signs, and paying particular attention to his eyes, shining a tiny light into them, and asking him to track it. Everything checked out OK. Then, he got out of bed, in his red plaid boxer shorts from Wall Mart, and tested his gait, and his balance. He started out slowly, and picked up speed, walking back and forth across the room. He felt slightly unsteady, and his head and his side hurt, but he was OK. He and Don had been talking for quite a while, and he had been feeling better and better the whole time.

As she examined him, and as David tested his legs, Don stood behind her, off to one side, and recounted the highlights of David's story in the measured tone of a teacher giving a lecture. He sounded like a subliminal tape, broadcasting into one ear, while the rest of her attended to David. And she seemed quite adept at doing these two things at once, her eyes calm, yet focused, the peaceful smile planted on her face.

Don said that his name was David Rhodes, and he was crucial to their cause, like the last piece of the puzzle. He said that David had special gifts, and that his story confirmed what they all suspected, and had heard from so many other sources. The controllers were not of this world. David was able to see through their mask, and see them in their true form. He was also in direct contact with spiritual and other etheric beings, both in this dimension and others, who were also playing a critical part in the struggle against the forces of darkness, and who would become their powerful allies at some point. But first, they would need to lay the foundation, in this dimension. He told her that David had been very high on the controller's most wanted list, and had been hiding out on an Indian Reservation in South Dakota for three years, while awaiting a sign from the powers that guide him on what to do next. He and his girlfriend Kelly had received that sign in the form of a vision of Don, and had come to Oakland to find him. He came flying out of that window, and into their hands, after he had been stopped by two policemen, who he detected as alien beings, and who in turn could see that he saw them as they really were. Hence, the chase.

Sherri was sitting on the side of the bed, as David completed another trip across the room. She listened to Don's entire discourse without changing her expression, and without saying a word.

David placed his hand on the table to steady himself, and looked at her beseechingly.

"You know, I'm definitely a little shaky, and my body hurts like hell, but this is exceedingly important. I've got to get to the Hilton to tell my girlfriend and my other friends that I'm OK. If I don't, who knows what they might do. And they've gotta know what happened. I can't use the phone. And nobody can call for me. It just wouldn't work. Too many things can go wrong. Especially now, now that they've probably figured out I'm back in the picture, and in Oakland. They'll definitely put the pieces together. I've been dealing with them for a long time, and I've got a real sense for these things. We're dealing with awesome powers here. Kelly's in more danger than she even knows. She's got to know."

Sherri calmly looked at Don, then back at David.

"Normally, I'd definitely say no. But there's nothing normal about any of this."

Her eyes returned to Don.

"Don, you go with him, OK? And you drive. Definitely no driving. And don't leave him alone, not even for an instant. And if you take a turn for the worse, if you start feeling even a little bit weird, I want you to get back here as quickly as possible, and call me. Bring your girlfriend with you. If this was the old days, you'd be in the hospital, for sure."

Her eyes glanced off into space for an instant, then darted back to him.

"Come to think of it, come back here as soon as possible anyway, and bring your girlfriend with you. Spend the night here. I'd much rather have you close by. And then I can come and see you in the morning. OK?"

David nodded.

Then he broke into a smile, and started giggling, as he looked at Don.

"I can't wait to see the look on her face when she sees you."

It was about eight o'clock, and about a twenty-minute drive to the hotel.

While they drove, Dr. Donald Morrisee filled in most of the blanks from his story. David was somewhat surprised that he had never heard of him before. For over twenty years, he had been a pioneer in the research and exploration for new sources of alternative energy to replace petroleum. He had started and was president of a foundation in Massachusetts, and was the editor of a foremost magazine in this area, as well as the author of several books. His primary focus was cold fusion, which is based on the very simple principle that when an electric current is passed through water, there is a significant increase in heat phenomena, as well as other nuclear phenomena. Cold fusion was always rejected by the scientific establishment, at least ostensibly, because these findings could never be explained on the basis of any of the existing scientific paradigms. Clearly, the real reason was the threat that it posed to the international oil monopoly, and the stranglehold that it had over the people of the world.

Dr. Morrisee had gone as far as inventing a cold fusion device, about the size of a hot water heater, which could supply all the energy needs of the average household, including automobiles, and far more. All that was needed was sufficient funding for mass production, and overcoming all of the other political, special interest and practical obstacles associated with anything that would totally revolutionize the lifestyle of the entire world. Then, the crash and the *New World Order* put an end to all this.

Dr. Morrisee was almost entirely blackballed by the mainstream media. In his magazine, lectures and books, he was a harsh critic of how established science had abandoned the true scientific method, and sold out to big money, most notably the oil, chemical and pharmaceutical cartels. He had always had clear insight into how the world really worked, behind the scenes, and though he was only recently learning about the role played by malevolent ET's, he had been aware for quite some time that there were forces of evil at work here that went far beyond mere greed.

Like David, he got too close to the real truth, making him a marked man. He was relentlessly spied upon in every aspect of his life. His website was continuously hacked, and brought down. He received anonymous death threats against his wife and children. On one occasion, an attempt was even made on his life, or at least to frighten him into backing off, when he was run off the road in his car.

He saw through the shenanigans of the *New World Order* instantly. He, his wife, Denise, and their son and daughter, both grown up, refused the *uni*, and went underground. He was a beloved man, with a vast network of friends and associates, some with the *uni*, some without. Survival was not a problem, but he had to be constantly on guard. The controllers would have liked nothing better than to find a reason, or to fabricate one, to take this man, so dangerous to their agenda, out.

Again like David and Kelly in South Dakota, he was in a holding pattern. He was waiting. He had a strong sense that he had a part to play in defeating the *New World Order*, but he had no idea what it was. He too believed that things were not as grim as they might appear. He was aware that there were other forces at work here, and that *The Shift* could quite likely fundamentally transform the battlefield upon which they were waging this struggle.

Then, one day he was handed a letter by a colleague from Dr. Gregory Wolfe, Chairman of the Geology Department at UC Berkeley. Dr. Wolfe was a double agent of sorts. On the one hand, he was a highly acclaimed academician, who had consented to the *uni*, and on the other, he was involved in the underground movement opposing the *New World Order*. He had been familiar with Dr. Morrisee's work for many years, and he knew his whereabouts through his underground sources. In the letter, he invited Don to join his eclectic group of scholars, professionals, artists and others in Oakland, who were seeking to find ways to overturn the *New World Order*, and create a different world.

The man who handed him the letter was driving back to Oakland the next day, and offered him a ride. Don knew instantly this was what he must do, and he and his wife were off to Oakland.

On the science side of things, Don had been moving away from his life-long allegiance to cold fusion in favor of zero point energy. All of the new paradigm science was converging around the hypothesis that the entire universe, including the vast amounts of so-called space in between material objects, consisted of an infinite field of interconnected energy. This energy was referred to as zero point energy. This was confirmed by the findings of Nikola Tesla at the beginning of the Twentieth Century, confirmed again in the forties and fifties by Wilhelm Reich, no relation to David Reich, with his theories about Orgone Energy, and more recently with the revolutionary discoveries in Quantum Physics. Zero point energy was not electromagnetic, though it did share many of its properties. It also had some of the properties of optic and sound waves, and others that the new scientists didn't understand at all. Zero point energy was something completely different, and many scientists believed they would never understand it, and perhaps weren't meant to. That didn't mean they couldn't put it to productive use.

Don was captivated by the writings on this topic by Dr. Maxwell Linder, a foremost Quantum Physicist, with whom he had a lot in common. Dr. Linder was also a renegade against established science, who had also disappeared after the imposition of the *New World Order*. His pet project was the invention of a simple motor, which used a conventional electric charge and a series of magnets to extract zero point energy from the quantum field. Don was enraptured. Here was a source of energy even more clean, efficient and infinite than the small amounts of water needed for cold fusion.

And best of all, when Don got to Dr. Wolfe's in Oakland, he was stunned and thrilled beyond measure that Max Linder was already there, and was a part of the group. They instantly become fast friends.

Don and most of the others in the Oakland group were also getting a real crash course in the fact that there were some very powerful and mysterious forces at work here, forces that seemed to be bringing them together, and working to shape a different future. For those who didn't believe in such things before, they did now. And they all agreed. This was one of the main things that spurred them on, and gave them hope.

David and Don agreed that zero point energy, or Orgone Energy, or quantum field energy, or whatever you chose to call it, was nothing new. The new paradigm science was simply catching up with what shamans, sorcerers, and indigenous spiritual traditions, not to mention most of the traditional Chinese, Japanese and Asian healing traditions, have known for thousands of years, and more accurately, at least for many of them, hundreds of thousands of years, perhaps longer. They knew that every nuance of the universe is an expression of energy, and they derived their awesome powers, akin to magic, from the fact that they learned how to see this energy directly, and they knew how to act in this world of energy. David's life had already been saved twice through his journeys in this world of energy.

They arrived at the hotel, and made their way up to David's room. He had told Don about the precautions he needed to take in public places. He also made sure that his Colorado Rockies baseball cap was covering the welt on his head to avoid undue attention. Don had also avoided public places such as these for quite some time, so he blended right in with David's routine. He was wearing his favorite straw Panama hat, with a chinstrap, and a sunglasses clip over his glasses. Together with his blue Hawaiian shirt, he looked like a Caribbean traveler.

God, I hope they haven't done anything, David thought, as he got out of the elevator. I hope they just waited.

They got to his room, and Kelly wasn't there. But all her stuff was.

They went next door, and knocked on Peter and Janice's door. David was relieved to hear Peter's voice inside, approaching the door.

Kelly was there with them. They were having dinner.

Hugs and kisses and tears followed.

David and Kelly held each other in silence for several minutes, eyes closed, breath sputtering. The others watched in silence, like statues. The love between David and Kelly stopped everything in its tracks.

"I knew you were OK," she said finally, her lips quivering. "I could just feel it. I knew it wasn't like Hickory Lake. I knew you weren't gone."

As they held each other, the three of them were aware of the stranger who had entered the room with David. But nobody said anything. First things first. David and Kelly had to have their moment.

They continued their embrace. It was like they had left their bodies, and their spirits were making love in a higher dimension.

"Boy, have I got a story to tell you," David whispered into her ear. "It's right up there with the best of em."

Kelly took a deep breath.

They were returning to this world.

Then the light went off in Kelly's head. She had only glanced at Don at first, but he was the last thing on her mind. But then it clicked. That shirt. She could never forget that shirt. But where had she seen it?

Arms still around David, her big blue eyes shot open into full circles, and focused on Don, who was standing right in front of her, next to the closed door.

Don returned her look, grinning serenely, impishly, still disguised in his hat and sunglasses. He felt like he had known her forever too, just like David. He wanted to join their embrace. He definitely belonged with these young people.

Kelly continued staring at him, and it all popped into place: that beard, that grin, that shirt, those scholarly glasses.

She pulled away from David, and glared into his eyes, their noses practically touching, her glistening eyes still bulging off her face.

"It' him! You found him!"

"It's him," he nodded, his face beaming. "I told you it was good."

FIVE ❦ THE FENCE

"We don't have to wait for *The Shift*," Patrice announced.

A murmur flowed like a wave through the audience.

"That's right," she went on. "We've been operating on the assumption, this whole time, that the only way we can get the upper hand, or at least be on an even playing field, would be for *The Shift* to throw everything into a state of complete chaos, as in a total crash of the technological infrastructure. That would put us on a more or less equal footing, at least until they figure out how to get their system up and running again, and it would provide us with possibly a great opportunity to reach lots of people, who would be completely disenchanted with the whole mess."

The audience had grown perfectly still, like the silence in between a flash of lightening and a crack of thunder.

"Not to mention all the other forces that would quite likely be at work that would throw them completely for a loop, and that could also work to our advantage."

She scanned the group that was packed into Dr. Gregory Wolfe's living room. Some were seated on couches and easy chairs, others on chairs that had been brought in from other rooms. Some were seated on the floor in front of her, and the rest were standing against the walls around the borders of the room.

She took a deep breath, and looked over her shoulder at Gemini, her colleague and partner in crime.

"Gemini and I believe we've found a way to push things forward. It's also a way that gives us control. Waiting for *The Shift* is like shooting craps. Not only do we not know precisely when it's going to happen, but when it does, we have no idea what we're going to be dealing with. Hell, there are those, like a very credible school of shamanic astrology, who believe that *The Shift* actually spans at least 144-years, and that at this time we're only a little over half way through it. They claim it started in 1926, and we have 59-years to go, at least. "

The crowd stirred again. It was like the tremor from a fast moving train. Where was she going with all this? What had they come up with?

"Oh, *The Shift* is happening, and it's happening now," she continued emphatically. "As Greg and so many of the other scientists here will confirm, the Earth's magnetic field continues to steadily decrease, at an increasing rate, and it's headed toward zero, and the Schumann Resonant Frequency, which is kind of like the Earth's heartbeat, has speeded up all the way to around 12 cycles per second. We're right on schedule here. According to our best estimates, the last time this happened was around 13,000 years ago, which was the last time the Earth experienced major cataclysms. At least that's what Daniel reports from his Hopi sources, and it's confirmed by the Mayans and countless others."

"And then there are things like the photon belt that we know are happening, but that we know practically nothing about. For those of you who don't know, the photon belt is a vast energy field that we are entering that is part of these cycles. Traditional, old-paradigm science really hits the wall with the photon belt because it appears to operate completely outside of any linear modality, and can really only be understood from a wholistic, holographic perspective, one that includes human consciousness. Most of what we know about the photon belt comes to us through channeling from our etheric sources. In the new paradigm, these are the new scientists. The photon belt too is happening, and it's happening now."

She looked at David and Kelly, and gestured toward them with her hand. They were sitting in the front row, on a couch, in between Donald Morrisee and Dr. Wolfe.

"And now your sources too tell us the same thing – shamans from a tribe in the jungles of South America, who have not been contaminated by western civilization, and Native Americans in South Dakota, who likewise have kept a grip on their true history, our true history, not to mention the late David Reich. The whole world branded Reich's ideas crazy, including, I dare say, many in this room, but virtually everything he said is turning out to be true."

David's eyes were glued on her. He was feeling a strange euphoria he had never experienced before. He had waited for this moment, for these people, for what seemed like his entire life. At everything he did, he had always been the youngest. He had always been the precocious one, the boy genius. Ever since his mother was murdered, when he was four, he never belonged, at least not to a group, or to anybody. Then, he met Kelly, and he belonged to her, and after that David Reich, who was like a father, though for all too brief a time. And he had been ripped away too.

And now, in this moment, he belonged to this group, to these people. And they belonged to each other. He was no longer a freak of nature. He was one of them.

And they had all been drawn together by forces none of them understood. He was certain that virtually all of them were feeling this too. He knew Kelly was. Their bond was far beyond the need to say anything. And he could feel it in the rest of them. He could feel it in the atmosphere around him. He hadn't met all of them, but in those he had, he could see it in their eyes, and feel it in their energy.

And best of all, this mysterious and novel feeling, this feeling of belonging, this feeling of like-minded thoughts, of kindred souls, of unified energy and vision, had power. There was power in this room, in this group, that was palpable. There was power that could move mountains, and perform the unimaginable. There was the power that enabled the Biblical David to slay the mighty Goliath with a tiny stone.

David thought of Hibutu, Mahnya and the Togi. He remembered feeling this way, this feeling of belonging, when he was with them, if only for a fleeting moment. He felt that he was one of them also. And Hibutu or Mahnya, or whoever it was that addressed the totality of his being on that journey, had sent the message that when the time was right, and they had fulfilled their task, these groups, and others from the spirit world, would come together, and be as one.

David wondered if Hibutu and Mahnya were there with them now, watching, eavesdropping, if they had made the trip on wings of light.

Of course they are, he thought. They had taught him well. That's why he was thinking about them. They had placed themselves in his mind.

He looked at Kelly. Their eyes met. He gestured to the space around them with his eyes, his eyeballs gazing around out of the tops of their sockets.

She understood instantly, and she followed him, doing the same.

Then, for the briefest of instants, he felt lighter, like his physical boundaries were dissipating, and the entire room, and everybody in it, glowed, just a momentary flicker.

Yes, they were there with them.

As quickly as it came, it went. It was important that they stay in the moment, with their group.

Message received.

They looked back at each other, nodded, and smiled. Then, they returned their eyes to Patrice.

She and Gemini certainly didn't give the appearance of two of the world's foremost computer geeks. Like David and Kelly, they were younger than most of the rest. Patrice was probably around Kelly's age, mid-thirties, early forties, and Gemini looked even younger, maybe early thirties. David thought they both looked like kids. Patrice was very pretty, in a plain and unpretentious, almost sloppy way, with long, straight, unkept, dark hair, and smooth classic features. She was wearing a light blue turtleneck top and wrinkled, beige pants that draped loosely around her small, slight frame. It was like she was attractive, in spite of herself. Gemini, in his faded jeans and white, short sleeve shirt, with a collar, had a rascally look, with straight, fiery red hair, a glint in his dark eyes, and a devilish smile.

They could all feel it. David was certain. The room was supercharged, and Hibutu and Mahnya, and who knows who else, were hovering about in its ethers. Belonging, unity, power, and it was also the exhilaration of discovery, of learning new things at an exponential rate. Along with all the other features of *The Shift* that were occurring in the world, this too was obviously speeding up, at least for those who were open to it, like the people in this room. And this learning, this awakening, also seemed to have a power that was unprecedented, and could not be denied, like David's tiny stone. For so many, learning the truth about how the world really worked was frightening, depressing and overwhelming. But for this group, connected as they were to the source of their power, it was like the verse from the Bible: "Ye shall know the truth, and the truth shall set you free."

The meeting was already over two hours old, and yet it hadn't lost a speck of its vitality. The time had zoomed by, and if it kept going the way it was, they could go all night. Nobody was tired. Nobody was bored. Nobody was looking at their watch, wanting to go home. Each moment burst with fresh illumination. It was like a natural stimulant, an orgy of enlightenment. Nourished with energy like this, none of them would ever need food anymore.

The first two hours were devoted to introducing David and Kelly, and telling their story. David and Kelly had spent the entire day and the previous night at Dr. Wolfe's, and had already met many of them. Don had been spreading the word ever since David crash-landed on the scene, and many of them stopped by that day to meet them.

David and Kelly were struck by the fact that everybody they met that day had one unique thing in common. They were all not the slightest bit startled by the unusual and spectacular nature of their story. They all accepted David's amazing meeting with Don, and the portentous nature of David and Kelly's odyssey from South Dakota, as a matter of course. That's the way things had been working for them for quite some time, and they all had experienced similar things themselves. They were all keenly aware that there were powerful forces at work, though many of them didn't fully understood what they were.

There was one other thing too. David and Kelly even discussed it, and they both had a hard time coming up with the words to describe it. It was as though everybody they met was expecting them, in a peculiar way. Like Don had said, the group was quite comprehensive, and they seemed to have all their bases covered, and yet they all gave the impression that David and Kelly were a perfect fit for the final empty slot. And prior to meeting them, they didn't even know what this slot was. All they knew was they were not complete. A piece was missing. And now, with David and Kelly's arrival, this was fixed. They were now a whole unit. David and Kelly still had to find their place within this, but the time for preparation was over. The time to act had arrived.

And whatever Patrice and Gemini were about to announce looked like it was going to be the first step.

The group didn't have an official leader or spokesperson. It was an experiment in spontaneous group dynamics. In other words, they all just went with the flow. Whoever wanted to speak did so, and whatever happened happened. Each took responsibility based upon their own unique contribution. They all viewed their mission as something they shared. Each had a clear part to play, and everybody seemed to know what their part was. Nobody was there for a free ride. Nobody was there to control or dominate.

One thing was for certain: it worked. And it worked because they trusted each other. They all agreed that the problem with most groups had nothing to do with structure or hierarchy. It had to do with people. If the people involved had their shit together individually, then the group worked.

However, when they looked to somebody to orchestrate their proceedings, that part seemed to fall to Don, and another gentleman, named Chris Buckley. Chris had stopped by the house early that day, and he was one of the first to meet David and Kelly. He was in his early seventies, and he still had jet-black hair, smooth skin, browned from the sun, and the appearance of a man thirty years younger. Like Don and several of the others, Chris had achieved mini-celebrity status in the alternative culture prior to the crash and the imposition of the *New World Order*. He was a no-holds-barred writer, investigative journalist, and public speaker, whose niche was exposing how the world really worked, behind the scenes. The world, of course, labeled him a conspiracy nut, and yet, like David Reich, just about everything he wrote about turned out to be true. He warned the public about the *New World Order* over a decade and a half before it came to be. His website was a foremost source of alternative news and information, exposing the deceit and manipulation of the government and those who owned it. He had also been a long-time friend and colleague of both Don and Reich. Like so many of his ilk, when free speech became the equivalent of a crime against the state, he became a marked man. He and his wife Laura, a natural healer, refused the chip, and went underground.

The entire day was a whirlwind of new names and faces for David and Kelly. It would take some time to get them all straight. Peter and Janice had also decided to join them. The night before at the hotel, David informed Don that they were chipped, and told him what invaluable allies they had been. Don invited them to the meeting. Peter couldn't resist the temptation to play sick for that day's meeting, and he and Janice spent the entire day at Dr. Wolfe's. It was getting infectious.

Several of the others had also received the *uni*. This facilitated matters tremendously, as it gave them access to virtually everything in the mainstream system, including computers, the Internet, and drivers' licenses, not to mention purchasing power. Those with the *uni* then served as double agents, with one foot in each world. Needless to say this placed them in great danger, making it mandatory to keep an extremely low profile, and not to attract the slightest suspicion. It was no secret, at least to those who knew how the game was played, that the *uni* could be used for far more than mere scanning, identification, and accessing a person's database. It could also be used to track by satellite a person's physical location, as well as to electronically control a person's thoughts and emotions. Anybody with the *uni* was at risk of becoming a total robot, a slave to whatever its programmers desired. This was actually done to a very small percentage of the population on a random basis, but primarily for the purpose of testing and experimentation. Since the vast majority of the population had already willingly given their minds away, it was only necessary to use these methods with those who were perceived as serious enemies of the *New World Order*.

The most painful irony for those with the *uni* was the peril it placed them in if they won the battle. They were safe as long as they weren't detected, and as long as the current system was in place. Once it wasn't, who knows what might happen. The controllers had the power to throw the switch, and kill them all.

Dr. Wolfe and his wife were chipped. As the Chairman of the Geology Department at the University of California, Berkeley, he had no choice. On the surface, he was a traditional geologist. Behind the scenes, he was a foremost expert on *The Great Shift of the Ages*, and what was really happening to the planet Earth, information that was carefully and systematically concealed from the public. When he was questioned on these matters in a public forum, Dr. Wolfe played his part, and discredited any scientific data supporting *The Shift*.

Dr. Sherri Tennyson was also chipped. She was a physician, with a medical license issued by the American Region of The United Union, or Union (U), which consisted of the former US, Canada, Mexico, and Central and South America. *Unis* were mandatory for all physicians. Medical licenses were no longer issued by the states, such as California, and a plan was in the works for them to eventually be issued by the U. She was also a provider for the Universal Health Insurance (*uhi*) of the American Region, which was also mandatory for all physicians in order to have a license. Without a license, it was illegal to practice any form of health care, even something as innocuous as the pastoral counseling traditionally done by the churches.

Jumping through all these hoops was demanding, but Sherri knew how to play the game, and she played it impeccably. To the world, she was a general practitioner, who operated her practice from an office in her home. She did deviate slightly from the norm because her specialty was vitamins and nutritional supplements, all of which were now under the control of the U, and which required a prescription by a medical doctor. The regulation of vitamins and supplements had also resulted in the significant dilution of the potency of most of these substances, as well as the substitution of synthetic ingredients for natural ones, thereby paving the way for their eventual replacement by pharmaceuticals.

Sherri's practice was about as unconventional as it got in the *New World Order* medical system, so her patients did tend to be looking for alternatives to the drugs and high-tech surgery of established medicine. Once the door closed, and when she had a patient she could trust, Sherri practiced various forms of natural and energy healing. Here again, she never took any chances. If there was the slightest doubt, she played the game, and toed the party line. She always had to be on the lookout for undercover agents, posing as patients, who were particularly plentiful in her specialty area, and who liked nothing better than busting a doctor for violating protocol. Word of mouth also spread through the underground culture about the kind of work Sherri did, and most of her patients came by this route.

There was also a married couple, named Francis and John Lapham. Their niche was organic food, farming, and sustainable agriculture, which meant free and independent farmers who replenished the soil, and raised farm animals for dairy products and meat the good, old-fashioned way - naturally. They wrote several well-known books on these topics, and published a foremost journal on organic gardening and farming. Francis and John were newcomers to the underground scene. They never thought twice about getting the *uni*. For a long time, they knew that there was something terribly wrong with the version of the world that was handed to them by the mainstream, but they couldn't pin down what it was. Then, about a year ago, a friend introduced them to the writings of Chris Buckley and David Reich, and the light went off. All the pieces finally fit together, and there was no turning back.

Under the *New World Order*, agriculture was totally dominated by a cartel of a few huge multi-national corporations, with an exclusive emphasis on food that was grown and developed through the use of chemicals, high technology and genetic engineering. Family farms had been driven out of business, and were a thing of the past. Food, then, consisting primarily of mind-altering chemicals, became another means of suppressing the emotions and the will of the people, and yet another method of mind-control.

Ostensibly, these corporate farms were under the control of the U, but in fact, it was the hierarchies of these corporations, and banks, in every sector of the business world, that called the shots. As you ascended the pyramid of power, it became clear that it was the same people, or beings, who were in charge. At the highest levels, the hierarchies of all these corporations and professions interlocked, and consisted of the same people/beings. And the higher up the pyramid of power you went the more invisible those who actually held the reins of power became, preferring to delegate authority to subordinates, or operating through a vast network of international secret societies, where *the global elite* gathered to make their most important decisions. For the precious few with the most power, at the very top of the pyramid, holding a position in the government was unthinkable. They looked upon even the highest Union officials as puppets or paid stooges.

One of the more intriguing characters David and Kelly met that day was a renegade cop, Lieutenant Frank Jacoby of the San Francisco Police Department. Like every other branch of the traditional system, law enforcement had also sold out to the *New World Order*, and the farther up the hierarchy you went the more true this was. The police too were virtually hired guns for the *New World Order*. And at its highest levels, intelligence agencies like the CIA and the FBI were bastions for the alien beings, shapeshifters, and those who served the dark agenda. The CIA and the FBI were unchanged with the advent of the *New World Order*. They served *the global elite* and the fascist agenda before. They served it after.

But not Frank Jacoby. Frank Jacoby was an old fashioned cop, who believed his oath of office was a sacred pact between him and the people. He understood the law, in its most strict and organic terms, and he believed he was morally bound to uphold it, and to protect the inherent rights of the people from injustice. Obviously, Frank understood the depravity of what was going on around him in the PD. He believed he could do the most good as a double agent, and he had the benefit of all the PD's access to those citizens who were considered serious threats to the *New World Order* agenda. Frank was well connected in the underground. That's how he met Dr. Wolfe.

Frank had no idea that David and Kelly were at Dr. Wolfe's. Because of the precariousness of his role, Dr. Wolfe's group did not contact Frank like they did the others. They left him alone to do his own thing. Yet, he was guided to Dr. Wolfe's that day, in the same manner as so many of the rest. He had heard about the incident with David at The Chip-Free Zone. He was intrigued at the attention this apparently minor fracas was receiving, and that it was even being investigated by some relatively high officials in the CIA. So, Frank decided to do some homework, privately, and he discovered the identities of Mr. David Rhodes and Ms. Kelly Archer.

David and Kelly were chatting with Dr. Wolfe and a few of the others when Frank arrived. David noticed him, as this incredibly intense man, with fire in his eyes, marched resolutely up to their group, like he was on a mission, never taking his eyes off David and Kelly for an instant. Frank's frame was imposing, with a tall, stocky build, and a robust expression, with large dimples. He was bald on the top, with short dark brown hair on the sides, and thick eyebrows. His clothes were totally Ivy League – a brown, tweed sports jacket, a white shirt, with a button down collar, and newish blue jeans, with a crease.

David felt a twinge of fear as this stranger approached.

Dr. Wolfe turned around. He greeted Frank, and started to officially introduce him, but Frank bluntly interrupted.

"I know. I know. I know who they are. I've been looking at mug shots all morning. Though I must say you two are very good at changing your appearance."

Frank turned to Dr. Wolfe, and shook his hand.

"You know you've got public enemies numbers one and two here. The big boys definitely want to take these two fine looking young people out. I must say I'm impressed. It's interesting too just who they consider to be serious threats, is it not? These two young folks don't look like they could fight their way out of a paper bag. But it's got nothing to do with that anymore, does it?"

A huge grin flashed across Frank's face, his dimples showing. They all laughed.

Dr. Wolfe invited Frank to stay for the meeting, and he accepted.

Daniel Black Horse, the young Hopi Indian, with a distinguished lineage to the Hopi elders of yesteryear, also stopped by early that day. He had come from Sedona, Arizona, having been called almost identically as David and Kelly, by spirit guides in a dream journey. He had a vision of Chris Buckley, who he had never seen or heard of, on a beach off the Pacific Coast Highway just south of San Francisco. He found the beach, and there were Chris and Laura, sitting on a blanket, as if they were waiting for him.

Meeting Daniel was like discovering a long lost brother. The connection was instantaneous and profound, a true meeting of spirits. He was strikingly handsome, with well-chiseled features, long, thin, jet-black hair, in a ponytail, and an intensely serious, yet peaceful, expression. He too was a shaman and transformational healer, a gifted wood flutist and hand drummer, and well versed in sacred Hopi chants. They swapped yarns about their spirit guides, and even though one was from the Southwest US and the other South America, their stories were practically identical. Daniel was in complete agreement that the merging of these indigenous people and the spirit world with the world of these white folks, who were waking up to the truth and to the true nature of things, was essential to bringing about *The Shift*, and would become a major source of their power. He too saw his role as a link between these worlds.

Tara Bradley was one of the others who had stopped by early to meet them. Everybody seemed to have their niche, their part to play, and hers was traditional religion. She was a beautiful, young black woman, with fire in her eyes, and a red scarf wrapped around her head that was adorned with black, primitive, African symbols. She had been a Presbyterian minister, with her own church in Madison, Wisconsin.

She too had been outspoken critic of the government's fascist direction, as well as many traditional Christian dogmas, and she was under constant pressure from the church hierarchy to soften her ways. Most notably, she rebelled against both the concept of original sin and Jesus Christ as savior, maintaining that neither was consistent with the real teachings of Jesus. She preached that human beings were born into this world pure and good, and didn't need to be saved from anything. She also taught the members of her church that ultimately they didn't need an intermediary between God and themselves, such as a minister or a church, and that it was each person's responsibility to discover God in their own way, in particular the divine that is within each of us, and throughout this glorious world and universe. Rather than alienate her congregation, this message exploded her church membership, and she began to attract media attention, and mini-celebrity status. When Tara refused the *uni*, and encouraged her congregation to do the same, it was front-page news in Madison. The church revoked her ministry, and fired her.

This was precisely how the system was designed to work, and it was working perfectly. Under the *New World Order*, the traditional churches, which in America consisted primarily of all the various sects of Christianity and Judaism, were among the rare institutions that were left entirely alone. The power elite had complete trust that the church hierarchies, like the corporate hierarchies, could police themselves, and keep their member branches in line with the *New World Order* agenda. In fact, this was assured because, once again, these church hierarchies, at their highest levels, consisted of clergymen who were nothing more than agents of *the global elite*. This is how it had been for thousands of years, as with, for example, the Vatican, one of the wealthiest institutions in the world, whose true agenda never had anything to do with Catholicism, but was rather one of power and control. The same principle held here as everywhere else. The farther up the pyramid of power you went, the more you would find that all these ruling hierarchies interlocked. It was all the same people, merely wearing different masks. Since the beginning of time, institutional religion has been one of the power elite's primary vehicles of mind control.

As afternoon shifted into evening, and the meeting time approached, Dr. Wolfe's house filled up with these extraordinary people, all with such extraordinary stories. One by one, David and Kelly met them. The vibe was always the same. They were enthralled with David and Kelly's story, and they acted like they were expecting them, like they were the final piece of the puzzle.

There was Dr. Max Linder, quantum physicist, mentor to Dr. Donald Morrisee, proponent of zero point energy, and inventor of a simple motor that extracted this energy from quantum space. There was Andrew Asher, a French Canadian musician from Quebec, who played guitar, and sang sacred chants from religions and indigenous spiritual traditions spanning the globe, and his partner, Tamisha, a beautiful young East Indian woman, who played a variety of hand drums, and performed ancient sacred dances to this music. There was Steven Babcock, 2004 Presidential Candidate from the Libertarian Party, and foremost authority on how the world would work with minimal government, and work better. There was Clay Finley, an economist, a black man, with an expertise on alternative forms of private money. There was Michael Hoover, a survivalist, whose knowledge of self-subsistence and living off the land would come in very handy if there was any sort of planetary catastrophe accompanying *The Shift*. There was Dr. Arthur Griggs, previous head of an organization that researched and studied extraterrestrial and UFO contacts over the years, as well as the military and government cover-ups of this by virtually all the major nations. Dr. Griggs also currently claimed to have contacts with several benevolent ET sources.

And a host of others, and yes, they did appear to have all the bases covered.

At the start of the meeting, Dr. Donald Morrisee did the honors of introducing David and Kelly, and Peter and Janice, to the whole group. They didn't intend to take a full two hours, but once they got rolling, there was no stopping it. And the group couldn't get enough of their magnificent and mysterious odyssey. This was clearly a match made in heaven.

Don started by telling them about his dream, and the fact that he just knew that he and Denise had to go to the corner of Evans and Fountain that evening. If they didn't, they would probably miss out on something of critical importance.

"And it was all so preposterously easy and straightforward. I had no idea what was happening, and yet it was clear as a bell what I had to do. Guns were going off inside the old hotel, pounding and yelling, and David comes smashing headfirst out of the window, and lands just a couple of feet from me and the car, out cold. I didn't even hesitate. There was no thinking involved. I picked him up, and threw him into the back seat, and off we went. The cops never had a chance. David locked the door to the room before he jumped, and that's all the time we needed. I know Denise probably felt differently, but I wasn't worried about the cops at all. I was just worried about David."

He started talking about the vision David and Kelly had of him in his makeshift lab that brought them to Oakland, but he stopped himself.

"I think it would be better if they told you about that themselves. But what I'd like to try to do is sum up a couple of the extraordinarily important things that they bring to us, things that just might kick us into the next gear. First of all, they both have an ability that will put to an end, once and for all, to the debate we've been having for such a long time. They have the ability to see our adversaries in a different form, dare I say, in their true form. And it appears as though it's true, as many of us have suspected, that what we're dealing with here is not human. We've all agreed all along that we're dealing with forces of evil of the most wicked and even satanic kind. What David and Kelly report puts an end to that most troublesome question: How could human beings be capable of this? We have our answer. They're not."

He scanned his audience. They were perfectly still, all eyes fastened on him, riveted on his every word. As unbelievable as what he was saying sounded, they trusted him. They had been moving in this direction anyway, and now this just capped if off.

"And secondly, they have other special abilities that transcend the material world. These are the types of abilities, the types of power, that we're going to need to meet the great challenge before us, and to use the great forces that are quite likely going to be unleashed by *The Shift* to our advantage. This is a world that Dr. Linder and the quantum physicists tell us about because it's the world they play around in. It's a world where our familiar laws of cause and effect no longer hold, where our ordinary boundaries of space and time can be exceeded, and where the unimaginable becomes the order of the day. It's a world Black Horse tells us about because it's the world his Hopi ancestors lived in, great sorcerers of yesteryear, a world where they performed magical and stupendous feats."

He closed his eyes, and breathed deeply. The audience before him was like a becalmed lake on a benign summer day – still, but replete with hidden power down to its deepest depths.

He hadn't planned on saying all these things. He didn't know where the words were coming from. He felt like he was being possessed by the energy that pervaded the space around him.

He opened his eyes, and words kept flowing, like waves of light through the lens of his spirit.

"And alliances. David and Kelly bring to us vital alliances, alliances without which we cannot persevere in this great challenge. Like the alliance Black Horse brings us with the Hopi elders and his immortal ancestors in the spirit world, David and Kelly bring to us an alliance with indigenous people throughout the world, people who have contacted them, people who have kept their connection with the ancient wisdom. It is also an alliance with higher, etheric worlds or dimensions, a spirit world, a world that radiates from the source, and with which these indigenous people, like Black Horse's Hopis, stay in contact. Though these indigenous people live in jungles and in the outback and in primitive locations around the world, some of them as yet untouched by civilization, they know that there's something wrong with the world. They can feel it in the Earth's vibrations, and their spirit connections let them know. They know that there are forces of evil at work, disturbing nature's precious balance, and tampering with the human race. And they can feel our presence, human beings who are doing our utmost to stay connected with the ancient wisdom. They know we're here. And they want to help. They want to play their part in keeping the Earth alive. This is big medicine, my friends."

He looked at David and Kelly with his kind, playful eyes.

David didn't think he possibly could have said what he did any more beautifully and eloquently.

Don beckoned to them with his hand.

"Come. Come up. Say a few words."

They stepped forward, and faced the audience.

There were probably close to a hundred people crammed into the room, and spilling out into the hallway. They felt like one. It was stunning how quiet they all were. It was like the entire world, and everything in it, had stopped, and was listening at this precious moment.

David and Kelly's eyes met. She gazed up into the space around them, her eyes rotating around in the tops of their sockets. They were feeling it again. They were not alone.

She faced the crowd, made eye contact with all of them, or so it seemed, and smiled angelically, her big blue eyes glittering.

"Can you feel it?" she said in her sweet and melodious tone.

When Kelly spoke from the heart, which was always, it sounded like she was singing, like a sacred celestial chant.

She scanned them all again in a single glance. They were still. Nobody moved. Even though they didn't know what she was talking about, she could see in their vibrant eyes and peaceful expressions that they understood, or would shortly.

She continued her song.

"A little over a week ago, David and I were visited late one night by a light traveler, a sorcerer from deep within the jungles of South America. His name was Hibutu. Hibutu took us on a dream journey, an inter-dimensional light journey, to his village, which has never had any direct contact with the civilized world. He introduced us to his wife, also a sorcerer, whose name was Mahnya, and to many of his relatives and friends in their community. They didn't speak to us in words, but in sounds, and they knew how to create pictures in our minds, which conveyed what they wanted to communicate far more clearly than words ever could. They told us that they used their ability to light travel to observe and learn about what was going on in the world outside of their village. That's how they discovered David and I, living in the wilderness on an Indian reservation in South Dakota. That's how they discovered Donald Morrisee, and they took us on another light journey, where we watched Don in his lab here in Oakland. They told us we had to find this man, and meet him, so we could work together to defeat the powers of darkness. I'm also certain that they, and many others like them, have watched and discovered many, if not all, of you in the same manner."

She took them all in with another glance. Now they knew. Once you got your feet through the door, as they all had, it was easy to fit all the pieces together. And once you were through that door, there was no turning back. The world would never be the same again.

Kelly was creating a picture in them, the same as Mahnya and Hibutu had done in her. Once you started riding this wave, the more these things started falling in place.

Her music played on.

"They're here with us now."

She nodded her head, and smiled beatifically.

"Can you feel it?"

She kept nodding, touching them all with her eyes.

"Hibutu and Mahnya are here with us right now, and who knows who else. They're watching us, and yes, guiding us. They wouldn't have missed this meeting for anything. And pretty soon, when the time is right, and we've completed our task, they'll be joining us – along with many others from other dimensions and etheric realms – the cosmic good guys, who can't wait to start playing their part in this great struggle. But first, we human beings have to reach critical mass. We have to demonstrate our willingness to take full responsibility to take back the planet from the cosmic bad guys. Without this, without us, none of the rest of it works."

The power of the silence and stillness in the room was palpable. They were like one being, with one heartbeat, all beating to the rhythm of the same drum.

Any questions about where Kelly and David fit in were answered in this moment.

Kelly took them all in with her eyes again, and the beat continued.

"Play along with me here. Let's welcome them. Everybody, all together, are you ready? Repeat after me."

They nodded as one, another wave passing through them.

"Namaste Hibutu."

"Namaste Hibutu," they intoned, like a choir filling the room.

"Namaste Mahnya."

"Namaste Mahnya," they echoed.

Nobody was shy. Everybody took part. They all believed. They were all feeling it.

They sounded like a chorus of Buddhist monks.

Perfect, even eerie, silence and stillness again, like the world outside had gone asleep.

It was twilight, and at that moment, a hummingbird brushed up against the screen of one of the open windows, its invisible wings vibrating like a finely tuned motor, suspended in one spot in the air, floating, defying gravity. It looked into the room with its beady little eyes, its tiny beak touching the screen. Then it was joined by another, most certainly its mate. They whirred together for an instant, purring like two celestial felines, peering into the room. They too were part of the meeting. Then they whizzed away, and were gone.

Perfect silence again.

Nobody budged. They all understood. Nobody had to say anything.

Kelly's eyes sparkled into them, touching them all with a single glance, as she finished her song.

"What a blessing to be alive in these sacred times, and sharing this with all of you on this perfect night."

She put her palms together, her fingers pointing into the air, and bowed in gratitude.

She stepped back.

Perfect silence reigned.

A dog barked in the distance. A horn honked on the street outside.

The spell was broken, for now.

David stepped forward, grinning like the cat that had swallowed the canary.

"Tough act to follow," he said in a hush.

They all laughed as one.

David then spoke, doing his best to fill in the blanks of their wild odyssey, and pretty soon Kelly jumped in, and joined him, filling in what he didn't. It was a challenge, but they covered it all, starting with the murder of David's mother, and her letter beseeching him to complete her quest, and going all the way through Kelly's rescue of him, and their magical escape from volcanic destruction of Martinelle, their subsequent hiatus in the wilderness of the Pine Ridge Reservation, and their recent inter-dimensional, light journeys with Hibutu and Mahnya.

"It makes a great story, doesn't it?" David commented when they finished. "Somebody should make a novel out of this. And a movie too. I'd pay to see it. Well, maybe not – no *uni*."

They all chuckled.

Patrice and Gemini were next. There was no break. It wasn't necessary. The energy they were generating created its own momentum, and carried them right through. It was nourishment, food, a natural drug. They were all pumped up, and ready for their next helping.

"Yes, *The Shift* is definitely happening," Patrice went on. "But we don't need to wait for it in its full force, whatever that will entail. We believe we've found a way to jump-start this whole thing, get a head start on our adversaries, and throw them a major curve ball at the same time, something we don't think there's any way they could anticipate. And something that could really throw things out of whack, at least for a little while. Something that could really swing things in our direction."

She was so excited she was out of breath. She placed her hand against the middle of her chest, and her tiny frame involuntarily swelled with air. She exhaled audibly out of her mouth.

"Forgive me," she said with a grin. "I'm more excited about all this than I thought."

"Gemini and I think we definitely have found a breakthrough," she went on. "I think most of you have probably heard of the frequency fence. But just in case, for those who maybe haven't, the Earth has been encased in a vibrational fence or net for a very long time. This amounts to a vibrational prison. Needless to say, we don't know a lot about this for sure because, like so many other things, it's top secret, and because our history has been so mucked up that it's difficult to know anything for certain. But it's our best guess that the frequency fence has been in place for far longer than what passes for our known history, and probably dates back at least to Atlantis and Lemuria, and the ancient civilizations that predated the cataclysms of 10-11,000 BC, roughly. Probably a lot longer because there's plenty of archaeological evidence to indicate that there were advanced forms of life here hundreds of thousands, perhaps even millions of years ago, and it's just as reasonable to believe that it was put in place as far back as then."

She had gathered herself. She was starting to roll.

"It appears as though the frequency fence, this vibrational prison, is primarily directed at human beings, and specifically human consciousness, higher consciousness, with the purpose of blocking human beings from reaching their full multi-dimensional and spiritual potential. It was necessary for the extraterrestrials who colonized this planet to keep human beings in their place. There have always been more of us than them, and they've always feared the possibility that we would reproduce to numbers they could not manage. They have always feared possible rebellions, still do, even though they're getting pretty damn cocky, and they were keenly aware that human beings, if allowed to evolve and develop fully, would not accept their servitude, and eventually would present a serious threat to them."

"The frequency fence is, of course, just one of many ways they do this. We've heard the compelling evidence that human beings have been genetically tampered with, again hundreds of thousands of years ago, resulting in many of our strands of DNA being permanently switched off. And more recently, of course, you get into some of the more obvious ways, such as the mind control exercised by the media, the government and the educational systems, and the biochemical tampering through the use of pharmaceuticals and all the other toxic substances human beings are subjected to on a routine basis."

David was surprised at the depth of her knowledge. She was supposed to be a computer geek. Obviously, this was a geek with an eclectic base of knowledge. As she talked, it seemed to him that this tiny, young woman, with the shabby clothes and the unkept look, was growing in stature and beauty.

"To the best of our knowledge, what the frequency fence does is block a broad range of frequencies of energy that are an essential aspect of a human being's connection to the universe at large and to the totality of life. Again, there's a lot we don't know about this because we're dealing with forms of energy here that we don't understand. This is not the electromagnetic energy that the old paradigm science is so familiar with. It shares many of its properties, but it's also a lot more. It has the characteristics of other forms of energy, such as sound waves, optics, and quanta, or quantum particles or waves. It's probably closer to the zero point energy that folks like Max and Don are exploring, and yet it's also quite likely that there are aspects of this energy that we will never understand, at least not with our reason, and not with the methodology of old paradigm science, nor were we meant to."

"Spiritual and esoteric traditions have had many names for it throughout our history. The acupuncturists called it Chi. The Hindus called it Prana. An ingenious western scientist by the name of Wilhelm Reich, no relation to our buddy David Reich, way ahead of his time, and buried in the trash bin of our history, called it Orgone Energy. And there are a host of others. And when we talk about it in this way, I think we get closer to what it really is. It's the only way we can make sense out of it. And when we do, the world of science overlaps the world of spirituality. We can't talk about this mysterious energy without talking about the unseen intelligence at work in the universe that gives it its various shapes and forms, like all the various forms of organic life here on Earth, or every form in the universe for that matter. It always comes back to the same thing. The universe, and the energy that makes it up, are alive, and have awareness, intelligence. It's only when we understand this that these things begin to make sense."

She looked at David and Kelly on the couch in front, sitting in between Dr. Donald Morrisee and Max Linder. Then she looked at Black Horse, who was leaning against the wall in front.

"Our two new allies, David and Kelly, with their amazing stories of inter-dimensional, light travel, and seeing into dimensions that are outside the scope of ordinary perception, are perfect embodiments of these concepts."

She took a drink from a plastic bottle of water, and then a deep breath. Her tiny body now swelled comfortably and naturally with air.

"It may seem like I digress from the frequency fence, but I don't. You see, human beings, along with everything else in the universe, are designed by this unseen intelligence, this divine spirit, to be an integral part of this vast quantum energy field. This infinite field is governed by the unseen intelligence, and everything in it is connected, energetically, vibrationally, with everything else. In this way, human beings have an inherent energetic or vibrational connection with the divine spirit, the source of all creation. This connection is the source of our greatest power, our full potential. When we make this connection, we are capable of living and acting in this world of energy, let's call it the quantum world, in which the customary rules of cause and effect no longer hold, and in which there are essentially no limits, instead of the material world, which is one of strict boundaries and limitations."

"David and Kelly, and the sorcerers from South America who guided them, as well as the sorcerers from Black Horse's Hopi lineage, are able to do their light traveling, and the other incredible things they have done, because they have made this connection, and they act in this other world, this other dimension, the world of pure energy and spirit. This is often referred to as our magical heritage, and it is something from which we have been disconnected. We are learning quite a bit more about all this technically, such as the role our DNA plays as an antenna or receiver for these energy frequencies, but I think that's a little beyond what we need to be talking about tonight."

"The frequency fence is one of their primary mechanisms to cause this disconnection. Again, we don't know that much about how it actually works, but based on what we do know, it's safe to assume that the fence interferes with, or scrambles, or totally blocks, many of these higher energetic frequencies, thereby cutting human beings off from the source of their full power. This is one of the factors that has led to the current division in human consciousness between spirit and matter, with most humans imprisoned in a meaningless and dead-end world of materiality, while being robbed of life's fullness. The Bible and many of the other ancient religious texts talk about the fall of mankind, and symbolically represent it in their dogma. In all likelihood, this disconnect from the divine spirit, from the source of all creation, which, after all, is energy with awareness, is the true fall of humanity."

"And yes, it is true that this energy, these higher frequencies, because they are everywhere and in everything, still do exist down here, on the planet, beneath the fence. They can't be cut off completely, and they can still be accessed. David and Kelly, and all the other folks we mentioned, demonstrate this, and I'm certain virtually all of the rest of you have experienced certain aspects of this in your lives, particularly lately, with all the amazing stories about how most of us were drawn here. But it's nowhere near as huge as it would be without the frequency fence. Take away the frequency fence, particularly when you consider all the eons it's probably been there, and the world would bear absolutely no resemblance to what we see today."

She swelled with air again, and grinned placidly. She glanced back at Gemini, sitting on the couch behind her, and nodded. He got up, and stood next to her.

"OK, there's the background. Now Gemini's going to finish up, and get to the juicy part."

She sat down.

Gemini spoke in a gravelly baritone, like an orator or an opera singer, his deep, resonant tone filling the room. Like Patrice, he looked like a child compared to the others, like one of Dr. Wolfe's students. He was of average height, with a lean, yet solid, build, and his booming voice was disproportionate to his body.

"I'll get right to the bottom line," he started, with a mischievous glint in his eyes. "We believe we've found a way to bring down the frequency fence."

The crowd buzzed. It was like the entire room quivered for an instant. And it was contagious. David could feel it pass through his body, a prickly sensation that danced up his spine to the top of his head.

Gemini waited for the room to settle down. He looked like he was enjoying this, blowing peoples' minds, with his ever-present, rascally smirk. He looked like the naughty kid in school, who had just put a tack on the teacher's chair.

"That's right," he went on. "You heard me. This could be huge. But let me back up. I'm getting a little ahead of myself."

His fiery eyes shot off into space for an instant, then darted back to his audience.

"When the fence was initially put in place, whenever that was, it was probably done from outer space, either from another planet, probably outside our solar system, or from a mother ship of some kind. Over time, as the ET's settled here, and made this their home, the operation and maintenance of the fence was switched over to an extremely high-tech network of satellites that surround the Earth. They're nearly impossible to detect because they're very small, and they're quite a ways farther out than all the other satellites. They're not held in place by the Earth's gravity, but by their own propulsion systems. Just to give you an idea of the level of technology we're dealing with here, these satellites have been this same size, about the size of your average kitchen stove, since the beginning, tens or hundreds, maybe even millions of years ago."

"This satellite network is operated by the same central computer that operates all the other programs in their system – the *uni*, all the other chips they've got planted all over the place, the *univision* system, all the other satellites, all of their zillions of surveillance devices, everything. For those of you who don't know, they call their central computer *The Beast*, and it's located in Belgium, Brussels to be exact. Gives new meaning to *mark of The Beast*, huh?"

The room was once again as silent as a tomb.

"They've always been obsessed with the idea of having one central computer running the whole show here on Earth. This can be traced way, way back. Now they've got it, and it's funny how this source of their greatest strength, at least in their eyes, is also a source of considerable vulnerability. It's a total good news-bad news situation. The good news is everything's in one unit, in one place, and the whole system is easy to control. The right foot always knows what the left foot is doing. The bad news is everything's in one unit, in one place, which makes it easier to find, and, at least potentially, depending on a lot of factors, easier to hack, which is what we think we're now able to do, at least in this one area, the frequency fence. And once we're in, we can wreak all kinds of havoc."

The smirk was off his face, but his eyes still glowed. This was serious business. His voice even lowered an octave.

"Patrice and I have our sources, informants, who are on the inside. Needless to say this is very sensitive territory, and we wouldn't even think of divulging their identities, even to a group like this. In many cases, we don't even know who they are. It's all done in code, and there's no way we can trace who we're dealing with. And I say they're on the inside. This doesn't mean they're actually in the belly of *The Beast,* so to speak, but they're pretty darn close, at least a lot closer than we could ever get by any other means. There's probably only a handful of people in the whole world who have access to *The Beast* itself. It's pretty much designed to run itself, at least eventually, the prototype of artificial intelligence, another one of their obsessions, their deities, kind of like Frankenstein's monster. And if I was one of those precious few folks with access, I definitely wouldn't feel like the safest guy in the world. Ultimately, this is probably information that goes off planet. Nobody on Earth has direct access. We've been given lots of clues and leads over the last year or so, and we've tried like the dickens to hack this thing, but it's always the same thing. We hit a stone wall. This thing is incredibly well protected. You'd have to have our level of technical knowledge, and you'd have to see it for yourself to believe it. It is truly not of this world."

His face twinkled once again with his devilish look, and his deeper octave kicked back in.

"But we got lucky – freakishly lucky. You might even say we were being watched over by somebody, someplace. You might even say we were guided by some of those same forces that so many of you say guided you here. If there's such a thing as a spirit in the computer world, then it was definitely watching over us, kind of like a benevolent spiritual spy. It was a friggin miracle, but we broke through. And we're pretty certain we can bring down the frequency fence."

He was still grinning playfully, as he glanced back at Patrice. She got up, and stood next to him.

"OK, Patrice and I are going to try to talk about what all this means, at least as much as we can, because basically we don't know. And then we'd like to open it up for discussion, and perhaps do some brainstorming about how we might be able to use this to our advantage. We're definitely treading in some very unfamiliar territory here."

Patrice was quick to jump in, her eyes opened wide, and her breathing shallow and rapid again.

"There is one thing Gemini forgot to mention. This isn't going to last very long. We'll be able to pull it off because we're going to catch them by surprise, but there's only a limited amount we can do technically. We're going to be able to throw their system out of whack, but once they realize what's happening, they will be able to figure it out, and get it corrected. They'll be able to get the fence back up again. We figure we've got maybe a day, maybe longer."

She shook her head, raising her eyebrows.

"So!" Gemini boomed. "The question we all now have is: What will the world be like without the frequency fence for the first time in hundreds of thousands of years? The answer is: we don't have a clue. But because we think we're dealing with more subtle kinds of energies here, it's our best guess that the technological infrastructure will stay up. It won't crash; at least we don't think it will. There probably will be minor disturbances, enough to cause a good deal of chaos – isolated outages, static phenomena, a crash of a system or two. But it probably won't be much more than what we experience during the most severe electrical storm you can imagine, or a period of intense solar flare activity. Maybe more. Who knows?"

He shrugged his shoulders. They looked at each other, then back at the audience.

"Like I said at the beginning," Patrice continued, "the frequency fence is aimed primarily at human beings, at human consciousness, our higher consciousness, at our vibrational connection with higher frequency energy in the universe. This is what we think will be the most affected. And there are all kinds of possibilities here. And a lot of it will probably depend on the level of consciousness we're talking about. For the average person, whose consciousness has been dumbed down to such a low level to begin with, who doesn't feel much of anything anyway, there may not be much of a difference. They may not experience much of anything. Or, maybe, for these kinds of people, people for whom higher consciousness is completely foreign, it'll blow their mental circuits all together. They'll feel like they're going crazy, or perhaps they will go crazy. That's a distinct possibility."

"Then, for those who do have some degree of higher consciousness, they may break through into even higher aspects of this. I was thinking about this when David and Kelly were telling their story. Perhaps, for many of those with higher consciousness, for those who do have a spiritual connection, and there's an army of them out there, they'll be able to experience the kinds of things David and Kelly were telling us about. Perhaps they'll be able to see the quantum field. Perhaps they'll be able to break free of their material boundaries. Perhaps they'll be able to do things that previously they were only able to imagine."

Her shoulders heaved, as she filled with air.

"Just imagine a whole army of people like this. Just imagine a whole army of people like the sorcerers from South America who contacted David and Kelly – sorcerers who are here in this room with us right now."

She gestured to the space around them, and grinned.

"Just imagine. There's nothing that could stop them."

Silence – the whole world again seemed under a spell.

Gemini jumped back in.

"Another thing, Patrice. There's no way to know for sure. It's just another of the many maybes. But if there is shapeshifting going on out there, and it seems like we have more and more evidence all the time that there is. If our world is filled with genetic hybrids, particularly at the higher levels of power, hybrids with a combination of human and ET genes, who can shift back and forth from one form to the other, then there's a possibility that this new influx of frequencies, with the fence down, might effect this in some way. This will catch them off guard too. Shapeshifting, if I understand it correctly, is primarily a function of consciousness and energy, like everything else at these higher levels. It's the relationship between the energy, which everything consists of, and the consciousness, which acts upon this energy to give it whatever form it takes. When the fence comes down, they might not be able to hold their shape, and the whole world will be able to see them in their true form. This might be only temporary, but it could happen. Either that, or the people with higher consciousness, under the influence of these new frequencies, might be able to see them in their other form, like David and Kelly do. Either way, it would be way cool."

They looked at each other again, then back at the audience.

They were finished.

The crowd stirred as one, the becalmed lake rippled by the wind.

"OK, we want to hear from you guys now," Patrice said, shaking her head, and extending her tiny hands. "But let me say one last thing. There's a lot more here that we don't know than we do. But there's one thing we think we can say with pretty much certainty. When the fence comes down, a lot of people, and I mean a lot of people, are going to be seeing things, perceiving things, feeling things, and quite possibly doing things that they've never seen, felt or done before. The world is going to be different, at least for a short period of time. Some people are probably going to freak out. But people are already freaking out, with all the shifts that are already happening. So, what's the difference? We talk a lot about reaching critical mass, how crucial that is, and how when we reach it, the dominos will start to fall, and the scales will tip in our direction. This could be the thing that gets us there. When the fence is down, we believe we will have access to power we've never had before, higher power. And ultimately, this is the kind of power it will take to shift to a new world."

"So!" Gemini boomed again, "Do you guys think we can use this event to tip the scales?"

Six ⚜ The Reunion

It was a bright, sunny day. The sky was deep blue perfection, without a speck of clouds.

David and Kelly were walking on a crowded sidewalk, on the sunny side of the street, of a small town. They were both wearing brightly colored, short-sleeve shirts, shorts and sandals. The crystal clear air was cool and damp, but the sun shined warmly on the skin of their faces and arms.

The sidewalk was wider than usual, like a mall, and composed of dark, red-clay bricks that absorbed the heat. The narrow, two-lane street was lined, on both sides, with small shops, with brightly colored awnings, and outdoor cafes. The sidewalk was tastefully landscaped with small pools with fountains, thick wooden benches, and a wide variety of trees, plants and flowers. The automobiles on the lightly trafficked street were barely noticeable. There were more bicycles than cars.

The crowd was cheerful and festive. The atmosphere was more like a fair. It was a sea of flowery dresses, Hawaiian shirts, fancy T-shirts, volleyball shorts, and beaming faces. Nobody rushed. Nobody was in a hurry. People were acting like everybody knew everybody else, making eye contact, nodding, smiling, saying hello, politely getting out of each other's way. Some stopped, and talked. Children frolicked and played. The sidewalk cafes were filled with chatter, and people were eating, drinking and enjoying themselves.

As they walked along, David had a feeling he had many times before. It dawned on him that it was so easy to fly. How could he, or anybody, lose sight of such of thing? All you had to do was will it, and break free from the shackles that hold you down. Our bodies are nowhere near as heavy as we imagine them to be. They are as light as a feather. Why don't we do it more often? It all seemed so silly and simple.

He knew Kelly was thinking the same thing. They'd been down this road now many times before.

He turned to look at her, and she turned toward him with perfect synchronicity, like a reflection.

Their eyes merged. They clasped hands, smiling beatifically, and they floated straight up into the air. When they were several feet above the crowd, they rotated their bodies in an arc to a horizontal position, and they passed slowly over the crowd, still gradually rising, hand in hand.

It was always at this point, when they had this experience, that they realized they were dreaming. However, these were not ordinary dreams in the traditional sense. They had learned to distinguish between ordinary dreams and dreaming. Ordinary dreams are the kind we learn about in Psychology 101, the Freudian variety. An ordinary dream is the equivalent of watching a movie of what's going on in our subconscious mind. It is a projection of our innermost, subconscious material into a symbolic or visual form. Ordinary dreaming is a totally valid concept and real phenomenon, and it can be a very valuable tool of self-understanding. David and Kelly still had ordinary dreams, lots of them.

However, the kind of dreaming they were currently experiencing was completely different. It was an actual journey, the result of a shift in our perception, which empowers us to enter totally different dimensions or worlds, or to travel anywhere in the universe in the blink of an eye. It is the equivalent of leaving our physical body, and taking a trip on the wings of our consciousness.

Shamans, mystics and sorcerers from cultures spanning the globe, for thousands of years, have been aware that the world of everyday life is only one of a multitude of worlds that are available to human perception. Their system of metaphysics, which has been confirmed by quantum science, is built upon the foundation that everything in the universe consists of energy. This energy is in a state of lightening fast movement or vibration, and every aspect of this infinite energy field is connected to every other aspect. There is also an unseen intelligence or spirit at work in this world, which governs the behavior of this energy, and the various physical forms it takes.

One of the defining characteristics of these sorcerers is what they call *seeing*, which is their ability, in altered states of consciousness, to *see* this energy directly as it flows in the universe. When they are engaged in *seeing*, they *see* human beings as luminous spheres, in the shape of an egg. Directly behind this luminous human sphere, at a distance of about an arm's length, at the height of the shoulders, is another smaller luminous sphere, about the size of a tennis ball, which they call the *assemblage point*. It is at this point where energy from outside the luminous egg, in the form of lines or fibers, converges, and human perception is assembled.

The *assemblage point* of human beings tends to be fixed at this point behind the shoulders, and as long as it is, human beings perceive the ordinary world of material, third dimensional reality we are all accustomed to. However, these sorcerers also *see* that in certain states, such as sleep, physical illness, or under the influence of hallucinogenic plants, the *assemblage point* moves, and when it does, human perception is altered. The art of sorcery, then, and the source of their magic and stupendous feats that defy normal reality, is learning how to voluntarily move the *assemblage point*, thereby gaining entry into totally different worlds of perception, where none of the customary rules apply. All of these worlds are just as real as any of the others. They are worlds in which people can live and die.

Dreaming is a fundamental tool of sorcerers for journeying to these other dimensions or worlds of altered perception, and the art of dreaming is one of the first things a sorcerer teaches an apprentice. Since it is common for the *assemblage point* to move during sleep, this is also one of the most advantageous states in which extraterrestrials or other entities or life forms from other dimensions can make contact with humans. It is a misconception that extraterrestrials travel around the universe exclusively in flying machines composed of matter, like flying saucers or huge mother ships. If they did, humans would see them more often. Another means of their travel, like shamans and sorcerers, is through their use of higher consciousness. It's far more effective, faster, and a hell of lot more fuel-efficient. In fact, most so-called human abductions and ET contacts take place in dream-like states of consciousness, and most humans who have had such contacts have learned how to achieve altered states of consciousness that are conducive to it.

A major difference between this kind of dream journey and ordinary dreaming is the fact that the person is fully aware that they are dreaming, and they have volitional control over their actions in the dream. They have the capability to choose to remain in this world of altered perception, or to wake up, which means returning their perception to the ordinary world of everyday life.

David and Kelly flew over the crowd at a very slow speed, gradually rising in elevation. They wanted to be seen. They wanted people to know this was possible. As was usually the case, only a few people noticed, or pointed, or seemed surprised. The majority of them simply continued on their way, going about their business. It was like David and Kelly were now separate from them, and couldn't be seen at all. Either that, or it just wasn't that big a deal. Nobody joined them. Nobody ever had. They always took these journeys alone. They often met with other people or entities on these journeys, but never in the act of flying.

They continued to rise into the air. Higher and higher.

The people became tiny dots in a sea of color below them. The full panorama of their surroundings started to come into view. What had appeared to be a small town was, in fact, the suburban outskirts of a huge city. Soon, the bay, the bridges, the skyline, the rugged, rolling terrain, and the Pacific Ocean off in the distance, with its bank of ever-present fog blanketing the horizon, came into view. This was still Oakland. San Francisco.

They flew over the city for a few moments in the direction of the ocean, still hand in hand, not going anywhere in particular. The thought of crashing no longer occurred to them. In the past, when they were novices at dreaming, it did. In those days, their flying was often quite a bite more uncertain and unsteady, and on a few occasions, they did lose their control to stay aloft, but they quickly learned that they weren't in any danger. They either woke up in their bed, or they crashed, went into the ground, and entered another aspect of the dream, which they learned to enjoy.

The thought of waking up was also remote, at least this early in the dream. They had advanced to the point where they could usually control when they departed from the dream journey. They either knew when it was time to return, or after it had lasted a while, the energy of the dream-state would begin to dissipate, like water evaporating, and they would lose their hold over it.

As they sailed through the air, a thought popped into both their minds simultaneously. It felt like it came from nowhere, from outer space, but they knew that this was a seed that had germinated, and had been growing inside them both.

Greyhound Rock.

Now was the time to return to Greyhound Rock. That was why all this was happening, why they were doing it. That was this dream's purpose.

Instantly, they both knew. When they dream journeyed together, their minds worked like one. They didn't need to say anything. They didn't even need to look at each other.

They rarely looked at each other when they flew. It wasn't necessary. At these moments, the world around them was what mattered. They would have plenty of time for each other when they returned.

As the ocean drew nearer, and as the glorious sun was beginning its late afternoon descent above the glittering sea, they veered to the left, and headed in the direction of Santa Cruz.

When they reached the water's edge, the crashing waves now visible, they headed down the rugged coastline, with the Pacific Coast Highway beneath, as it snaked to the south.

Then, almost instantly, as if time and space had been bypassed, Greyhound Rock came into view – the massive sandstone cliffs, the crescent beach at their base, and the massive rock, with the spine of a giant greyhound, poking its nose into the rolling surf.

Time and space skipped, once again.

They were standing on their spot, at the end of the rock, overlooking the infinite expanse of water. They were like wraiths to each other, mirages. It was like they were there, but they weren't. They weren't looking at each other, and they were no longer clasping hands, and yet each permeated the other with their presence, like the ocean mist that filled the air.

The scene was a perfect snapshot of the last time they were there – the surf roaring around them, spouts of water shooting into the air, the huge rock quivering beneath their feet.

Then it all stopped, like a cosmic switch had been turned.

Everything went silent. It was impeccably still.

The ocean was as calm as glass. There wasn't a breath of wind. The fog had disappeared, and the horizon stretched in a perfect line before them, tracing the curve of the Earth ever so slightly with a golden hue. The sun bathed them in warmth.

Perfect, serene silence.

Then all at once, they heard it.

Uhh! Uhh! Uhh!

It was a chorus of barking seals.

Uhh! Uhh! Uhh!

The sound came from below, and filled the air around them.

They could see the rocks below, on all sides, including those that were blocked from their field of vision. It was like being in more than two places at the same time. It was like all the frames of a movie playing simultaneously in front of their eyes, and being able to see them all with one look.

The rocks were covered with seals. Some were perched on the tops, and others were clinging to the sides, as they stuck their snouts and long whiskers into the air, and proudly bellowed their gruff, yet harmonious song. The surrounding water too was ruffled with hundreds more, as they rolled about, and playfully swam.

A beautifully synchronized gala played out before them. The seals were taking turns, sharing their ecstatic celebration. As one finished its part from atop the rock, it plunged headfirst into the sea, and the next would waddle up to take its place, continuing the melody uninterrupted. Then another would shoot up out of the water, plop onto the open space just vacated, poke its snoot into the air, and take up its part in the choir.

Around and around they went.

David and Kelly were enveloped in this sweet serenade.

This performance was obviously for them. All these seals, from who knows where, had joined their dream journey, gathering in this one magical spot, at this most propitious time, and they were telling them something.

As quickly as it started, this too stopped.

Silence again.

The seals kept their spots on the rocks, and turned to face the open sea. They were still. The ones in the water stopped swimming, treading water, and poked their small black heads through its surface, their eyes also turned toward the horizon. There were so many, and they were so close together, they looked like an island of smooth black rocks.

The water was like a pane of glass again, all the way to the horizon. Although the sun was shining brightly, the water took on a dark blue, almost murky black color.

The instant the seals stopped their barking their sound was replaced with another. It started faintly, and grew steadily in volume. It came from above, from both sides, down both coastlines, and it also came from the sea.

Eee! Eee!

It was the high-pitched squeal of seagulls, countless seagulls.

Eee! Eee!

Louder and louder.

The sky was filled with seagulls, in every direction, so many they cast a shadow upon the sea. They too had flown to this spot from whereabouts unknown. They too were singing their song. They too had a message.

Their squawking was not as much a song as it was a herald, a proclamation. They knew something was about to happen. They knew what it was, and they were screaming to David and Kelly, and to the world, to pay attention. They would show the way.

The seagulls also had a definite course and a destination. Those that flew along the coasts reached the tip of Greyhound Rock, right above where David and Kelly were standing, and turned out to sea, where they met with the others, coming from every direction. They formed a thin, swirling cloud, several hundred feet from shore, stretching from one end of the golden horizon to the other.

They too acted with precise synchronicity, performing incredible feats of aerodynamics. The cloud moved with a downward current, birds fluttering straight down to the water, touching it with their feet, or landing for the briefest of instants, and then flying off to the side. They too were taking turns. Those that flew off were immediately replaced with the next wave that dropped down to touch the water. Above them, the next wave hovered, waiting their turn to descend.

Around and around they swirled, screeching their high-pitched chorus to the heavens, and the sea.

The still, dark water was like a magnet pulling them down, and they touched it with such care and delicacy that its glassy surface was undisturbed.

David and Kelly then saw what was drawing them.

The dark water started to come to life, trembling ever so slightly, sending colliding ripples in every direction. The sea was like a living being, quivering like a mass of protoplasm.

It started as just one – the smooth, arched back of a dolphin, gliding through the water, the small dorsal fin trailing behind, as it disappeared back into the water. The instant it was gone, another followed behind with a perfectly symmetrical motion, only its shiny, arched back and dorsal fin coming out of the water, its head and tail staying submerged. Then another, and another, and another after that. Pretty soon, a chain of dolphins was stretching out before them, noses and tails practically touching, like a snake slithering through the water, half above the surface, and the other half below.

On either side of this, others started gliding in and out the water, and other chains started to form. In no time, the entire sea before them was speckled with countless dolphins, a mirror image of the cloud of seagulls swirling above, stretching from several hundred feet offshore to as far as the eye could see, in every direction.

They too appeared to have reached their destination. Their swimming slowed down, and practically stopped, as they skimmed, floated and sloshed about close to the surface of the dark water. They looked like they were mingling, communing. They too began to look like a huge, undulating land mass. Obviously, they were gathering here for a purpose. They too had a message.

The swirling cloud of seagulls continued to be drawn downward, brushing the dolphins with their webbed feet, like a gentle caress, and then shrieking ecstatically as they flew away, making room for the next wave.

The seals joined in the festivities, as they continued barking their song, taking turns leaping on and off of the rocks below, and frolicking about in the water.

David and Kelly acquiesced to this spectacle, to these forces. They were outside of themselves. They were one with it.

Then, a human voice popped into their reverie, or rather, merged with it, reverberating in the space around them.

"Quite a show, wouldn't you say?"

The voice seemed to come from everywhere at once. It was behind them, on the rock above them. It was also inside their own heads, and coming from the sky above. It had the hint of an echo, like it was coming from inside a huge cavern.

David recognized it instantly. It was a voice that had etched itself into the fibers of his being. He could never forget it.

If this had been the world of everyday life, it probably would have scared the shit out of him. But he had grown accustomed to dream journeys, and he knew that anything could happen. Nothing came as a shock.

He turned around.

David Reich and his wife, Linda, were standing on the rock above them, smiling ebulliently, glowing in the late afternoon sunshine. They appeared exactly as they were on the day David first met them, almost four years ago, at Reich's cabin on Basalt Mountain in Colorado. Reich was wearing his gardening clothes - faded blue jean cutoffs, white tennis shoes with no socks, and a grayish blue T-shirt with the name of Reich's publishing company, *Cosmic Connections Publishing*, printed on it in white letters. His light green eyes had their usual twinkle. His long, dishwater, brownish blond hair, with the slightest streaks of gray, was parted in the middle. His tiny nose was offset by his huge mouth that was filled with big, perfectly shaped teeth. Linda had long thick red hair, light blue eyes, and a full face, with faint freckles. She was wearing beige running shorts, a tight, sleeveless, white T-shirt, and sandals.

David couldn't help but notice that she wasn't wearing a bra, and the nipples of her smallish breasts were poking through the thin material of her shirt. He noticed this at Basalt Mountain, and he noticed it now, like a snapshot in time.

He laughed to himself. Were these images reproduced from his own memory banks? And why this one? He had seen them so many other times.

Even though Kelly had never met Reich in person, she knew instantly who was standing before them. She had been to a couple of Reich's lectures, read several of his books, and seen pictures of him, but none of that had anything to do with her knowing. She picked it up from David. She saw it in his mind. And she saw the same image.

"You're not dead?"

David said these words without actually speaking. He heard himself talk, and the words had the same faint echo as Reich's, but his voice was separate from him, and he had no sense of moving his mouth. His mouth, entire body for that matter, was indistinct, like it was there, but it wasn't. In this state, his physical body, or what passed as it, was unsubstantial. It was like an image that was projected onto this spot for the sake of convenience or expediency – little else.

It was the same for all of them.

"Kind of hard to say," Reich replied in the same manner, his voice in the space around them, separate from his body. "We're kind of in between gigs."

As they heard the words, the boundaries of their bodies, or these physical images of them, seemed to dissolve, and they all became one person. They all listened to the words together in a kind of dark space, like looking at the back of their eyelids.

When David heard Reich's words, he, or what passed as him, smiled, and had the urge to laugh. This was so like Reich, making fun to the bitter end, even at a time like this. David never could have made this up. Whoever, or whatever, said this was definitely David Reich.

The voice of Reich continued.

"All kidding aside, we definitely bit the bullet that day in Martinelle. But somebody was looking over us. When our physical bodies died, our energy returned to the cosmic energy source from which it came. But before the other part of our totality, our essence, or our awareness, could do the same, we were beamed out of there, so to speak. The time will come when our awareness too will return to the source, and then we will no longer exist as what you see before you. But for now, this part of us is still consolidated, and it still exists in a higher dimension, the dimension you are visiting at this moment. Obviously, our work is not entirely finished. And we continue to watch over what's going on down on Earth, and what you guys are doing, with the greatest of interest. And if you complete your task, and if everything goes the way the divine spirit designed it, we will be able to help. We haven't helped yet because divine law forbids it. But what a thing it will be to behold. And believe me – we're not alone. There's an army of us."

When he finished, they all took their shapes again, like they had opened their eyes. Once again, they were standing at the tip of Greyhound Rock, in the sunshine, facing each other.

"Look out over the sea, my young friends," the voice of Reich continued.

David and Kelly turned around.

The spectacular scene played on.

The dolphins continued their orgy of communion.

The seagulls danced with them, singing ecstatically.

The seals barked their celestial chorus, circling in and out of the water.

"What does all this mean?" Reich asked. "What are they saying to you?"

For the first time, David and Kelly looked at each other directly. Their forms were vivid.

They spoke in perfect harmony, the words coming from their mouths this time, with crystal clarity.

"It's time."

They looked back up at Reich and Linda.

Their bodies too were distinct and colorful; reflecting the golden sunshine, and the words Reich spoke also came from the lips of the form that stood before them.

"That's right. That's what the animals are telling you. That's what this magnificent world is telling you. That's what this sacred journey is telling you. And that's what we are here to tell you. Critical mass has been reached. The vibration is at the proper resonance. The time is now. The time has come to complete your task. And the time has come for us to give our help."

David and Kelly looked back at each other.

David blinked.

The world went black.

When he opened his eyes, he was in his bed at Dr. Wolfe's house, holding Kelly in his arms, looking into her big blue eyes.

They didn't feel like they had been asleep. They had merely been instantaneously transported from one spot to another on the wings of perception.

"It's time," they whispered, again in harmony.

Seven ❧ Higher Frequency

Two days later.

Wednesday morning.

The first thing they noticed was the birds.

David and Kelly and most of the others from the meeting several nights ago, plus a bunch of newcomers, were again assembled at Dr. Wolfe's. They were watching a press conference on *univision*, with the President of the American Region of the United Union, William (Bill) Chase. Of course, in the *New World Order*, all the branches of the media were centrally controlled by the U, but the façade of a free press remained, as did these public spectacles. As strange as it seems, although most people, chipped and unchipped alike, knew this information was controlled, they still watched, and they still behaved as though it was news. Such is the essence of living in a fabricated and vicarious world, where you know something isn't real, but you treat it as though it is because you've lost sight of the other possibilities, and it's the only reality you have left.

The press conference was being held at the White House in Washington, DC, where the presidents of the United States had once resided. It was a beautiful day in late summer in Washington, and the event was being held outside on a terrace, adjacent to one of the many lush White House gardens.

As the President was responding to another rehearsed question, there was an abnormally loud screeching of birds in the bushes and trees surrounding him. It sounded like a flock of hundreds of tiny birds, in a frenzy. It was so loud the normally unflappable President was forced to stop. This was highly unusual. In all the years of press conferences at this site, nobody could remember this ever happening before.

The President, obviously thrown out of kilter, grinned at the audience of reporters and insiders, peering over the tops of his glasses.

"Must be Democrats," he chuckled snidely, doing his best to keep his cool.

The façade of the two-party system was also still in place, in spite of the fact that no president had been honestly elected by the vote of the people since the advent of electronic voting machines.

His voice was muffled amidst the clamor.

At that moment, the sound of dogs barking came from the White House behind him. It was well known that the President and his family had a chocolate lab and a basset hound. This too was not normal barking. It sounded agitated and crazed, like they were literally bouncing off the walls.

The President glanced back, over his shoulder, and then with perplexity at his closest aides at the side of the stage. He took a deep breath, and leaned forward, his mouth practically touching the microphone.

"Well, I know they're not Democrats," he practically shouted, attempting to look amused.

The racket continued.

He leaned forward into the microphone again, and did his best to talk above the noise, the sound of his breathe reverberating into it.

"I apologize. This is rather embarrassing. I'm certain they'll get the dogs under control in a second. And in the meantime, I'm going to do my best to continue. Now, where were we? Oh yes…"

He picked up where he was before.

As he continued, everybody at Dr. Wolfe's heard it, and they could hardly believe their ears.

The tone of the President's voice started to change. He was from the Northeast US, and any accent, at least by US standards, was negligible. His normal tone was deep and even, not unpleasant to the ear. Now it was suddenly gruff, course and condescending, like he was scolding or threatening his listeners. As he went on, this intensified, to the point where it was surreal, like he was growling.

His voice also gradually became disembodied, like it wasn't coming from him anymore. Pretty soon the words he was snarling obviously no longer matched the movement of his mouth. It sounded like it was coming from a loud speaker above him someplace. The words also started running together, becoming practically indiscernible, like a grating, guttural wave.

He finished his response, looking like he wasn't aware of anything unusual. As he scanned his audience, and pointed to another planted reporter for the next question, the President also looked different. His normally cool and placid face now looked sinister, with his brows furrowed, his eyes glaring, and his mouth stiff.

The dogs had stopped, but the birds continued their frenzied screeching.

The UV screen went black. The sound went off too.

They waited. Nothing changed.

After a moment of stunned silence, they rustled as one, and looked at each other.

Chris Buckley broke the silence.

"Wow," he exclaimed. "Did everybody else hear what I did?"

"Tell us what you heard, Chris," Donald Morrisee replied, "and let's see."

Chris described the whole bizarre scene. They all nodded. They had all seen and heard the same thing.

"OK. It's happening," Don proclaimed, shaking his head. "Things are happening."

"I think we can safely assume," Chris continued, "that if we all saw what we did, then a lot of other people out there did too. Probably not everybody, not the zombies, the mind-controlled ones, but enough to make a difference."

The frequency fence was down. It had been for almost an hour. Patrice and Gemini's contacts in Germany were the ones who initiated this on their system, and they reported that everything, at least from a technological point of view, went precisely according to plan.

They also planned it to coincide with the Presidential news conference, hoping that something would happen within the full glare of the media. They got their wish.

As soon as they received confirmation that the fence was officially down, Patrice and Gemini clicked off email blasts to a multitude of networks around the world. One of the group's tasks of the previous two days had been to compile massive lists of as many of their email contacts as they could accumulate. Once the fence was down, they fully realized that if bizarre things started happening, the Internet might be shut down completely. The central planners would need some time to get their stories straight before they could start posting news, or reporting it.

In the *New World Order*, freedom and privacy on the Internet, like everything else, were things of the past. The monopolization of the huge telephone companies, under the covert direction of the same international corporate powers that controlled everything else, had led to strict regulation, exorbitant fees and control of all Internet content. All of which, of course, had the complete blessing of the puppet governments, and the regulatory agencies that approved it. It was no longer possible for just anybody to put up a website, and say whatever they pleased. Content on the Internet was practically identical to that on *univision*. It was all propaganda, commercially endorsed, and it all toed the *New World Order* party line.

People could still email relatively freely. The government and the controllers didn't want to give this up because it was their easiest and most widely used method of spying on the private affairs of people. It was not uncommon for the emails of individuals deemed to be suspicious to be blocked, or for people to be arrested for using email to commit thought-crimes or other subversive acts. It was basically the same with telephone communication, except telephone surveillance wasn't as effortless.

Patrice and Gemini were, of course, well aware of all this. They were meticulously prudent in their use of email, and they used coded names and language that were carefully designed not to be detected by any of these technological traps. With their scrupulous use of such methods, they had managed to fall off of all the radar screens of the authorities. It was like they didn't exist.

However, in this one instance, under these once-in-a-lifetime circumstances, they threw caution to the wind. They were rolling the dice, and it was worth the risk. The opportunity to shift to a new paradigm doesn't come along everyday. And if it didn't work, their lives might not be worth much anyway.

The email blast went out to thousands of people around the world, people who they knew were aware of the forces at work, and who were eager to play their part in creating the new world. They didn't mince any words as far as the language they used. Without giving any of the specifics about the frequency fence, which might give them away, they announced that something had been successfully done to throw a monkey wrench into the *New World Order*. The time had come. Extraordinary things were about to happen, and it was necessary for everybody to keep their eyes open, to feel the vibrations, and to band together to do whatever needed to be done to defeat the powers of darkness. They were looking at the high probability of major chaos throughout the world, but this was no surprise. They were ready. They were strong. And they were up to the task.

The UV screen turned dark blue, and printed words appeared on the bottom of the screen.

"Technical difficulties...please stand by."

Then a voice, which sounded like a recording, made an announcement.

"We are currently experiencing technical difficulties. Please stand by. Our technicians are working on the problem. The broadcast will resume shortly."

Patrice and Gemini were both at their laptops, sitting at a table across from each other, intently typing and clicking.

"The Net's still up," Gemini announced to the room. "It'll probably take some time for any of this to get there."

He stopped, and peered over the top of his screen at Patrice.

"Shew!" He blew through his teeth, shaking his head and shoulders. "I really feel weird, like I'm high or something. I'm tingling. My body's tingling."

He rubbed his fingers in front of his face.

"My fingers – my head – my toes – everything's tingling."

Patrice returned his look, took a deep breath through her nose, and let it out through her open mouth.

"Me too," she said in a hushed voice.

She stood up, feeling her cheek bones with her fingers, and then stretching her arms out to the side, with her fingers extended. She also stretched open her mouth and her eyes into wide circles. She looked like she was checking to see if her body was still there, and if it worked in the way she was accustomed to.

It didn't.

Something was happening.

They could all feel it.

It started slowly. They could barely feel anything at first. Then it swelled like a balloon filling with air.

There were close to a hundred people in the room.

They were all stirring, like leaves being blown around in a wind storm. People were moving, standing up, stretching, feeling their bodies, and milling about.

A murmur filled the room, which quickly escalated to excited chatter.

Something was most definitely happening. The world felt different. They were all picking it up. And now they felt different.

The atmosphere in the room was a weird blend of looseness and joviality, mixed with highly charged nervous tension. There was the uninhibited giddiness of a fantastic party, where anything can happen, as well as the heart pounding, lump-in-the-throat anxiety of not knowing what the hell's going on.

The room was bristling with energy.

They seemed to have forgotten the serious business at hand, or didn't care. Exuberance was in the air. People were a twitter. People were aglow. People were scared shitless.

Only one thing was for certain: something had shifted. Things were not the same.

Don took charge, or at least tried to.

"OK! OK!" He shouted. "Let's settle down! Let's see if we can get back on track here."

They ignored him. The clamor continued.

Several of those closest to Don stopped, and gave him their attention.

He shrugged his shoulders, with his usual impish grin, his face flushed.

"Come to order!" He yelled as loudly as he could, pretending to be angry.

This was totally not Don.

They all laughed. It was laughter tinged with nervous energy. But he got their attention.

The room quieted, but it still rustled, crackling with electricity. Giggles and muffled talk rippled through them.

They were a seething cauldron. It was only a question of time before the lid blew off again.

There was a chorus of dogs barking and wailing outside. They too sounded frenzied, possessed by some alien force. Some were at the neighboring houses. Others were off in the distance. It sounded like every dog in the world was going nuts.

Don smiled irrepressibly.

"I feel like the parent at a slumber party here."

They laughed again.

"OK," he continued. "I hate to burst this bubble, but we've got some rather important work to do here."

The announcement started on *univision* again. The screen was still dark blue, with the same printed message on the bottom. They all listened. It was the same as before.

They rustled again.

"OK people," Don repeated, more authoritatively. "Talk to me. What's going on? Chase starts sounding like some kind of spook out of a horror movie. Then the UV goes off. Every dog in the universe is going berserk. And it looks like we're starting to feel some weird shit right here in this room. I know I am. Let's see if we can figure out what's happening, and then let's figure out what to do with it all."

During the news conference, David and Kelly were standing alongside the wall, next to Daniel Black Horse. They heard the same things as everybody else. However, David saw what he always saw. Kelly too. The President had the evil eye, with pupils that were vertical black slits, stretching the full length of his eyeball, and giving the whites of his eyes a flashing appearance. The skin of his face had that same sickening, light green, swamp-like hue, and there was an iridescent aura around the top part of his body of the same color.

David and Kelly also saw two other beings on the White House terrace that were not visible to the others. Standing impassively behind the President, on either side, like statues, were two abnormally tall men, who resembled the two policemen that David had encountered earlier. They were each about seven feet tall, with bald heads, and slim, well chiseled features. They were wearing plain grey suits, with white shirts and black ties. They too had the evil eye, and the same coloring. They gave the impression of being body guards from another world. David and Kelly had seen these same types of beings, and had encounters with them before. They affectionately referred to them as goons. The being Kelly shot on Martinelle, when she rescued David, which transformed into a reptilian creature as it lay dying on the floor, was a goon.

When the UV went off, and the group was frolicking and groping in the new, higher frequency vibes, David's perception shifted, and he *saw* the same world of energy he had *seen* on his dream journey with Hibutu. He didn't understand how this happened; only that it seemed very natural in this new frequency. It just happened, and this seemed like the place to be, like this world was more natural than the other one.

Like before, the entire world was a spectacular lattice of luminous fibers that pulsated like they were alive. The material world of his normal perception overlapped this world of energy, but it was faint and indistinct, like a ghost-like image in the background. This lattice of energy fibers was an indescribably intricate spider web of luminosity, in which the lines crisscrossed in every conceivable direction, without any of them actually touching.

The people were luminous beings in the shape of eggs. They were penetrated by an apparently infinite number of the fibers at two points. One was a point in the midsection of the egg, like a naval, and the other was the *assemblage point*, which was about the size of a tennis ball, and located on the opposite side, about an arm's length from the egg, at the height of the shoulders. The point at the naval was the contact point, where the luminous being experienced the energy from the outside world. This was the point where human feelings were generated, the point where humans felt the world. The *assemblage point* was where outside energy was transformed into the world that humans perceive. Humans had the capability to move their *assemblage points* to other points around their luminous egg, or to points internal to it. When their *assemblage points* moved, humans not only perceived the world differently, but they perceived different worlds entirely.

David *saw* all the luminous eggs in the room, and he perceived that the *assemblage point* was in this same position for all of them, with two exceptions – Kelly and Black Horse. In their cases, it had dropped to a position at the midsection of the egg, on the opposite side of the naval point. He also *saw* that his *assemblage point* was in the same position, in front of him. He was aware, therefore, that Kelly and Black Horse were perceiving exactly the same thing he was, and that everybody else was still in the world of normal perception.

As alluring as this luminous world was, David was also aware that he needed to return to the world of normal perception in order to participate in the task at hand. Just as he had so often intended to awaken from a dream journey, he thought about returning to the normal world, and willed it. Instantly, he was back in the material world with the others, with his normal material body.

David and Kelly looked at each other with perfect synchronicity, like shadows of each other. Again, they didn't need to speak. But this time it was different. Bathed in the higher frequency vibes, it was all so much clearer. They were aware of what they had just *seen*, and they were aware that they were there together, and came back together, by mutual intention. Words were a total waste of time and energy.

They looked at Black Horse, and he looked back, mirroring them.

"I've heard about this, but I've never *seen* it before," Black Horse said sedately. "I've had many visions. I've been on many journeys. I have visited realms that are far, far away. But that was new. And I know you were there with me."

David and Kelly nodded in unison.

"We've been there a few times…" Kelly started.

She looked at David, and instantly knew she could speak for him. She knew it was as true for him as for her.

"We've been there a few times, and what's different this time for us is we can return there whenever we choose, and come back here whenever we choose. All we have to do is intend it. Before, we were more in the control of outside forces, and we got there by acquiescing to them. Our volition didn't have that much to do with it. That's changed now, with this higher vibration."

David nodded. He could have said these words himself.

David, Kelly and Black Horse tuned back into the group.

After Don settled them down, he started by expressing some of the extraordinary things he was feeling, and then he asked others to do the same. There was a definite consensus that they were all experiencing thoughts and sensations of a highly intensified and unprecedented nature. Their minds were processing more information with greater acuity and less effort. Their bodies were experiencing feelings that were both accentuated and novel. Those of them with previous experiences with mind-altering substances or with naturally induced transcendental states reported that those states were the closest things to this. There was greater understanding, and it felt natural, intuitive. This understanding didn't come from their rational minds, but from the totality of themselves – mind, body and spirit.

Everything seemed so simple. Everything bristled with sensuality. Touch, taste, sound and smell were supercharged. Colors were brighter and more vivid. The entire world had more depth and life. Time itself seemed to stand still. Each moment was so full that other moments, past or future, were of no interest. They had no relevance. Everything was here and now, in its totality.

If their mission hadn't been so clearly established beforehand, it certainly would have been more difficult, nearly impossible, to focus on. But that was not even close to being the case. It would take far more than this to knock these folks off track.

Along with this completeness, this euphoria, came the feelings of anxiety and discomfort that normally accompany cognitive and sensory overload. This was truly a journey into the unknown, and it felt like it. Yes, it was wonderful, but it also stretched them to their limits. Many of them felt like they might jump out of their skin, like their internal circuits might blow, or like they might simply burst with the intensity of it all. A few of them reported that they felt like they were losing their fucking minds.

But again, with their higher purpose so deeply rooted in their souls, this too would not get in their way.

Everybody had a chance to speak their piece, and the room settled down again.

Don glanced at David, Kelly and Black Horse, leaning against the wall. "You guys want to add anything?" He asked.

They shook their heads in unison. They didn't want to dissipate their energy with words.

"It's happening," Kelly said plainly.

"If there ever was a time to connect with the divine spirit, and the spirit world," Black Horse added, "now's it."

The room was silent.

Dogs continued wailing.

Sirens could be heard in the distance.

Many of Dr. Wolfe's neighbors had gathered in their yards outside, and were muttering excitedly.

Chris Buckley's eyes were gazing off into space. He dropped them back to the group, and spoke wistfully.

"Gemini was right the other night. If we're feeling this way, and we know what's happening, just think about all the other people out there. Just think about the average poor schmuck, who doesn't have a clue. This could get intense."

The UV had been monotonously repeating the same recorded message.

But now, a different and very familiar voice came on the air.

"Good afternoon, Ladies and Gentlemen, this is Walter Reasoner reporting live from New York."

Walter Reasoner was the head honcho news anchorman on the *unichannel*, the U's primary 24-hour news and information channel. Walter was a worldwide celebrity, and whenever there was a crisis, he was the master of ceremonies, and he ran the show. It was often said that his was the voice of calm and reason in times of emergency and unrest. He was affectionately referred to as "Uncle Walter."

A picture of Walter flashed on the screen, with his name underneath it.

"Interesting. There not even going to show him live," Chris stated. "They're really not taking any chances here. You know they can."

Walter announced that while UV was experiencing technical difficulties, he would continue to do an audio report of the news. He also announced that the Internet was experiencing similar technical difficulties, but that the problems were not believed to be serious, and their technicians were working on it. Order would be restored soon.

Patrice and Gemini feverishly pecked at their keyboards.

"Yup," Gemini exclaimed. "All I get's the Explorer home page. None of the links are working. Browser's down. Search engine's down. It's stuck on the same old news. It's dead in the water."

Patrice was peering at him over the top of her screen.

"Check your email, Gem. I just sent you one."

Gemini clicked, and waited.

"Got it. Email's working."

"Somebody check your phone," Chris asked the crowd.

"Right here," Dr. Wolfe replied.

He pulled his mobile phone out of his pocket, and pressed a couple of keys.

"Working. Got my office."

"Me too," somebody yelled from the back. "I just got through to Denver."

Walter continued his report. His tone was paternal, almost patronizing, like he was speaking to a group of little children.

"Ladies and gentlemen, on behalf of the officials and technicians at *univision*, I want to assure you that the interruption of *univision* and the Internet is a routine technical matter, nothing more. Please don't be alarmed. Go about your normal business as best you can. We are already receiving reports that many people around the country and the world are panicking, and in some areas erroneous and malicious gossip is circulating. Please stay tuned to *univision* for all the latest developments. I will remain on the air, at the very least in this audio only format, with all the latest news. If you don't hear it here, it's just not happening. I repeat – this is a routine technical matter, and all these systems will be back up and running as soon as our technicians correct the problem. And we at *univision* want to come right out and report that none of the following things have happened. There has been no terrorist attack on the technological infrastructure of the world. There has been no act of international warfare.

There has been no outer space event, such as the destruction of key satellites, or abnormal cosmic ray or solar flare activity, or anything of that kind. I repeat – stay calm, go about your normal business, and we will stay on the air with all the latest developments."

"Ha! Yes, there has!" Gemini blurted playfully. "There has been a terrorist attack, and it's worked!"

Walter paused, and then he started narrating other news stories, on other topics, as if nothing unusual was happening.

"Wow!" Don exclaimed. "This is better than I ever imagined. They can't pretend like nothing's happening. People are going to see through this. They're going to be able to connect the dots. They're going to know something fishy's going on. They're going to have to come up with a cover story, and that could be rough. This is fucking fantastic!"

"We've got to get out there," David urged, "be a part of what's happening, channel all this energy in the proper direction."

The entire room buzzed again, like bees dizzy with pollen in the springtime. The pot was starting to boil again.

Don raised both his hands in the air, beckoning for one last silence.

"Yes! Yes! He's right. It's time for action. But we must come up with a plan."

They agreed that they had three ways to connect with the world out there, both close and distant. There was face to face, and as long as telephones and email were still working, they needed to use both of those also. They reasoned that there was a good chance that telephones and email would remain at least partly operational because they were indispensable to their adversaries also. They decided to keep four computers going, making as many email connections with the networks they had compiled as possible. Patrice and Gemini volunteered, as did Peter and Janice, who had their laptop out in the car, and Dr. Wolfe's wife, Jessica, who would use theirs in his office upstairs.

In addition to the email addresses they had compiled over the previous two days, they had also compiled lists of all the telephone numbers that they could come up with of all of their personal contacts throughout the US and the world. Several of them also volunteered to stay behind, and stay on the phones, calling and leaving messages to as many of these people as possible.

Everybody else was to go out, and make contact with flesh and blood people. They had no idea what to expect. So, there was no way to plan what they were going to say and do. They only knew one thing. Their task was to work to channel the energy of this higher frequency vibration in the direction of rescuing the planet Earth, and creating a new world.

As all this was being discussed, David again intended himself into the dimension of pure energy. He wanted to ask for guidance, and he wanted to do it in this world. The transition was instantaneous and effortless. How could this world, right at his fingertips, ever have seemed so far away? How could the portals to this world, so gaping, ever have seemed so cumbersome and inaccessible?

As before, he *saw* the indescribably intricate lattice of pulsating luminous fibers that connected everything there was, both close and infinitely distant. He *saw* the room full of luminous, egg-shaped spheres. And he *saw* that the *assemblage points* of Kelly and Black Horse had shifted to the same spots as before, at the midsection, opposite the naval point, confirming what he already intuitively knew. They were there with him again.

David felt lighter than air in this world. It was like he existed, yet didn't, both at the same time. He was not the same David Rhodes that existed in the normal, third dimensional world. The only parts of that him that existed in this world were his awareness and his energy. All the other parts of him were obliterated, scattered to the ethers from which they originated.

This David that was not David was also different as far as his emotions. Perhaps it was more reasonable to say that they couldn't even be called emotions in this world, and that emotions, as such, didn't exist. David felt light and dizzy, but not in an uncomfortable way. He felt like his luminous form might just float off into space at any moment. Yet, none of this really mattered anyway because everything in this world was a part of everything else. There was no life, no death, no time, no self. There was no separation of things into other things. There simply was. There was no fear, no anxiety. Nor was there joy or elation, in the customary way we feel them. His feelings were outside the scope of the words we use to describe them. The closest he could come was to call it a form of apathy, but in a pleasant and paradoxical way. Nothing really mattered, and yet, at the same time, everything had mind-boggling significance.

David acquiesced to these feelings, to the totality of this world.

Without thinking the thought, or saying the words in his head, he asked the question: *What now?*

The answer came instantly. It was inserted into the totality of his being in the same way Hibutu, Mahnya, and the Togi people had communicated to him. It was in the form of a picture that he *saw* and felt with all of his senses from his physical form in the third dimensional world, as well as his other senses from this new world.

David could sense the presence of his allies. He couldn't *see* them, not yet, but he knew they were with him in this luminous world. Their spirits were speaking with his spirit, in the language of the spirit. Hibutu, Mahnya and the Togi were there. David Reich and Linda were there. Red Cloud and

Flying Hawk from South Dakota were there. His mother, Celine, was there. And others, a multitude, a spiritual army. The Hopi elders and the Hopis from the spirit world, from Black Horse's experience, were there. And others, unknown, from places unknown, both in the physical world, and in higher etheric dimensions, were there.

The first thing David picked up was sound.

Boom, ba, ba, boom, ba! Boom, ba, ba, boom, ba!

It was drumming, primitive hand drumming – a circle of men and women, from different races, from different cultures, connecting with the divine spirit with their primal rhythm and vibration. Then, he *saw* the people, a crowd of people, giving themselves up to this vibration, merging with this vibration, and dancing ecstatically. They were dancing on the grass, at the water's edge. The spell was hypnotic. Many others were being drawn to them, and joining. On the other side were the buildings of the city. And piers jutting into the water, with lots of different kinds of boats docked, and big, fat seals lolling about.

He didn't recognize this place. He didn't think he'd ever been there. And yet he knew what it was. The words popped into his head, just like the rest of the message.

"Fisherman's Wharf."

Message received - no time to waste. It was time to intend himself back.

He thought the thought, and there he was, back in the material world with the others.

David and Kelly and Black Horse looked at each other, and nodded. They said nothing, in words.

Dr. Wolfe was announcing to the group that he was going to go to the University. He was going to come out of the closet at last, and share what he knew with as many students and faculty as possible. Dr. Tennyson and Max Linder, the quantum physicist, were going with him. He had a large lecture scheduled that afternoon, but he seriously doubted whether too many students would show up. He also wondered how many of the faculty would stick around. Only one thing was for certain: at times like this, people needed to congregate, and there was no better place for that than a large university.

Dr. Wolfe and Dr. Tennyson were both chipped. If things didn't go the way they hoped, and everything returned to normal, they stood to face grave peril. They didn't care. They knew what was happening. They knew what they were feeling. This was huge. This could be the day that changed the entire world. They were willing to risk it all. They were willing to die for what they believed.

The others with the chip felt exactly the same. They were too far down this path to turn back now. Peter and Janice were totally converted. To hell with his law practice. This was so much more important.

Donald Morrisee, Chris Buckley and Steven Babcock, the ex-Libertarian politician, were going to go to downtown San Francisco, to the financial district, to the Transamerica Building. They imagined there would be major mayhem there.

Tara Bradley, the ex-Presbyterian Minister, and Clay Finley, the monetary economist, both blacks, were going to go to the inner-city in Oakland. Andrew Asher and Tamisha, the Canadian musicians, asked if they could tag along. Andrew had a djembe drum on his back, harnessed to his shoulders, and Tamisha had a pair of maracas tied around her neck.

Tara saw this, and exclaimed, "Cool!"

And others would go to other places, the mission the same.

Donald Morrisee's eyes caught David, Kelly and Black Horse.

"What about you guys?" He asked.

"Fisherman's Wharf," Black Horse replied. "We have an appointment at Fisherman's Wharf."

"Far out!" Don bellowed.

EIGHT ❧ KINDRED SPIRITS

Boom, ba, ba, boom, ba! Boom, ba, ba, boom, ba!

The drums pounded their primitive rhythms into the heavens.

Boom, ba, ba, boom, ba! Boom, ba, ba, boom, ba!

David, Kelly, Black Horse and Peter could hear them all the way from the street in front of the huge, multi-tiered, indoor mall.

Boom, ba, ba, boom, ba! Boom, ba, ba, boom, ba!

The walkway weaved across the lawn in between the buildings, and down the hill to Fisherman's Wharf. As they turned the final corner, the throng came into view, silhouetted against San Francisco Bay.

It perfectly matched David's vision.

People were approaching the drummers along the walk-way adjacent to the Wharf in both directions. People were sitting on the grass on the hill in front of the mall. A large crowd was dancing in front of the semi-circle of drummers, who were positioned, some sitting, some standing, alongside the railing at the water's edge. Others encircled the dancers and the drummers - watching, moving, swaying, like they were being pulled into its vortex.

Only Kelly and Peter had been here before. But they had never seen anything like this. The drummers were always here - day and night. But usually there were three or four of them, sometimes a few more. And people usually didn't pay that much attention to them, while they went about their other business. Rarely did anybody ever dance - sometimes a few weirdos.

Now there were about thirty drummers - men and women, young and old, of every imaginable race and creed. A quick scan of the crowd told the same story. It was bursting with color and variation, a hodgepodge of all the people of the world. This didn't feel like the city of San Francisco in the United States of America. It felt like a place newly created in space and time.

And it felt pure. Here David and Kelly were, out in the world, in the middle of a major metropolitan city, and they didn't feel any of those sickening vibes they always felt in the presence of the alien beings. Normally, in this place, they'd have to be on their guard. But not now. It was clean. The vibes were pure. There were no alien beings here, or anywhere close by.

As David listened to the drums, he heard a faint echo, barely discernible to his heightened senses, coming from above, or from somewhere. He listened more closely. It wasn't an echo, but a separate chorus of drums - far, far off in the distance. And yes, it sounded like it was coming from the sky. The heavens themselves were joining in this symphony. The entire world was drumming.

Their spiritual allies were all there, the whole army. They too had made the crossing. Or more likely, they had been with them the whole time. And more - all the etheric beings and forces in the universe, which were now focusing their energies on the Planet Earth, at this potentially momentous time, were there.

The drive from Oakland had been like nothing any of them had ever experienced.

David, Kelly and Black Horse decided to bring Peter along because they needed somebody with a *uni* to pay the toll on the Bay Bridge. And whatever else that might come up. It was risky to be out there in the world without a chip.

The instant they walked out Dr. Wolfe's door, they knew this would not be any ordinary trip. The world outside felt bigger than before, more expansive, like its boundaries had been stretched far beyond their previous limits. While they were inside Dr. Wolfe's, in an enclosed space, there was a certain comfort in the closeness to so many others who understood what was happening, at least somewhat, and who were experiencing the same flood of novel thoughts and sensations. Now the very earth that they walked upon didn't feel as solid. The air they breathed felt more refined. This was a new and unknown world. All of the customary pillars they were accustomed to leaning upon had been pulled away.

This new world demanded a new vigilance. They had to pay painstaking attention to all of it. They could not afford to relax, at least not for a while, until things began to take some sort of shape again, if indeed they ever would.

Outside Dr. Wolfe's, dogs were howling. Sirens wailed in the distance. Many of his neighbors had gathered in their yards, and were huddled in small groups. Several others from Dr. Wolfe's had gone outside, and were talking to them.

What does one say at such a time?

"Sorry to inform you that the world you woke up to this morning, and which you have learned to rely on, for good or for bad, has fundamentally changed. And the crazy way you're feeling right now just might be the way it's going to be for awhile. But it's really nothing to worry about. Trust me."

The traffic was so light it was eerie. The Bay Bridge and the other freeways and streets were practically abandoned. Whatever people were doing, they weren't driving. David and the others were expecting just the opposite. They were afraid the trip might take hours due to gridlock. After all, it was early afternoon on Wednesday, and they figured that under these weird circumstances people would hightail it home where they felt the safest.

"Jesus Christ!" Peter shook his head. "This is California, for Christ's sake. People live in their silly-ass cars. Something else must be going on."

As it turned out, the light traffic was definitely a good thing. Peter was driving his Mercedes, and in his altered state, he had an excruciatingly difficult time focusing his attention on something as mundane as driving an automobile. His thinking was so plugged into his right brain, and the avalanche of novel thoughts and feelings he was experiencing in the moment, that he was having a difficult time getting his left brain in gear. It was an effort for him to coordinate all the simple activities of driving that we normally take granted. Performing more than one motor task at a time was a struggle.

They got no farther than the stop sign at the end of Dr. Wolfe's block, when Peter turned to face them.

"Guys, I'm gonna need some help. This is the hardest god damn thing I've done in a long time."

They all giggled like children. They couldn't help themselves.

With Kelly in the front, and David and Black Horse in the back, they worked like a team to navigate the car to the Bay Bridge, and then to Fisherman's Wharf. Kelly was in charge of the map, and it took all four of them to do what one person normally would do without hardly thinking.

Like kids on a road trip, they couldn't control their laughter. The situation was so absurd, and their emotions so preposterously mixed. One moment, they were feeling the ebullience of the higher frequency, and the euphoria of creating the new paradigm. And the next, the enormity and danger of what they were doing came crashing back in upon them, and everything felt like it might spin completely out of control. Sobering reminders of what was going on in the world quickly brought them back down to Earth.

The relatively few drivers who were brave enough, or stupid enough, to be out on the roads presented a serious danger to themselves and everybody else. Some cars were moving so slowly they were barely moving. Others were driving recklessly, at high speeds, weaving in and out of traffic, like they had totally lost their minds. Some cars had stopped all together, blocking their lanes on the freeway. Several drivers had even gotten out of their cars, and were wandering like zombies in the traffic. Many had good sense enough to pull off to the side of the road, and waited there. Groups of people had gathered alongside the road, apparently trying to figure out what the hell was happening. Most of the cars that continued on their way did so at speeds far below the speed limit, and they swerved from lane to lane like the dividing lines weren't there.

There were numerous wrecks. Most of them were of the fender-bender variety. Emergency vehicles were out in force - fire engines, EMT's, ambulances - with their sirens blaring and red lights flashing. However, policemen were conspicuous in their absence. During the entire trip, David and the others didn't notice a single police car.

Peter managed to get into the groove of the driving, with the constant help of his crew. He was the most comfortable going around thirty-five to forty miles per hour, as they meandered their way through this chaos. They had to continuously resist the urge to stop, and help all these poor souls along the way. It felt so weird being the only ones in the world who knew what was happening, but they had no control over that. They had a mission, and the mission had to come first. They could not allow themselves to get knocked off track.

They passed a hospital in Oakland, which was the scene of obvious commotion. It was a busy part of town anyway, but the sidewalks were much more crowed than you would expect. Everybody appeared headed in the direction of the hospital. The traffic was far heavier here, with cars lined up around the block, waiting to enter the hospital parking lot. An emergency vehicle was parked to one side of the building, its red light still flashing. Hospital personnel, in their grayish, blue, unisex uniforms, were scurrying in and out and about.

David and the others also did something none of them ever did - listen to the radio. Kelly was working the buttons on the complex, high-tech dashboard of the new car, and had a difficult time figuring out how it worked, particularly in her left-brain impaired state. Peter stated in no uncertain terms that if he helped Kelly with the radio, he would definitely crash the vehicle, killing them all. So, Black Horse helped her with that, as David continued to serve as a second pair of eyes for Peter as he drove.

They figured it out, and were pleasantly surprised at what they were hearing. Radio was obviously not as rigidly controlled and censored as was *univision* or the Internet. Knowing so little about radio they didn't understand why. Perhaps it had something to do with the frequencies, or the controllers figured it didn't have that much influence anyway, or maybe they just hadn't gotten around to it yet.

But clearly this was the case. Many channels were carrying Walter Reasoner, and many others were reporting the same strict *New World Order* party line. However, they also picked up other voices and channels that were obviously more independent. Many of them were taking telephone calls from listeners, and broadcasting these live, without showing any real concern for what was said. What it all boiled down to was gossip, the vast majority of which was either greatly sensationalized or simply incorrect. But for David and the gang, this was the most helpful source for what ordinary people were thinking that they had heard in a long time.

The disparity between what Walter Reasoner and the mainstream news sources were reporting and what people were observing and experiencing was immense. They continued to report that the only real problem was a major glitch in *univision* and the Internet, which the technical experts were in the process of attempting to repair, and that people needed to stay calm.

However, major corollary stories were arising that Reasoner and the mainstream sources were reporting. Or more likely, these news events were being engineered by the controllers, and were the beginning of the cover story they were inventing.

They reported that the Union Aviation Commission (UAC) for the American Region (AR) of the United Union (U), as an alleged safety precaution, had ordered the cessation of all air travel. All airline flights were postponed until further notice, and those flights that were in the air were required to land at their first opportunity. They reported that this was due to the possibility that unknown computer programming errors could be at work, which could affect the entire technological infrastructure. Similar actions were also taken by the aviation commissions in the other global regions.

The suspension of all rail travel and mass transit soon followed for the same reason. If programming errors were responsible, this could possibly effect chips throughout the infrastructure, including automobiles. A warning was issued by the Motor Vehicle Division (MVD) of the AR of the U, in which people were advised that they may be in danger driving their automobiles, and that they did so at their own risk. David and the gang heard this warning several times, and they agreed it was very ambiguously worded. It could easily have been interpreted as saying that driving a car was illegal, until further notice. But the cops appeared to have disappeared, so it didn't make any difference anyway.

Other shutdowns followed on the heals of these. Without the Internet, it was impossible for the international financial markets to operate, and they too were closed. At this rate, pretty soon the entire world would be shut down. It would be like one big snow day, which David and Kelly remembered from their winters in Wisconsin. However, there were no technical problems with the *uni*. So, people could continue to purchase basic goods and services, and the economy could continue to function.

As they listened to all this, David and the gang marveled at how tricky the controllers were, and how careful they were to cover their tracks. David and the gang knew that there weren't any programming or computer glitches, and that airliners, trains and cars were perfectly safe. They knew that *univision* and the Internet were shut down because the controllers were afraid of what people might see, and everything after that was part of their cover story. If the President can be so exposed, albeit so briefly, then who knows what else might be. David and the gang were also keenly aware that if the situation didn't change quickly, the controllers would definitely need to concoct a better cover story.

But all this mainstream news was tame compared to what David and the gang heard on the other channels. People in droves weren't buying it. People knew something monumental was happening. They could see it, and feel it. And the vast majority of them were terrified.

Huge numbers of people were reacting to the higher frequency energy by becoming physically ill or freaking out mentally, both in a wide variety of ways. One of the storylines that was gaining considerable momentum in this rumor mill was that this, as well as the peculiar way everybody was feeling, was being caused by a killer virus that had been foisted upon the public, perhaps as an act of terrorism, or bioterrorism. There were also those conspiracy nuts who maintained that this was perpetrated by the government, as a means of forcing new vaccines upon the populace, enforcing quarantines and higher levels of martial law, and strengthening the totalitarian stranglehold of the *New World Order*.

Many believed this virus had been delivered through the public water supply. Others believed it was airborne, and was a by-product of chemtrails. Chemtrails are a top secret government and military project that had been going on for almost twenty years. Chemtrails are the plethora of puffy fumes that are sprayed from jets, which crisscross the sky like a spider web, and which, on bad days, often turn clear days into cloudy ones. Of course, the authorities maintain that these are contrails, the normal exhaust and water vapor fumes that are expelled from jet engines. But it doesn't take a rocket scientist to understand that this is pure poppycock. Normal contrails quickly dissipate and disappear. They do not have the capability to expand, and develop into cloud formations. Something is being sprayed from those jets.

And it went on and on, with a myriad of other variations on the same theme.

The born-again Christian influence was also highly vocal on these airwaves. They believed that these were the "end-times," or the Second Coming of Jesus Christ, which were predicted in the Bible. They had been predicting this for a long time, and they believed it was happening. Unlike the infidels, these Christians didn't sound as frightened, but were more in a state of agitated rapture, as they feverishly quoted scripture in tones that bordered on hysteria. The themes were all the same. The Antichrist had had its day, and reached its apex. But the time had come for it all to end, and now it was Christ's turn to save those who had remained faithful.

As they flipped through the channels, they even heard one guy, a telephone caller, talk about the Mayan and Hopi prophecies for *The Shift* of the year 2012. He went on to say that what they were experiencing was probably the beginnings of the pole shift, and that things would probably get a whole lot worse before they got better.

As David listened, he had the eerie feeling he had heard this voice before. He knew it. He knew this man. But who was it?

Then it hit him.

"That's him! The guy from the barter shop in Oakland. I'm sure of it. Tom. Tom Brantweiler. That's him. I know that voice."

David thought of Tom often. Ever since that fateful night the goon cops almost killed him, David had a strong sense his path would cross with Tom's again. And hearing him on the radio wasn't it. It was only a hint. There was more to come. David knew that Tom must have fled that night, disappearing into the underground he knew so well, never to return to The Chip-Free Zone again. After what the cops had been through with David, they had the goods on Tom now for sure.

David and the gang heard others on the radio, but it was all variations on one major theme. People knew something extraordinary was happening, and they weren't buying what Walter Reasoner and the controllers were telling them.

They arrived at the other side of the bridge in San Francisco, and took the Fisherman's Wharf exit. They had been so preoccupied with driving, listening to the radio, and all the other crazy things that were going on, in their left-brain impaired state, that they had hardly noticed anything else. Peter had adapted well to the driving, and he was doing fine.

David glanced out the window, and noticed for the first time that the bright blue sky was filled with the lattice of pulsating luminous fibers or energy lines. Previously, he had only *seen* this when his perception had shifted totally out of the third dimensional material world, and into the dimension of pure energy. But this was different. His *assemblage point* had not shifted, and his perception was still exclusively in the material world. Previously also, when his perception shifted to the dimension of pure energy, this lattice of energy fibers was superimposed over the material world, which could be seen more faintly in the background, like a ghost-like silhouette.

This was not the case here. The blue sky and the energy lines were both in this dimension. The energy lines were in this world. Neither was in the foreground or background. Again, in a contradiction to linear logic, they were both in the sky and separate from it. They were both here and there, at the same time. They were both close and far away. They didn't cover up the sky, nor did the sky cover up them. And these energy lines were fainter than in the world of pure energy, like traces or wisps. And when they pulsated, they would almost disappear, only to expand back again, giving the impression that the sky was beating like a heart.

"Kelly, Daniel, look at the sky. Do you *see* them?"

"Yeah," Kelly exclaimed, in wonder.

"Me too," Black Horse replied more plainly. "Amazing."

David put his hand on Peter's shoulder.

"Peter, do me a favor. When you get a chance, without crashing the frigging car, just take a look at the sky, and tell me if you see anything unusual."

Peter glanced up through the windshield, without moving his head.

"Nope," Peter shook his head. "Nothing unusual. Just the sky."

Boom, ba, ba, boom, ba! Boom, ba, ba, boom, ba!

David and the gang continued down the walkway to the edge of the crowd. People were standing two or three deep in a semicircle around the dancers and drummers. Their numbers were growing, as others continued to approach from all directions.

Boom, ba, ba, boom, ba! Boom, ba, ba, boom, ba!

The energy of the drums and the dancers was irresistible. David and the gang felt its force pulling them in like a huge magnet. David took Kelly and Peter's hands, and Kelly took Black Horse's, so they wouldn't lose each other, and they slithered through the crowd, into this sea of vibrating humanity.

The irony of what they were doing wasn't lost upon any of them. Here they were on one of the most important days in the entire history of the planet Earth. And they were here to play their part in *The Great Shift of the Ages*, and to create the new paradigm. They had lived their entire lives for this day, for this moment. Everything they had ever done had been in preparation for this. And what were they doing? Dancing.

And yet there really was no choice in the matter. It was all perfectly clear. There really was only one thing to do - dance. At this moment, there was nothing more important than acquiescing to the rhythm and flow of the energy in which they were enveloped.

Boom, ba, ba, boom, ba! Boom, ba, ba, boom, ba!

As they moved into the swirl of pulsating humanity, David again could hear the voice of his dear friend, David Reich. He couldn't tell if this voice was part of the memory that echoed in his soul, or whether Reich was once again actually speaking to him from the spirit world. On this extraordinary day, with dimensions overlapping, like the energy lines in the sky, it was probably both - one and the same.

And the words were one of Reich's favorite mantras. David had heard him say this again and again.

"The best thing any of us can do to play our part in creating the new world is to put our vibration of peacefulness, joy and love into it. That's where it all starts."

So, they did.

David, Kelly, Black Horse and Peter merged with the rippling current of music and people.

Boom, ba, ba, boom, ba! Boom, ba, ba, boom, ba!

David had never danced before, but just like with anything natural, like breathing or sex, he picked it right up. He knew all this. It was just a question of calling it up from the depths of his being. The drums beat to the tune of his ancestral spirit, and his body moved to the primordial rhythms that were programmed into his cells, his protoplasm and his DNA.

Boom, ba, ba, boom, ba! Boom, ba, ba, boom, ba!

As David moved to the vibration of this scene, he was really far more interested in this sea of people. They looked different. They didn't look like the people back at the hotel in Oakland, or like the people on the street at the Chip-Free Zone, or like Dr. Wolfe's neighbors, or like the people they saw on the freeways. He felt like he did with the group back at Dr. Wolfe's. These people looked like they weren't afraid, and like they understood, like they had a sense of what was going on, in all its colossal magnitude, and scariness. This felt like a different world.

As he shook and swayed his body, David heard another voice. This one definitely didn't come from within him. This was clearly a message from the outside. And again, it was inserted into his being in the form of a picture.

The message was: *See it.*

He knew exactly what this meant.

Hibutu and Mahnya were up to their tricks again.

He intended himself into the luminous world of pure energy. His perception flipped into it instantly. It was as before - unchanging, yet eternally changing - permanent, yet fluid, all at the same time.

He also knew why he had been called into this world. He was here to *see* the people. They too were as before - luminous spheres in the shape of an egg. Yet, he *saw* something else that was out of the ordinary. The *assemblage points* of many of these egg-shaped spheres had shifted. In each case, the movement was only slight, but David knew that the slightest of movements resulted in radically different perception. These were no longer humans, in the ordinary sense.

That was all he needed to know. He intended himself back into the world of normal perception.

A young woman, whose *assemblage point* had shifted, was dancing rapturously in front of him. She was thirtyish, with long, curly, reddish brown hair, and she was wearing a long, full maroon skirt, with lots of colorful flowers on it, a white tank top, and sandals.

David knew instantly what he must do.

He sauntered up to her, still moving with the music. He placed his hand delicately on her shoulder, and looked at her with his mesmerizing, sparkling blue-green eyes.

"My name's David. May I ask you something?"

He had to lean forward, and speak into her ear in order to be heard above the drums.

She stopped dancing, but continued bobbing her shoulders, and wiggling her hips. Her light brown eyes were full of life, and they mirrored his.

"Hi, David. Sure," she replied, smiling joyfully.

"Do you know why you're here?" He asked, his eyes blazing into hers, their faces practically touching.

"I was called," she said, matter of factly.

David smiled at her euphorically. Pieces were starting to fit together.

"Do you know who called you, and why?"

She stopped dancing, still with her joyful smile.

"No! Call it channeling. Call it what you will. I go where the forces lead me. This morning that inner voice told me to come here. I had no idea why. I just knew I had to come."

She started bobbing her shoulders, and swinging her hips again. She continued with bulging eyes, shaking her head.

"And something's happening, for sure! I've been waiting for *The Shift* for a long time. Is this it? You can see the energy in the sky, can't you, David? The lines. I know not everybody can, but you can, can't you?"

He nodded, still beaming.

"You're a part of this, aren't you, David?" She bobbed and weaved, eyes still bulging. "You know what's going on, don't you? Tell me."

He moved closer to her, putting his hands on her shoulders, their faces practically touching again.

"All in due time. You're in the right place. Just keep dancing."

She smiled beatifically.

"What's your name?" He asked.

"Angela."

His eyes shined into hers, and she reflected them.

"I love you, Angela."

They embraced, their bodies held tightly against each other for several moments. He could feel her heart pounding behind her breasts.

"Mmm," she sighed ecstatically into his ear.

Boom, ba, ba, boom, ba! Boom, ba, ba, boom, ba!

The crowd surged with the music.

David turned around, and saw Kelly embracing a man, their bodies held tightly together. The man was sixtyish, with long, curly, silvery hair, combed back, a smooth, ruddy complexion, twinkly eyes, and a youthful, vibrant look. He was wearing faded blue jean cutoffs, and a red Hawaiian shirt, with tiny white flowers on it, with the collar open, and a necklace with small, sparkly beads and stones.

David danced over to them.

"Mmm," the man sighed into Kelly's ear. "I can feel your heart beating."

Kelly looked into the man's eyes, her arms around his back.

"What's your name?"

"Jack."

"I love you, Jack. We're all here for the same reason. And keep dancing."

"I know. And I will. Here's to *The Shift*."

Jack placed his hand out, his palm facing her, and they slapped hands.

David and Kelly faced each other.

Boom, ba, ba, boom, ba! Boom, ba, ba, boom, ba!

They both knew what was happening.

They didn't have to say anything, but Kelly did anyway.

"These people were called here, just like we were. And those that weren't were drawn here by those that were. You know what I mean. *Assemblage points* are shifting. Jack here can *see* the lines in the sky."

David nodded. Words were a waste of time.

They both noticed that Black Horse was standing next to them, like he had materialized out of thin air.

"There's a group of natives over there," Black Horse said in his plain and sober tone. "One of them's drumming."

He pointed with his eyes, and David and Kelly saw them.

"Different tribes - Cherokee, Lakota, Oneida. None of them knew each other before today. They all met here. And they all say they were called here by the spirit world, just like us. I *see* that their *assemblage points* have all shifted. They can all *see* the energy lines in the sky."

Boom, ba, ba, boom, ba! Boom, ba, ba, boom, ba!

Peter had joined them. He had been dancing, wildly, ecstatically. He was not the same person he was in South Dakota just several days before.

They looked at each other, back and forth, waves of energy flowing between them, waiting for their next signal.

David received it.

"We're supposed to be up there."

He pointed to the drummers with his eyes.

They all nodded, trusting.

As they weaved their way through the dancers toward the semi-circle of drummers, David's eyes caught those of one of the drummers. It was a woman, fortyish, with a heavy-set build, and long, thick brown hair, with streaks of gray. She had on a white, smock-like top, with multi-colored Native American designs, and jeans.

As David approached, their eyes were locked together. Her huge green eyes were exquisite, and drew him like a magnet.

He didn't have to use his rational mind. Forces were guiding him. All he did was acquiesce.

He reached her. She stopped drumming. Their eyes were enmeshed, as he stood over her.

David leaned down, placing his hand on her shoulder, and spoke into her ear.

"Do you always drum here?"

He squatted on his haunches in front of her.

She shook her head,

"First time! I'm from Santa Cruz. I drum all the time. I'm with a circle. But never here."

"Why today?"

A grin flashed across her face.

"I have no idea. I just felt like it. I woke up this morning, and wanted to get out of town. I hopped in my car, and ended up here."

Boom, ba, ba, boom, ba! Boom, ba, ba, boom, ba!

She reached out, and grabbed his hand, holding it firmly.

"You know something, don't you? Who are you? What's going on? Something's happening, isn't it? I feel different, like I'm high. Everybody does. The sky looks different. Something incredible's happening."

"I'm David, and you'll see. Yes, you're in the right place. Just keep drumming. What's your name?"

"Cheryl."

"I love you, Cheryl."

They hugged.

"I love you, David."

David stood up, and turned around. Kelly, Black Horse and Peter were right there, waiting for him to finish. Their eyes met. They didn't know what was next.

Yet, they all knew what to do - wait, wait for their next signal.

They waited, drums booming, people swirling around them

Boom, ba, ba, boom, ba! Boom, ba, ba, boom, ba!

Black Horse received it.

He motioned for the others to come closer. They huddled in front of the drummers, as he spoke.

"There's a Hopi chant that's perfect for this. It's done on occasions of monumental change. It celebrates these changes, which are always blessings. It's perfect for this moment."

They all nodded, trusting.

Black Horse straightened up, and faced the dancers. The others flanked him - David on one side, Kelly on the other, and Peter next to Kelly.

Boom, ba, ba, boom, ba! Boom, ba, ba, boom, ba!

Black Horse took a deep breath, puffing out his chest, and pushing his shoulders back, while he scanned the whole scene before him. He looked like he was absorbing it all with his breath, taking it into his body.

He started tapping his feet gently on the Earth in rhythm to the music, first on one side, three taps, and then on the other. Then, he raised his hands into the air, his palms up, about to the height of his abdomen, and he started shaking them gently, in rhythm to the tapping of his feet.

Cupping the world before him in his hands, he gazed hypnotically into the space above the crowd, and beyond.

"Hey, yah, hey, yah, hey, yah, hey! Yah, hey, yah, hey!"

His tone was deep and smooth. His melody was the perfect complement to the total vibration of this glorious scene.

David, Kelly and Peter mirrored his steps, as they chanted along, cupping their hands in front of them.

The sound rippled across the enraptured dancers, and they started to turn in its direction, like a whirlpool swirling around its vortex.

Black Horse's dark eyes scanned the crowd, merging with them. He raised his cupped hands above his head, and waved them, beckoning them to join him.

"Hey, yah, hey, yah, hey, yah, hey! Yah, hey, yah, hey!"

The movement of the human mass shifted, as the dancers started to dance along with Black Horse. Before their movement was random and wild. Now it was more uniform, as they faced him, with the coordinated tapping of their feet on the Earth.

The dancers joined the chant, faintly at first, barely discernible amidst the pounding of the drums.

"Hey, yah, hey, yah, hey, yah, hey! Yah, hey, yah, hey!"

Black Horse continued waving his hands in the air, like he was hailing the sky, inviting the heavens to join.

David again heard the distant echo, but this time, instead of drumming, a celestial chorus was chanting along with Black Horse.

The sound swelled.

"Hey, yah, hey, yah, hey, yah, hey! Yah, hey, yah, hey!"

Black Horse lowered his cupped hands back to the level of his abdomen, and continued to shake them gently with the rhythm of the drums and the chant. The crowd followed along in perfect unison.

The chant resounded in the space around them, and began to eclipse the drums.

One by one the drums stopped, as the drummers joined the chant.

Soon the only sound was the chanting.

"Hey, yah, hey, yah, hey, yah, hey! Yah, hey, yah, hey!"

Black Horse stopped his dance, but continued to hold his cupped hands before him, motionless. With his eyes closed, and head tilted back, he continued to sing his reverent melody to the heavens. The crowd chanted along in perfect harmony.

"Hey, yah, hey, yah, hey, yah, hey! Yah, hey, yah, hey!"

The chant resounded into the ethers. At this moment, it was all there was.

There was now total silence in the pauses between the chants. There were no barking seals, no wailing dogs, no sirens. The entire metropolis was still. There wasn't a breath of wind. Even the usually moody ocean was calm. If felt like the whole cosmos, and everything in it, was participating in their ceremony.

David felt the vibration of the chants ripple through his total body, taking it over. He too was a vibration. Like everything else in the universe, he was an antenna, meticulously designed by the source of creation, to send and receive energy. And in so doing, he was not only connected to the source, he was the source.

"Hey, yah, hey, yah, hey, yah, hey! Yah, hey, yah, hey!"

Black Horse took a deep breath, and dropped his head and his hands in one motion, as he exhaled. David could hear the air leaving his body.

The chant was finished.

The silence was absolute. It was the silence of eternity.

Black Horse was still, eyes closed, his face pointing to the ground.

Perfect silence.

David again had that sense of waiting for the next signal.

He wasn't picking anything up yet.

He patiently waited.

Maybe somebody else would receive it.

The huge crowd respected the silence, like the whole world was a sacred cathedral.

Black Horse opened his eyes. He looked up at David, out of the corners of his dark, intense eyes, and nodded.

The message popped into David's total being with perfect clarity. Again, it was a picture, not mere words. The picture was his entire life, his entire reason for being.

But the words said: *It's your time.*

He looked at Kelly. She too nodded, and her eyes said the same thing.

David faced the crowd. All eyes were upon him. The message was as clear as a heavenly chime. He was a total stranger to them. And yet, in this magnificent moment, they saw something in him. And like cosmic lovers in a sacred dance, they were waiting to take his lead.

Time stood still.

Another message popped in. This one was in words. They were the words of Celine, his mother, who had departed this world on her definitive journey over twenty years ago. The spirit world was moving closer, overlapping with this one. David heard her voice as clearly as when she lived. The words were the same as her final words to him, which she wrote in the letter that he read nine years after her physical body left this world. She was murdered because her power had become too great.

Yet her voice and her words were alive. He heard her in the space around him.

"I was forced to depart this life before my work was complete. Everything happens for a reason. The reason, then, must be you. You are my most important legacy. Continue the work to set humanity free. As you complete yourself, remember you are completing me. I am with you always."

David's eyes returned to the crowd. It was his time to speak.

He didn't have to think. He simply acquiesced to the forces and the power that now hovered so close. He allowed these forces and this power to flow through him, like the cosmic antenna he was, and his words flowed from this source.

David had never been an orator. He had never spoken to a large crowd, particularly without a microphone. Yet, his voice carried like the air itself was thinner, and reverberated through the space around all these people. They all heard him, perfectly.

"We don't know each other, and yet we do. We are all here for the same reason. We have all been called here, whether we are aware of it, or not, to be together for the purpose of creating a vibration that will change the world."

"I know that every one of you knows exactly what I'm talking about. I also know that every one of you can feel the power of what we're creating here. I also know for certain that most of you can see and feel that something very unusual is going on, right now, at this moment. You can feel it in your bodies and in your minds, and you can see it in a lot of crazy things that have been happening today in the world. As a matter of fact, something very remarkable happened this morning at around 10 AM, something that could be the trigger to bring down the old world, and create the new one. And maybe not - it's all up to us."

"This is where I fit in, and my friends here. There's only a very small group of us who knows what happened this morning. You have all been called here, as have we, to hear about it, from us, and then you will know too. And then the next step will be to spread the message, and to continue to create this incredible vibration we are creating here. This vibe, along with the truth, are the most powerful weapons we have to change the world, stronger than all the guns and bombs and money that our adversaries have. As an army of spiritual warriors, armed with these weapons, there's no way we can be stopped."

"And no - what happened this morning is not a killer virus. It's not an act of bioterrorism. It's not Judgment Day. It's not an invasion by ET's. Or any of the other rumors that are going around. And it's not the shifting of the Earth's north and south magnetic poles, at least not yet, but that's getting a little warmer."

"It's something else, and it's something extremely positive, if we can all just handle it properly, as we're doing here. But in order to make sense out of this, I have to back up a little. Another one of the things we all have in common here is we all know there is something terribly wrong with the world. Many of you may not know exactly what it is, but you know it's so. There are forces at work in the world today, whose primary objective is to enslave the human race, physically, mentally and spiritually, and feed upon its energy. I realize this is not a pretty picture. These are dark forces indeed. But in order for us to correct this, it is imperative that we know the truth about what we are dealing with."

"And this is not a modern-day phenomenon. It's been going on for thousands of years, and if truth be told, it's been going on for hundreds of thousands, perhaps millions of years. In order to enslave the human race, it's necessary to get control of the human mind and the human spirit. One of the methods the dark forces use to do this is propaganda, which creates a world of illusion that humans believe is real. Human history is one of the most important illusions. Conventional history is used to cover up the fact that the dark forces arrived on this planet from other worlds long, long ago, way before what passes as the beginning of our history. They came here for the purpose of colonization, and to exploit the Earth's extremely rich natural resources. Many highly advanced civilizations, far more advanced than what we see currently, existed on this planet during these times, and these civilizations were destroyed by forces very similar to those that are on the verge of destroying this one."

"OK, this brings us back to what happened this morning, and the unusual things we have all been thinking and feeling today. In order for the dark forces to enslave us, when they first arrived here, it was necessary for them to cut us off from the primary source of our power. As all of you who have been called here know, the primary source of our power as human beings is our spirituality, which means our connection with the divine spirit of a living universe. And we make this connection with the totality of ourselves - mind, body and spirit. We make this connection with our vibration, which is what we are doing here today."

"One of the ways the dark forces succeeded in cutting off human beings from the full range of their spiritual power was through the erection of a frequency fence. Many of you have heard of this. The frequency fence is a high-tech, vibrational barrier, maintained by a central computer and a system of satellites, which surrounds the Earth, and which blocks vital energy from the universe from reaching us. The frequency fence, for all these hundreds of thousands of years, has turned the Earth into a vibrational prison."

"My friends here and I were guided by some very powerful forces, the same kinds of forces that guided you all here today, to come to this area, Oakland specifically, so we could connect with a group of people, who are aware of these things, and who are committed to creating the new paradigm. We are also blessed to have among our ranks some of the foremost computer geeks and hackers in the entire world. These geeks, our allies, also under the guidance of these etheric forces, miraculously figured out how to hack into this central computer, and bring down the frequency fence. That is what happened this morning at around 10 AM."

"I'm certain you can figure out the rest for yourselves. What you are feeling and experiencing today are the higher frequency energy vibrations from the creative source of the universe that are your birthright. And we can all see how we can connect with this energy communally, in mass, to embellish it, and create an even more powerful vibration."

"We are not alone. Other groups, like us, are doing this same thing, right now, at this moment, in other places, in this country, and around the world. The word is spreading. And the vibe is spreading to all those millions of people, like us, who are not afraid, and who are open to these forces, to this energy, and whose mission it is to create the new paradigm. And what we're seeking is critical mass, something very simple, and yet very profound. Once this truth, and once this vibe reaches a certain critical mass of people around the world, they'll be no stopping it. This is not something we can understand with our rational mind. It is an energetic and spiritual principle. It won't take all of us, not even a majority, not even close to that. But we will reach a point energetically, where the old will drop away, and the new will start to be created in ways we cannot even imagine."

"That's right. That's another thing I know about all of you, all of us, who were called here today. We're not afraid. We're not afraid of the strange and unusual and wonderful things we're feeling today. We're not afraid of the dark forces. We're not afraid of the unknown. We welcome it. We're not afraid to die for what we know is right. We're not afraid to live in a world that is totally different from the one we know."

"This is not the case for the vast majority of our fellow human beings, those who have submitted to their bondage, and who even cling to it. Most people won't be able to handle this higher frequency energy. Many people will freak out mentally. Many people will get physically sick, and many people will probably die. This could also trigger quite a bit of chaos. Most of us were seeing quite a bit of that sort of thing before we arrived here today. This is not a pleasant thing to say, and it is an unfortunate thing to watch. It is most tragic that so many people have so lost their way. However, these are things that are outside of our control. We are only able to help people who are willing to try to help themselves. And again tragically, the fate they suffer is a choice they have made."

"Many of you also may find it odd that I am saying these things in a public forum. We lost our right to freely talk about such matters many years ago. But where are the cops that are always so prevalent, particularly in places like this, where the tourist trade must be protected? Why aren't they hauling my ass off to jail for saying such seditious things, things that present such an obvious danger to the established order? Things are shifting, my friends. Weird things are happening. Look around. Do you see any cops? No. Not one. Anywhere. I'll bet there aren't even any lurking around in plain clothes. Why? Because I can feel it. And you can too. It's just people like us, people who were called here, drawn here by this energy. Where are the cops? I don't know. Not here. Weird things are happening, my friends, weird and wonderful things. What about the sirens, all the sirens we were hearing just a short time ago? And the dogs? Gone. They've stopped. It's perfectly silent."

"So what's going to happen? What's going to come of all this? We have no idea. We have no idea how long the frequency fence will remain down, and how long this situation will last. Even if they do manage to get it right back up, it's a pretty good guess that things aren't going to just immediately return to normal. An awful lot has come down here, today. A lot of people know what they've seen and felt since ten o'clock this morning. And people can see through the bullshit they're hearing on *univision*. There's only one thing we know for certain. An amazing window of opportunity has been created here. This is a once-in-a-lifetime affair. This is not *The Shift* that so many of us hear about, and so many of us know about. We are currently in the midst of *The Shift*, but the most dramatic aspects of it, on a planetary basis, such as the pole shift and the full impact of the photon belt, are yet to come. But what we are experiencing now, today, can certainly set the stage for *The Shift*, and point us in the proper direction, so that when the most dramatic aspects of *The Shift* are upon us, we will be ready, and we can use this shifting energy to create the new world."

"And finally, what can we all do, now, today? I know we'd all like to continue drumming and dancing and chanting. The vibe we're creating here is magical. But we were all called here for a reason. And our work here is now done. Time is of the essence, and it's necessary for us all to take the next step. We must now all do our utmost to spread this message, and to spread this vibration, to as many others as possible. If you have a network of friends or other people who are open to what we're talking about, share this with them. Help us reach critical mass. Every person, every spirit, counts. And do it in whatever way works best for you. If it's possible to do it in person, that's always best. But the last I heard telephones and email were still up and working, and a lot of people were doing a lot of yakking on the radio."

"When you're finished, or if you don't have a network, my friends and I invite you to join us, and our group, in Oakland. Let me give you the address. Remember this. Write it down. And if you don't get it, just come up here when we're done, and ask us. We're at the home of Dr. Gregory Wolfe. The address is 3477 N. Hilliard, in Oakland. That's 3477 N. Hilliard. And come to think of it - we've got room for a few in our car. So, if you want to drive back with us, you're welcome."

"As I said, time is of the essence, and our work here is done, but let's say farewell to this moment by drumming and dancing some more. Let's get our energy back up to where it was, and then go out there, and share all this."

"Cheryl. Go for it!"

"Ba, ba, boom, ba, ba! Ba, ba, boom, ba, ba!"

NINE ❧ CRITICAL MASS

"It was like the only people who were there were the ones who were meant to be there," Chris Buckley exclaimed, shaking his head excitedly. "Weirdest damn thing. Most of them had the *uni*, but they all understood all the crap that's going on in the world, and they don't like it. They weren't blown away by what's happening today. They were feeling extremely weird, like all of us are, but it was almost like they were expecting it, and they were capable of handling it. And they were all drawn there in ways they couldn't understand. They just felt like being there. And they were looking for answers, looking for what to do next."

It was early evening, and the late summer sun was sinking toward the horizon.

David, Kelly, Black Horse and Peter had just returned to Dr. Wolfe's. The crowd at Fisherman's Wharf wouldn't let go of them, and they practically had to rip themselves away. The people there were excited and scared. They had zillions of questions, and nobody wanted to leave. With the Earth pulled from beneath them, they craved grounding.

David and the gang had also brought Cheryl, the drummer from Santa Cruz, with them. She drove with them, leaving her car in San Francisco. "To hell with it!" she said. "This is more important." That attitude seemed to sum up quite well what was happening on this amazing day.

Dr. Wolfe' was attracting a crowd. David and the gang couldn't find anywhere to park, and ended up over two blocks away. As they approached they saw people sitting in their cars in front of the house, and milling about on the sidewalk and in the front yard. A group of them was standing around the window to the large living room where the meetings were held.

David had that same feeling again, the one he had at Fisherman's Wharf. These people looked different from the norm. They looked alive and purposeful. And this place felt different, like an enclave in a sea of chaos and sickness.

And again, it felt pure. There were none of the sickening feelings of revulsion. It was unmistakable. There were no alien beings here, no spies.

Jessica Wolfe was tending the front door.

"Come on in, guys," she greeted. "I can't let them all in. We don't have room."

Most of the core group had returned, plus many others who David didn't recognize. Everyone seemed to be in their spot. Chris, Don Morrisee and Dr. Wolfe were sitting in front. Patrice and Gemini was sitting in front of their laptops. The entire room was crammed with people, who spilled into vestibule and the adjoining rooms.

As David and the gang entered, all eyes turned in their direction. This group too looked different than they did just several hours ago. The vibration in the room felt different. It was like everything in life on this day had been accelerated in ways they couldn't imagine. As a group, they looked warm and flushed, like they had just come from a rejuvenating sauna, like their blood was finding new ways to circulate. And the look in their eyes was a combination of exhilaration and fatigue. They were like children at a slumber party, with lenient parents. They could fall asleep in an instant from exhaustion, but would not dare allow themselves. They were having too much fun, and they didn't want to miss anything.

David received another message, a picture.

The light travelers and the spirit world were here also. Their energy was palpable.

See them.

David flipped his perception. He *saw* the luminous egg-shaped spheres, and he *saw* that many more *assemblage points* had shifted, including Chris and Don's. People were changing.

That was all he needed to *see*.

He flipped back.

Chris Buckley continued, quivering with animation.

"We didn't know what we were doing. I just had this irresistible urge to go downtown. I had to. I express this to Don, and he says, 'OK, let's go.' He tells Steven. Steven's in, and we're off. George here's got a car and a *uni*, so he drives us. I don't know San Francisco. All I know's the Transamerica Building, with the pyramid. That's part of this urge. So that's where we head."

"We get there, and there's this crowd of people on the sidewalk, about a hundred people, business men and women types, you know, suits, from all the offices, banks and department stores down there. So, we double park. George stays with the car, and the three of us are off, like the Three Musketeers. We'd been listening to the radio on the way, so we have a sense of the buzz that's going around."

"So, we dive into this crowd, and start mingling. And it's all the same. 'What's going on?' 'I'm feeling really weird.' 'Do you feel it too?' 'Why are we here?' 'They're lying to us.' 'Something incredible's going on, and they're not telling us what it is.' 'Maybe they don't even know.' 'First the crash, and then the chip, and now this.' 'What the hell's going on, and what can we do about it?'"

"And then the most frigging amazing thing happens. Don and Steven and I are huddling, comparing notes, trying to figure out what to do next, and the whole place goes dead quiet, like a god damn cemetery at midnight, right there in the middle of downtown. We look up, and they're all looking at us, like we've got the answers, and it's time to deliver the goods. Don and Steven both look at me, and I guess it's my turn. I just start talking. I start explaining what's happening, doing my best to unravel it all, as difficult as that is. I talk for about ten or fifteen minutes. I think I do a pretty good job of covering it all. And when I get to the end, as astounding as it all is, they all seem to get it. It all just clicks right in."

"It's like those hundred people, in that place, at that time, were hand picked. They were the ones who could get it. They were the ones who could handle it, the ones who could help to take the next step. Yes, what we told them got them all stirred up and agitated and frightened, but it wasn't anything they couldn't deal with. And we told them to spread the word, and where they could find us in Oakland. Several of them are here now."

"And, oh yeah - one other thing - I almost forgot. All those people had noticed something most unusual, and it seemed to be happening everyplace. All the top brass, the executives and head honchos of these companies, these businesses, were suddenly AWOL. The day started out just like any other, and they came in as usual. But then as soon as all this weird shit started coming down, with the frequency fence, they were gone, nowhere to be found, disappeared. People much farther down the chain of command were forced to make some very important decisions, like whether or not these companies would even stay open."

"And you know, the most amazing thing of all, there was nothing there, in the middle of downtown San Francisco, that stood in the way of us delivering our message. There were no cops. There were no hecklers. We saw lots of chaos and people freaking out on the way, but when we were there, nothing, nothing to distract us. It was like the entire city, the entire world, just left us alone, in that place, in that moment, to do what we needed to do. And we did."

The crowd rumbled, heads nodding affirmatively, like a wave of confirmation passing through them.

"Absolutely amazing!" Dr. Wolfe chimed in. "Exactly the same thing happened with us at the University. Time is of the essence here, and I don't need to take up a lot of it because that was practically word for word what happened to Sherri, Max and I. We went to my lecture hall. Very few students showed up, so we said, 'Come with us.' And we walked over to the student union together. There were lots of people there, students, faculty, civilians. There was quite a bit of commotion, some panic. A lot of people weren't handling this very well. Some were losing it."

"There was one particular group of people, on the lawn outside, again about a hundred, that had a glow to them, a vibe. They seemed more sedate and sane. We were drawn to them, and just like Chris said, we started to mingle, and they were OK, shaky like all of us, but open, looking for answers. Then, the same thing - they went silent, and looked to us, and then to me. So, I explained everything I know, and gave an action plan. And it worked. Everybody got it. Several of them are here now."

David, Kelly and Black Horse looked at each other.

Kelly spoke

"Exactly the same with us at Fisherman's Wharf. Ditto to everything - right down the line. We too met with a band of spiritual warriors, and most of them are out there right now spreading the message. And we brought back Cheryl here, and there will be many more to follow."

The room was still. Like plants sending their shoots into the earth, the enormity of what was happening was taking root.

"We are not alone, my friends," Kelly went on, "not only on the excursions we took into the outside world today, but right now, here, in this room. We are in the presence of guidance, from very powerful forces, and very powerful entities. These unseen realms are our staunchest allies. All we have to do is ask, ask for their help, and be open, include them in what we are doing. They share our mission to cleanse the Earth."

Silence.

A solitary bird sang frenetically in the branches of the tree outside. Like them, it sounded both frazzled and euphoric.

David looked at the picture window overlooking the front yard. People were lined up in front of it from one end to the other, peering intently into the room. They were in two layers. Those in front were kneeling or squatting, and above them another row was standing. Behind these, others hovered, trying to peek through the gaps.

"OK!" Don assumed command. "What else is there to report?"

The room rumbled again, like everybody was about to explode. Obviously, there was.

"What about you guys on the home front?" Don continued, "Anything going on on the phones and email?"

Patrice and Gemini had been communicating by email with the group's various networks all day. Francis and John Lapham, the organic food and sustainable agriculture folks, had been on the phones. And Jessica Wolfe and Janice Hoagland had been doing both.

Don's eyes landed on Janice, who was standing behind Patrice and Gemini, pecking away at their keyboards, next to the window.

Janice's chest filled with air, her eyes popping open, and rolling back in her head.

"Ah…yes," she replied, like this was the stupidest question she had ever heard.

She gathered herself.

"Well…needless to say, some pretty amazing things are happening out there. We've gotten many reports, from all over the country, and the world, that things are happening in small groups, much like what we've heard today. It's the same basic pattern, so I don't think I need to elaborate - the same numbers, the same forces at work, everything. The only difference between them and us is they don't understand the particulars about the frequency fence. But ultimately it doesn't matter. They can see what's happening. They know this is an extraordinary moment, and they know enough about *The Shift* to know that now's the time."

"As far as all the other stuff is concerned, there's a lot going on that most of you are probably not aware of. The mainstream media is just reporting a bunch of crap. And it really appears as though they've lost their grip, like they really don't know how to handle this situation. People, and I mean everybody, are seeing through this. Things really look like they're falling apart. Normally, they're such good liars, and they're so good at coming up with cover stories to explain anything. But this time it looks like none of the big boys are writing the scripts. And without their scripts, the yes-men, like Walter Reasoner, just can't cut it. He's making a blooming idiot out of himself."

"President Chase has made no public statement. He's quoted as having made statements, but it's all just the same drivel - nothing to worry about - don't panic - we'll get it fixed - and everybody can get back to their normal business of being mindless robots. But people know something's fishy. Do they really expect people to believe that Walter Reasoner can speak to the American people, but the President can't? Plus, a lot of people saw what happened with Chase on *univision* earlier today, and word's getting around. People are definitely wondering about all this. That was totally weird, like sci-fi. Is the President really who he says he is?"

"And Congress too - both houses of Congress adjourned shortly after all this happened. The media's not reporting this, but this is what our sources on Washington are telling us. Congress doesn't have to adjourn, and people know this. Congress doesn't need *univision* and the Internet to conduct their business. Sooner or later, but not right away. But that's what they did, particularly the Senate. Within minutes of the fiasco with Chase and *univision* going down, the Senate adjourned. It was like those bastards had some secret pipeline into what was happening, and those good old boys and girls wanted to get out of there, quickly. It was like they really didn't want some kind of a repeat of what had happened with Chase, right there in front of the public. And the House too, but they stuck around for awhile. They weren't in quite as big a hurry."

"And the hospitals too - you guys should probably know about what's going on with the hospitals, and the doctors. The hospitals are being absolutely overrun, everywhere, all across the country. Most people are not handling this higher frequency well at all. People in droves are getting physically sick, and they're going crazy, and they're flooding to the hospitals, and to their doctors. Under the best of circumstances the hospitals wouldn't be able to deal with this, but we have it from very reliable sources that all of a sudden there is a serious shortage of doctors, and other hospital personnel, but most notably doctors. Kind of like the President and the Senators, suddenly, they're nowhere to be found. Our sources also are telling us this seems to be most true for the bigwigs, the well established ones. So much for their Hippocratic Oath. It seems that many interns and nurses and paramedics and those types are sticking around, and are doing their best, but the situation is way past hopeless. Most of them are flipping out too. Things are most definitely falling apart, and it's not going to be long before people start dying in numbers we're not accustomed to, at least not in this country."

The bird outside continued to sing its frazzled, euphoric song.

Don closed his eyes, took a deep breath, and groaned.

"We knew it would come to this," he said sadly. "We knew this part would be hard to take. And it is. How tragic that things were allowed to degenerate to this point."

"Don, may I say something please?" a voice came from the back.

It was Dr. Sherri Tennyson.

She took a few steps forward, into the crowd.

"As a physician, I can't begin to describe how much this pains me. It just rubs so hard against every fiber of my being as a healer. There's this part of me that just wants to run out there and help people. But I can't allow myself to think that way. None of us can. It's completely detrimental to our objective, and we wouldn't be helping those people anyway. We would simply be getting sucked into their dependency game. And Don's right. We knew this day would come, if not in this circumstance, then in the next one, or in the one after that, or the one after that. It was inevitable because this system is rotten to the core. And what's happening now, with all these people getting sick and dying, really doesn't change anything. I've been watching this system kill people for decades. This isn't any different. It's only normal for people like us, with a conscience, to struggle with this. But we must keep reminding ourselves that these people who are getting sick and dying are doing so because of choices they made, just like we are here now, in this room, doing what we are doing because this is a choice we made. The best thing we can do for suffering humanity is exactly what we are doing."

Silence.

"Thanks, Sherri," Don said softly.

Silence.

The only sound was the muttering of the people outside.

The silence struck a perfect chord in David's being. It was just what they needed. They had had enough talk. Everybody knew what was happening. More talk would dissipate their energy. He sensed that the vapors surrounding them were thick with other worldly presences, their allies. What they needed now was silence. And they needed to wait. This was the proper medium to open the portals to these allies, who were eager to help.

Just as David was about to say this to the others, he heard the exact words he was about to say come from Kelly.

"May I make a suggestion please, Don?" she said. "Time is of the essence. We don't need to discuss this any further. I think we all get the picture. The most important thing right now is this moment. This moment will tell us what's next. It will guide us. But we must sit quietly, and wait. It will come."

Don nodded. He trusted her.

Chatter could still be heard from outside.

Kelly looked at the people peering in through the picture window.

"Tell them to be quiet, please, out in the yard. We need silence, please."

Janice was standing next to the window. She knocked on the glass.

"Quiet please! No talking!"

Several of those peering in the window turned around.

"Quiet please!" came from outside. "Silence please!" "No talking!"

The talking stopped.

Even the bird was silent.

Now all they had to do was wait.

Everybody closed their eyes.

And breathed.

They were enveloped in silence and darkness.

It didn't take long.

It was barely audible at first, far off in the distance. But moving, coming closer, slowly growing louder.

Ba, ba, boom, boom, boom! "Hey!"

It was the beat of a drum, followed by a chorus of human voices, lots of human voices, shouting in rhythm to the beat.

At first, David wasn't certain they could all hear it. He thought it might be another round of celestial drumming, like he heard at Fisherman's Wharf, only perceptible to those whose *assemblage points* had shifted.

But eyes started popping open, and everybody in the room was looking at each other. They could all hear it.

Ba, ba, boom, boom, boom! "Hey!" Ba, ba, boom, boom, boom! "Hey!"

It was moving in their direction, closer and closer, louder and louder.

It was a happy sound, the sound of people reveling in celebration.

"What the hell?" Don exclaimed.

"Let's go see," Chris shook his head.

They all got up, and filed outside. It took several minutes for the room to empty.

Dr. Wolfe's front yard and the sidewalk were now jammed with people. They spilled over into the street, where there was virtually no traffic, and into the yards of his neighbors on both sides. His neighbors must have joined this throng because nobody seemed to care.

As David stood among them, he had that feeling again. These people looked different. They looked vibrant and alive. They looked unafraid. And there was connection. Hardly anybody knew anybody else, and yet they were all connected, connected by their higher purpose. Hardly anybody knew anybody else, and yet they all knew each other perfectly. They always had.

Angela from Fisherman's Wharf was there.

Black Horse's native friends from Fisherman's Wharf were there. One had brought his drum.

They were all different people, and yet they formed one homogeneous unit. The collective energy generated by this synchronistic mass was enormous. In the midst of all this radiance, David felt like he did on dream journeys. The boundaries of his physical body felt more fluid, translucent. He felt like they would dissolve in an instant, if he willed it, and he, or his energy, would merge with the energy of this mass, and they would all fly away together to other worlds.

But he had to stay in this world now. He had to will himself to stay rooted here. This was where the work needed to be done. And they had to do it together.

Ba, ba, boom, boom, boom! "Hey!" Ba, ba, boom, boom, boom! "Hey!"

Closer it moved. It was coming toward them, just a few blocks away now. It sounded like one drum and maracas, and an army of exuberant voices.

David and Kelly's eyes met, like reflections of each other.

Again, she spoke the thoughts he was thinking.

"It's a different world. It's happening! We're doing it! This is critical mass. You can feel it. And to think this same thing is happening all over the country, and the world. And our other-dimensional allies are here with us, watching over us, guiding us. They're moving closer too, all the time. The greater the energy, the closer they come. Dimensions are overlapping. The frequency fence is down, and the whole planet is enveloped in this cocoon of energy. You can feel it! You can *see* it!"

She pointed at the sky.

It was twilight. The sun was setting below the level of the houses.

David could still *see* the energy lines in the sky. As the sky darkened, they looked different. They no longer had the appearance of a lattice of fibers, and they weren't as wispy and subtle. Now they were far more corporeal, looking like patches of highly charged cirrus clouds, which took several different shapes. They had both the appearance of luminous streaks and swirls. There was also a wraith-like impermanence about them. One minute they were there, and the next the weren't. Yet, the dark blue sky was always filled with them. Unlike cirrus clouds, they weren't fixed in the upper atmosphere. They were both close and far away. Sometimes it seemed like they were only a few feet in the air above, like you could reach out and touch them.

David wondered if this energy was actually intensifying, or whether it was his perception of it that was changing. Could they all *see* it? He hadn't shifted his perception in a while now. But, it wasn't necessary. He looked around at all these people, and it was obvious. Many sets of eyes were raised to the heavens, and the spectacular light show in the sky was a major point of focus. They all *saw* it. Dimensions were indeed overlapping.

Ba, ba, boom, boom, boom! "Hey!" Ba, ba, boom, boom, boom! "Hey!"

Closer, closer. It was almost there. But who and what?

The sound had arrived at the end of Dr. Wolfe's street, which extended two short blocks to a dead-end, where it intersected at right angles with another street.

All eyes looked in that direction.

Around the corner, like drum majors leading the homecoming band, came Tara Bradley, the African American, ex-Presbyterian Minister, and Clay Finley, the African American, alternative money expert. Behind them came Andrew Asher and Tamisha, the Canadian musicians. Andrew was playing his djembe drum, which was harnessed around his shoulders, and Tamisha was shaking her maracas, while she danced exotically. Behind them came a throng of people, mostly blacks, who were laughing, dancing, throwing their arms into the air, and shouting to the rhythm of the drum and maracas.

As David watched them come around the corner, they just kept coming. There must have been over a hundred. David remembered that Tara and Clay were going to the inner-city in Oakland, and that is exactly what this looked like. These were definitely people who were very, very poor. Their clothes were tattered and dirty, yet their spirits soared.

And behind this throng, but not a part of the pack, others followed, mostly white people. They were not partaking in the dancing and the reveling, but they were straggling along anyway, hanging around the fringes, and following, just to see where all this went, like this energy was pulling them on strings like puppets.

When the entire pack was around the corner, David's eyes returned to Tara and Clay in the front. Tara was completely lost in the primitive beat and energy, her glazed eyes shifting from the Earth below to the heavens above. She danced wildly, ecstatically, shaking her body, swinging her hips, and waving her hands in the air. Clay's dancing was far more subdued, but he wasn't having any less fun. His eyes were pointed straight ahead at the crowd in front of Dr. Wolfe's, a huge grin planted on his face, his big white teeth offset against his black skin, which said, "Can you fucking believe this!?"

The crowd that followed behind was swinging and shaking and shouting like they had all just been released from prison, which, in a way, they had. Whatever was happening on this weirdest of days couldn't possibly be any worse than what they were coming from. When you've got nothing, you've got nothing to lose. So, why not enjoy it?

Ba, ba, boom, boom, boom! "Hey!" Ba, ba, boom, boom, boom! "Hey!"

Cheryl took her drum, and sat on the cement ledge adjacent to the sidewalk. She began to drum along to the beat. She was quickly joined by Black Horse's native friend, who had a strap for his drum, and played standing up.

The crowd in front of Dr. Wolfe's joined in the collective shout at the end of the beat.

"Hey!"

"Hey!"

Many of them started dancing along.

Tara and Clay's troupe advanced down the street. They reached the outer fringes of the other group, and the two groups merged. Tara and Clays's troupe was like a joyous river flowing into this ocean of people. As they danced and marched into the crowd, they gave high fives to everybody.

"Ba, ba, boom, boom, boom! Hey! Ba, ba, boom, boom, boom! Hey!"

The entire crowd heaved, like a giant amoeba, sending a wave of energy out, and then in, as it pulsated.

Don, Chris and Dr. Wolfe, David, Kelly and Black Horse were standing at the end of Dr. Wolfe's driveway.

The sea of humanity separated, making way for Tara and Clay, Andrew and Tamisha, who continued to dance and play, as they moved toward them through the crowd.

Tara's energy was contagious.

David, Kelly and Black Horse, laughing uncontrollably, with tears in their eyes, danced along. Don and Chris, both former hippies, were soon to follow. Clay, still grinning like he couldn't believe what was right in front of his eyes, started clapping his hands to the beat. The rest of the crowd clapped and danced along.

Ba, ba, boom, boom, boom! "Hey!" Ba, ba, boom, boom, boom! "Hey!"

They all danced together for a moment

Then Tara stopped, dropping her head and her arms, and stood draped like a statue. She was breathing heavily, her chest heaving.

The drumming and maracas stopped.

The huge crowd went totally silent. This wasn't some raucous fraternity party. Silence in the new paradigm was the order of the day, and all these people, the chosen ones, understood this. They understood the power of silence. They understood that this was their medium.

Tara looked up at Don and the others, like she just remembered who she was, and broke into a radiant smile.

"Wow," she exclaimed, in a hush.

She was out of breath, as she talked.

"We've been doing this for hours. We came all the way from the hood in Oakland - ten, fifteen miles, I don't know. We weren't having much luck talking with the brothers and sisters, so we just started drumming and dancing. We've been drumming and dancing all the way. When we started out, there were about ten of us. Now look. We've been gathering folks along the way. A lot of folks joined, and then dropped out. Got it into their heads that this was a whole lot more than just a party. The people you see here now - this is the hard core.

These are the folks whose hearts are in the right place, the folks who were meant to be here with us."

As he watched her, David's heart was bursting love. When she stopped speaking, he walked over to her, put his arms around her, and hugged her, their bodies pressed tightly together. They could feel each other's heart beating.

"I love you," he said softly.

"I love you, David."

Kelly was right behind. She put her arms around both of them.

The others, Don, Chris and Dr. Wolfe, Black Horse, Clay, Andrew and Tamisha huddled around them in a circle. They all put their arms around each other, and felt the love.

The huge crowd encircling them was perfectly silent. There must have been five or six-hundred of them now, and they were huddled together, shoulder to shoulder, with David, Don and the gang their nucleus. Many of them also put their arms around each other, or held hands. Others continued to straggle in around its periphery, but once they arrived, they too pressed against this cell, pulled by its vortex.

The world around them was perfectly silent. They were in the midst of one of the largest cities in the world, and there was hardly a sound. The power of this silence was spreading. Something was obviously happening out there in the world, but they had no idea what yet.

Again, there was only one thing to do - wait.

Wait for their next signal.

This was yet one more moment in a progression of moments they had come to know so well. This was not a time for talk. It was not even a time for doing. It was a time to acquiesce. Their message would come to them.

The rest of the cell understood this perfectly. Nobody had to tell them what to do.

They watched and waited, in silence.

This time it was Black Horse who was touched, touched by the Hopi spirits, just as he was at Fisherman's Wharf.

This moment was begging to be celebrated.

Black Horse's voice caressed the silence in a soft and gentle tone.

"Hey, yah, hey, yah, hey, yah, hey. Yah, hey, yah, hey."

His chanting was barely above a whisper.

David and Kelly joined him, in the same delicate tone. Their trust in him, and his source, was absolute.

They were followed by Andrew, Tamisha, and the rest of the nucleus.

The sound rippled through the amoeba, and soon the entire cell was singing softly together.

There were no drums, no maracas, and no dancing.

The cell swayed, like tall grass in a gentle breeze.

They sounded like a choir of angels, their sweet, beatific melody reverberating through the neighborhood, and beyond, into the heavens.

They chanted until it was dark.

The configurations of energy in the sky had changed again, and were now even more spectacular. There was no moon, and the entire nighttime sky was filled with lights that resembled the aurora borealis at its most dramatic. Some of these configurations were crystalline streaks, and others were swirling, misty, ionized clouds. And all of this energy was constantly flickering and shifting, growing in intensity, then vanishing, and appearing somewhere else. Like before, sometimes it seemed infinitely far away, and at others, so close you could almost touch it.

Through this luminous tapestry blazed numerous abnormally large shooting stars, with tails like comets. Were they meteorites, UFO's, or something else all together? And all of this was against the backdrop of the normal nighttime sky, with its stars, planets, Milky Way and constellations, except all of these lights too were now magnified fantastically. The evening star, Venus, was so gigantic it looked like a second sun had been born.

Within this awesome display, several solid bands of light also appeared, which created distinct lines in the sky. Adjacent to these lines, on the other side of them, there were strips that were totally black, with no light or stars or energy of any kind. These gave the appearance of doorways, doorways to other dimensions, to other worlds.

Everybody could *see* these things. This was totally clear. As they chanted, the eyes of the cell were turned toward the heavens. And when something dramatic happened, like one of the huge shooting stars, you could feel the cell shudder, like an undulation of its protoplasm.

Once again, David received the message: *See it.*

Hibutu was in this light, watching over him.

Trusting absolutely, David intended the flip of his perception into the world of pure energy.

It was, as before, timeless, unchanging, and yet constantly fluid.

But there was one huge difference. All of the *assemblage points* of the luminous spheres had shifted, and their boundaries or shells had lost their distinctness. They had become diffuse, and they were merging or blending with the ones next to them. So, rather than *seeing* separate forms, what David *saw* was more like a single mass of luminous energy that shined like the sun.

This crowd, as they chanted, hand in hand, mesmerized by the cosmic light show in the nighttime sky, had become, energetically, vibrationally, one being.

David didn't need to *see* anymore. He flipped himself back into the material world.

He looked at Kelly. Her eyes mirrored his, and she nodded. She had *seen* it too.

She leaned toward him, and whispered in his ear:

"*Critical mass.*"

They laughed uncontrollably, euphorically. It was happening. The world was changing.

David's bliss was beyond the scope of words. He no longer felt like a human being. He felt like a quivering mass of primal, orgasmic energy. Again, he felt like his human form could dissolve at any moment, and be absorbed by the luminous amoeba surrounding him. Or, simply fly away on the beams of light in the sky.

But he still had to hang on, hold himself back. He needed to be here now to finish their work. When it was complete, there would be plenty of time for the rest.

The chant continued.

"Hey, yah, hey, yah, hey, yah, hey. Yah, hey, yah, hey."

The ionized amoeba pulsated.

"Hey, yah, hey, yah, hey, yah, hey. Yah, hey, yah, hey."

The lights in the sky streaked and swirled and shifted. Portals to other worlds yawned.

"Hey, yah, hey, yah, hey, yah, hey. Yah, hey, yah, hey."

More and more people came, not knowing why, pulled into this magnetized cell - seven-hundred - eight-hundred - who knows?

"Hey, yah, hey, yah, hey, yah, hey. Yah, hey, yah, hey."

And then it happened.

The lights in Dr. Wolfe's house and the rest of the neighborhood went out.

Black Horse stopped chanting.

The cell stopped chanting

Silence again.

Now they were standing in darkness, with the sky ablaze overhead.

David broke the silence.

"I think we just got our next message."

They couldn't even see each other. All they could see were their silhouettes against the fiery sky.

"Somehow I don't think there's any point in calling the electric company," Dr. Wolfe said.

They all chuckled.

The cell was still. Nobody panicked. They were still in waiting mode. They all knew that what was happening was happening for a reason. It was all part of the divine plan. It was all a blessing.

A voice came from the back, followed by others.

"Phone's out! No signal!"

"Mine too! Dead!"

"Yup! Phones are out!"

Several of the people who were parked on the street in front went to their cars, and turned on the lights. Now they could see a little.

The cell remained still. Nobody left. There was no electrical power, and no telephones. And yet, they all knew this was where they were meant to be.

Dr. Wolfe took charge.

"All right everybody, listen up! A little darkness never hurt anybody. We've been in the dark since the crash. A little more won't hurt. Besides, Jessica and I have been preparing for something like this for a long time. We've got lots of candles and flashlights and battery powered lanterns inside."

Jessica was standing above him, on the landing at the end of the walkway to their house. She turned around, and went inside, not saying a word.

"OK. We'll get that stuff fired up. And any of you who are neighbors of ours, please go back to your homes, and do the same thing. Help us out with candles, flashlights, battery powered lights, or anything else you have around. Mike and Patty, you're out there. Steve and Susie, I saw you guys. Steve, I know you've got a ton of camping gear, and Mike, you've got gadgets for everything. Go get it."

A man made his way through the crowd, from the street, with a flashlight, and gave it to Dr. Wolfe.

"Here. Use this. I had it in my car."

"All right!" Dr. Wolfe exclaimed. "Thanks. Now we're in business."

Dr. Wolfe took the flashlight, walked up his driveway, and opened his garage door. He clattered around inside, and the garage filled up with light. He reemerged, holding two bright camping lanterns by their wire handles.

"Hey, help me with these chairs, would you?" He asked the people closest to the garage door. "All of them."

A group of people scurried in, and followed him into the front yard carrying a bunch of folding, yard chairs.

Lights began to flicker on in the windows of Dr. Wolfe's house, and those of most of his neighbors.

David and Kelly looked at each other with their usual synchronicity.

They were both feeling something they had never felt before. They felt it the instant the lights went out. Their look communicated this. On this day of such heightened and unworldly feelings, here was yet another. And yet this one felt much more mundane. Neither of them knew what it was yet. So, again, they didn't have the words for it. But something about this world felt different. All they knew was it felt unimaginably good.

Another message popped into David.

"They're gone."

With their eyes locked together, Kelly said the words:

"They're gone."

David nodded.

Another message popped in.

"They've left."

This time David spoke:

"They've left."

Kelly nodded.

Tears came to their eyes, and they embraced, their bodies trembling with convulsive joy.

Standing in the darkness, beneath the blazing sky, on the face of their beloved Earth, fresh insight flashed into them. South Dakota. That's why. Now they understood. They always had understood, but not like this, not with such crystal clarity. This was why the powers and forces that guide the universe had led them to South Dakota. At the time, it seemed like the only place they could go. Such are the workings of the divine spirit, who does, in fact, work in fantastically mysterious ways. They just didn't fit into the normal world anymore. They would have to learn to fend for themselves in the wilderness.

Now, here they were again - in the wilderness - alone in the darkness of the universe with nothing but their beloved Earth and their connection with the divine spirit to guide them. But that was all that was needed, all that was ever needed.

Dr. Wolfe had placed the two lanterns in the middle of his lawn, and arranged the chairs around them in a circle.

"Don, Chris, come!" He beckoned to the cell around him. "David, Kelly, Daniel, we need to have a pow wow. Tara, Clay, Patrice, Gemini, all you guys, your presence is requested. We need to talk."

The nucleus gathered, sitting in a circle around the lanterns.

Before they could begin, the horn of an automobile started honking at the end of the block. It was at the fringe of the crowd, which now filled the street, and it was trying to get through.

Honk! Honk!

The crowd made way, and the headlights started inching through the throng down the street in their direction.

"What the hell?" Dr. Wolfe exclaimed.

The honking stopped, but the car continued to nudge against the tightly packed crowd, forcing them to move out of its way.

"Make way, please!" A voice commanded from the car. "Very important business here! Make way!"

The car got closer, and Dr. Wolfe recognized the black, Buick Le Sabre of Lieutenant Frank Jacoby, San Francisco P.D. - the renegade cop David and Kelly had met at the meeting a few nights before.

"Ha! It's Frank."

The closer the car got, the harder it was for the people to move. It finally arrived at the end of the driveway, and parked in the street.

Frank thrust the car door open, sprang out, and marched around the front of the car, swinging his arms, like he was going to battle, his eyes glaring over the car at Dr. Wolfe's. He was dressed in his customary outfit: a brown, tweed sports jacket, a white shirt, with a button-down collar, and newish blue jeans, with a crease.

Frank's eyes picked out Dr. Wolfe in the light of the lanterns, in the nucleus of the cell, as he moved through the crowd.

"Looks like an unlawful assembly, Dr. Wolfe!" he barked.. "You must be violating about twenty ordinances here!"

"Fuck off, Frank!" Dr. Wolfe laughed. "The world's coming to an end. You know where you can stick your fucking ordinances!"

The whole crowd laughed. Whatever tension there was was discharged. Many of them probably didn't get it at first, but they did now. Frank was playing a game. He was one of them.

Frank flashed a gigantic, toothy smile, dimples poking into his cheeks, as he continued his march up the walkway to where Dr. Wolfe and the others were sitting. With his dimples, suddenly he was cute, a big teddy bear.

David then noticed there was another man in the car with Frank. The man opened his door less obtrusively, and followed several feet behind Frank.

It was Tom Brantweiler.

He looked identical to the last night they were together - stubbly gray beard, blue jean overalls, with suspenders, and a white T-shirt. He looked like he hadn't shaved, or changed his clothes since then.

David laughed, a chill going down his spine.

What else? he thought.

He got up, and jostled his way through the people. When he got to Tom, he didn't say anything. He just threw his arms around him.

"Hey, young fella," Tom greeted warmly, returning his hug. "Somehow I had a feeling you'd be in the middle of all this. Some exciting things going on, eh?"

David let go, and peered deeply into Tom's green eyes, which still had their lively sparkle. All the incredible things that happened since he flew out that window, and was scooped up off the sidewalk by Don Morrisee, flashed through David's mind. He was speechless.

"I knew you made it," Tom said softly. "I had to get the hell out of there. They'd be coming for me next, for sure. Left the store. Never went back. But I had some friends on the scene that told me you got out. Went into that old building, and disappeared. Agents Smith and Smith came out with a lot of nothing. And those dudes aren't chopped liver. Pretty neat trick, young fella. What are you - some kind of magician?"

"Sort of," David beamed.

He was still speechless. He asked the first thing that popped into his mind.

"What? You and Frank Jacoby?"

"Yeah, go figure," Tom chuckled. "We go way back, partners in crime for ages. I was his informant, and he was mine. He protected me, tipped me off - couldn't have done it without him. And just think about it for a minute. Now he's willing to be seen with me in public. There's definitely some big shit coming down here."

He gestured with his hand at the lights in the sky.

David affably grabbed his hand out of the air.

"Come. Come and meet Kelly."

Frank reached the edge of the nucleus. Dr. Wolfe, Don, Chris and the rest were seated around the lanterns.

Frank stood, his hands on his hips, the light from the lanterns gleaming off his bald head. He spoke in a booming tone, like a general addressing his troops. It was almost like he was doing a caricature of himself - the cop, the law enforcer.

"Looks like the whole city's out. And I wouldn't be surprised if it's a lot more than that. I don't know. I'm just guessing. We had a really good view of it when it happened, the whole city, across the bay. It all went out - pitch black. And it was the same thing all the way here, in Oakland. Total blackout. Come to think of it, this is the most light we've seen since it happened."

"What's happening, Frank? Any idea?" Dr. Wolfe asked.

Frank smiled more placidly. He took a few steps to an empty chair in the front of the circle, and sat down. The chair creaked under the stress of his robust body. He sat carefully on its front, on the thin metal frame, his body leaning forward.

"Seems I might ask you the same thing," he said more calmly, like a normal person. "You guys did it, didn't you? The frequency fence. That's what this whole day has been all about, isn't it?"

They all nodded, as one.

"I knew it," Frank said in a hush.

He took a deep breath, and started speaking in his bombastic tone again.

"Well, yes, there are a few things I think you all would be very interested to know. The shit has completely hit the fan out there. I left the department an hour or two ago. That was when the lights were still on, and the phones were still working. And there weren't many of us left. The ship had been pretty completely abandoned. So much for our sacred oath to serve the public trust. Mostly every cop, at every level, had abandoned their post, and was taking care of their personal business. At least that's what it looked like. I don't know where they all went."

"And nobody could be reached. Nobody was in charge. We tried calling the Chief. No answer. And we went right down the pecking order. Couldn't reach anybody. We tried other precincts - San Jose, Oakland, Berkeley. Same thing. Nobody can be reached. All we got was the foot soldiers. Couldn't get any of the brass. It's total chaos. So, we call Sacramento, L.A. Same thing. We tried the State boys. Same thing. The top brass are all AWOL. So, I get creative, and call a buddy of mine, a guy like me, a straight shooter, a lieutenant in the L.A.P.D., a guy who I normally wouldn't even talk on an open phone line with. He tells me they have serious problems in the inner city, and they tried to reach the Governor. Unavailable. The Lieutenant Governor. Same deal. The rats have all abandoned the ship. Nobody's running the show."

"So, I decide to throw in the towel. If I'm going to be someplace, I want to be here, with you all. I want to be someplace sane, where there's some hope. But on the way I decide to drop in, and see my friend Tom here. Tom's been forced into the underground by the Gestapo, like so many of you. But Tom's got sources you wouldn't believe. Tom knows everything. He knows about stuff that's going on on other planets, for Christ's sake. And he tells me this same kind of stuff is going on everywhere, throughout the rest of the country, throughout the world. There are rumors in Washington that the President and the Vice-President are incommunicado. Same thing with the Joint Chiefs of Staff. And now all the electrical power and the telephone signals go down. There's no way to confirm any of this anymore because there's no more communication, but we would be crazy not to believe that this blackout isn't a lot bigger than just this. I'll bet it's the whole country, maybe the whole world."

"Folks, something very weird is going on here. This crisis is completely different, and the big boys aren't handling it the way they normally do. Normally, they use any crisis to impose more martial law, and grab more power. And invariably they're one step ahead of the game because it was them who manufactured the crisis to begin with. But this one's completely different. It almost seems like they're afraid to do anything, afraid they'll be caught in the act, and their whole gig will be up. It's like they're waiting, and hoping the whole thing will just go away. And things just keep getting worse and worse. Totally weird!"

Black Horse had walked up alongside David, Kelly and Tom. They looked at each other, their eyes glancing back and forth. Black Horse's eyes conveyed that he had received the same message as them.

Silence, again, reigned supreme. The entire cell respected it.

Kelly and Black Horse fixed their eyes on David.

Their message was unmistakable.

It was his time - again - another of those moments he was born for.

"We're pretty sure we know what's happened, Kelly, Daniel and I," David proclaimed. "We also have some folks in other dimensions and the spirit world, who've been speaking to us, and they too are telling us what's happened."

Silence. A thousand eyes were upon him, and countless others from those other dimensions he spoke of. The air, again, seemed rarified, and David's voice carried effortlessly to the far edges of the cell.

"They're gone."

He scanned them all with his mesmerizing eyes, front and back.

"They've left. Can't you feel it?"

"Gone!?" Dr. Wolfe blurted, his eyes bulging out of his head.

The cell rumbled, its protoplasm again quivering.

Many of them instinctively trusted that this was true. They could sense it with their heightened awareness. They could feel it in their bodies. They could see it in the dazzling lights in the sky. And they could feel it in their connection with each other.

The cell quieted, as David continued.

"Yes, they've left. It's all very simple really. We hit critical mass, and we defeated them. We forced them to leave. We created a vibration that they couldn't tolerate, a vibration with a frequency that's completely out of phase with what they need to survive. They were like vampires in the ascending sunlight. And that's more literally true than you might think. For hundreds of thousands of years, or however long they've infested this planet, they fed off the negative energy that they stirred up in human beings - fear, anger, hatred, aggression, killing, wars, all those kinds of things. When the frequency fence went down, we were able to create energy with a vibration of such proportions that it not only threatened their power structure, on a practical level, but far more importantly, on an energetic level, it threatened their food supply. They just couldn't stand it. Like a kid who gags when his parents force him to eat Brussels sprouts, they had to get up, and leave the table. But in their case, they'll never come back."

"And obviously, quite hastily. They had to get the hell out of here, and find some other planet they could infect. There was absolutely no reason to linger. Even if they did manage to get the frequency fence back up, such chaos had been created, all around the world, and such doubt in the minds of even the most brainwashed people, that it would have been impossible for them to reestablish their control."

"But much more importantly, we had reached critical mass, and that's irrevocable - energetically irrevocable. They could see that once the pendulum started swinging in the other direction, there was no way it could be stopped. Our vibration was ascending, and the old vibration was descending, and would begin to die out. This place really didn't feel good to them anymore, and if they stuck around, they would die."

Silence.

Close to one-thousand people, and their heads were all spinning, their emotions preposterously mixed. They had just received the best news imaginable. They were free. Their planet was free. No more *New World Order*. They would no longer have to dance to the tune of *the global elite*. Their lives now belonged unconditionally to them.

And yet here they were, in the darkness, surrounding two battery powered lanterns, candles flickering in the windows of the houses around them. Lights they had never *seen* before danced and shifted and shot through the sky. For an entire day now, their thoughts and feelings had ventured into strange new realms, realms that from now on would be the new norm. Everything from their familiar and mundane world of everyday life had been stripped away. They had no electrical power. There was no longer any money. They had no jobs. They didn't know where their next food would come from. The gas in their cars would run out, as would the batteries that powered these lanterns, and the wax that held the wicks of their candles.

Standing in the midst of this nucleus, David had never been more clear on his calling. Everything he had ever done in his life was a preparation for this place, this moment. It was divine perfection.

He took a moment, to soak it all in.

"So what's next?" He went on serenely. "They've left us. They've left us in the darkness, apparently with nothing, but that's really not the way it is at all. What they've left us with is the most monumental blessing imaginable. They've left us with the perfect opportunity to participate in *The Great Shift of the Ages*, and to create an entirely new world, a world that's not contaminated by them in any way. I don't know why they turned off the power before they left. They probably thought it would do us in. But if they wanted to destroy us, they could have used the *uni* that so many of you have. They certainly had the technological capability for that. Maybe they didn't think they needed to. Maybe they needed the power. But that's unlikely because where they're going they won't be traveling in space ships that utilize this kind of power. They're way beyond that. They have the know-how to travel inter-dimensionally, and they can cover vast distances across the universe in this manner. Maybe they were rushed, and they weren't thinking too clearly. I don't know."

"But the fact that they left us with no power, and virtually no infrastructure of any kind, is an unimaginable blessing because it forces us to do the one thing we needed to do anyway. It forces us to do the one thing we must do in order to survive. And I'm talking here about surviving in the face of the colossal energies that will be unleashed by *The Great Shift of the Ages*. It forces us to start over. If we are going to create a new world, we must start from scratch. We cannot set out to rebuild the system as it was because that system was rotten to the core. The new world we will create must be built upon the foundation of the energy and the vibration that we have created today. I'm certain we can now all see how immeasurably powerful this is, so powerful that it allowed us to reclaim the planet."

"Leaving us the way they did is an unimaginable blessing because they left us with the only two things we really need. One is our beloved planet Earth, whose heart I can feel beating very rapidly beneath us at this very moment. The Earth hasn't been free of these malevolent forces in a long, long time. The beings and spirits in the other dimensions and worlds that I speak of are rejoicing wildly at this moment, as is this beloved, sentient being we are standing upon. The entire universe is cheering our victory. These beings and spirits will be joining us shortly in ways we can't imagine. They're going to be coming through those portals we can see opening in the sky."

"The other blessing they've left us with is our connection with the divine spirit of a living universe. This is something nobody can ever take from us. And this is something that we, and many others like us throughout this country and the rest of the world, have elevated on this day to get to where we are now."

He reached out for Kelly's hand. She took it, and they drew close to each other.

"Kelly and I have lived in the wilderness, on an Indian reservation in South Dakota, for the last three years. We lived there because we had to. The outside world was no longer a safe place for us. We went there with nothing, and we left there with what we have now - nothing. All we had were the seeds to grow the food in our garden. The Indians gave us our first seeds, and taught us how to reproduce them. We can now use these seeds to grow the first generation of food in the new paradigm."

"And we were blessed with a wonderful teacher, a young shaman, a Sioux named Flying Hawk. Flying Hawk taught us how to survive by living in harmony with the Earth. These are things that we, and others like us, can now teach you. But there was really only one lesson to be learned from this. It is the secret of all manifestation, and the secret of all that is created in harmony with the divine spirit. And I will share it with you now. It is the one thing we all need to know to create the new world. If we are in tune with the Earth, and if we are in tune with the divine spirit, then the Earth and the divine spirit will shower us with unimaginable blessings."

"This is not the first time this has happened. The human race has been faced with colossal Earth changes on several other occasions. And each time it has led to extinction, or practically to extinction, and rebuilding from practically nothing. But this time is totally different, and once again, here is where we are so blessed. This time we are pure. We are pure because the energy of the malevolent beings is no longer here. The malevolent beings were not in tune with the Earth, and they were not in tune with the divine spirit. Their intent was always to control the forces of nature, rather than harmonize with them. This is why they were always overcome when the forces of nature reached such vast proportions. This was one battle they could never win. And this time wouldn't be any different."

"Every native American tribe and virtually every indigenous culture on Earth has predicted, in their ancient and sacred lore, these colossal Earth changes at this time. They also teach something that is the key to why this time is different, and why this time we will make it. They taught that those humans who were not in tune with the Earth, and who were not in tune with the divine spirit, would be destroyed by these forces. Those who were in tune would not only have the capability to survive, but to flourish. This, again, is why we are so blessed. Now that we are pure we can ride the wave of these colossal Earth changes, instead of fight them. And the Earth and the divine spirit will shower us with unimaginable blessings."

ABOUT THE AUTHOR

Jack Allis is the author of the blockbuster novel *Infinity's Flower - A Tale of 2012 & the Great Shift of the Ages* (www.jackallis.com), and since its publication in September 2007, he has become the living embodiment of its message. *Infinity's Flower* is an epic thriller, dealing with these monumental times of shifting energy, and the challenge facing the forces of light to create the new world. Its message echoes the ancient prophecies from indigenous cultures spanning the globe, telling us that our higher consciousness and spirituality are the primary source of our protection in the face of these colossal Earth changes, and the primary source of our power to create the new world of light and spirit.

Jack now travels the country, and delivers this message to as many awakening souls as he can reach, with his groundbreaking powerpoint presentation and sacred chants, which are based on *Infinity's Flower*, and entitled *2012 & the Shift – Transforming Challenges into Blessings*, in addition to an ever-expanding number of TV and radio interviews.

Jack practices what he preaches, living minimally and close to nature in a tiny cottage on Little Okauchee Lake in Wisconsin. He has written two other novels, *Infinity's Children* and *Masters of Destiny*, as well as his popular monthly e-newsletter.

In addition to his writing, Jack is also a personal growth and spiritual teacher, working with people in person, by telephone, and over the Internet, in addition to his seminars and workshops. In his healing work, Jack emphasizes the harmony of the body, mind and spirit, and he teaches people how to experience peacefulness and joy in their lives, and manifest their dreams.

Jack's formal education consists of earning a California Marriage & Family Therapy License in 1989 and a Masters Degree in Clinical Psychology from

Antioch University in Santa Barbara, California in 1987. He was in private practice in cognitive psychotherapy (mind/body) in Santa Barbara and Ventura from 1989 until 2001, when he moved to Wisconsin.

A true Renaissance man, Jack has dedicated the last forty years of his life to seeking out diverse and non-traditional knowledge, which touch virtually every area of life, including holistic health, philosophy and spirituality. On his journey, Jack has acquired in-depth knowledge of Taoism and the philosophies and spiritual teachings of the Far East, meditation and martial arts techniques from a variety of cultures, the philosophical and spiritual teachings of shamans and indigenous spiritual cultures spanning the globe, both past and present, the revolutionary discoveries of quantum physics, organic gardening and farming, astrology, the philosophy of Objectivism, sovereignty and our vanishing freedoms, alternative theories of money, economics and history, and a variety of esoteric teachings.

If you enjoyed *Infinity's Flower*, and would like to experience some of Jack Allis's other creations, we invite you to check out the following at **www.jackallis.com.**

Before there was *Infinity's Flower*, there was *Infinity's Children*.

Suspense reaches the same dizzying heights, as David evolves from a precocious young boy, miraculously meets and falls in love with Kelly, and they join together on their quest to defeat the powers of darkness, and create the new world.

Jack & the Shift on DVD

2012 & the Shift
Transforming Challenges into Blessings

Filmed at the 2008 Mount Shasta Summer Conference, this DVD includes a 90 minute Powerpoint presentation and sacred chant based on Jack's epic thriller, *Infinity's Flower*.

www.ingramcontent.com/pod-product-compliance
Lightning Source LLC
Chambersburg PA
CBHW070022260626
47159CB00005B/1927